as brave as you

as brave as you

JASON REYNOLDS

THORNDIKE PRESS
A part of Gale, a Cengage Company

Farmington Hills, Mich • San Francisco • New York • Waterville, Maine
Meriden, Conn • Mason, Ohio • Chicago

GALE
A Cengage Company

LIBRARY OF CONGRESS CIP DATA ON FILE.
CATALOGUING IN PUBLICATION FOR THIS BOOK
IS AVAILABLE FROM THE LIBRARY OF CONGRESS

ISBN-13: 978-1-4328-4931-3 (hardcover)
ISBN-10: 1-4328-4931-X (hardcover)

ISBN 13: 978-1-4328-5024-1 (pbk).

Published in 2018 by arrangement with Atheneum Books for Young Readers, an imprint of Simon & Schuster Children's Publishing Division.

Printed in Mexico
1 2 3 4 5 6 7 22 21 20 19 18

For my grandfather Brooke Reynolds and my dear friend Brook Stephenson. You both brought so much light to the world.

#437: the stupidest name for a sport is football. Why isn't it called tackleball? Real football is soccer. Soccer is the second-stupidest name for a sport, unless it was the name for female boxing. But female boxing is already called boxing, even though boxing should be the sport to see who can pack up stuff, like clothes, the fastest. Why isn't that a sport? If it was a sport, Ma would be a world-champion boxer.

#438: another weird word is season. Like winter, spring, summer, fall. but why does it also mean adding flavor to food? that makes no sense, but I wonder what it would be like if I could season my food with the seasons. Like if you sprinkled some winter on peas, they'd probably taste like . . . cold peas. but if you sprinkled some summer on them, maybe they'd taste like pizza or something.

ONE

#460: Poop. Poop is stupid. Stupid poop. Stupid. Poopid. Poopidity. Is poopidity a word?

Genie stood a few feet away from Samantha's shabby old doghouse, scribbling a mess of words in his notebook. His older brother, Ernie, was luring the mutt to a cleaner spot in the yard with a big pot of leftover chicken, bacon, grits, greens, and whatever else was for doggy breakfast.

"Okay, that should keep her busy for a few minutes," Ernie said, successful. He walked over to the side of Grandma and Grandpop's house, grabbed a rusty shovel, then came back to Genie and started scooping up crusty piles of dog poop.

"What I wanna know is what you 'bout to do with that mess?" Genie asked, pinching and pulling his shorts out of his butt. Ma must not have noticed how much he had grown since the year before when she packed all his old summer clothes.

"If you put that notebook down, you'll see," Ernie said, holding the shovel out and walking toward the back of the house where all the trees were. When he got close enough to the wood line, he looked over his shoulder. Genie shoved the small notebook into his back pocket. "You watchin'?" Ernie called out, making sure all eyes were on him.

Genie hustled over. "Yeah." Ernie flashed a sly grin, one that worked perfectly with his dark shades. Then, without giving any kind of warning, he cocked the shovel back and flung it forward. The poop flew into the air and out into the woods, slapping against the trees and exploding.

"Ooh yeah!" Ernie cheered, holding his shovel up as if he had just scored a touchdown.

Genie gaped, his mouth falling open as Ernie came back to scoop up more dog crud. "You just gon' stand there, or you gon' get in on this?" Ernie asked, chin-pointing to the other shovel leaning against the side of the house.

No way was Genie going to miss out on slinging poop. On *poopidity*? No. Way. How often does anybody get to catapult doo-doo into a forest? Never. Genie ran and grabbed

10

the other shovel.

"Get this one," Ernie said, stabbing at a gross mound, still stinky.

Genie grimaced, but he slid the shovel under the poop, grimaced again at the scratchy sound of metal on dirt, then lifted it and followed Ernie back to the tree line.

"Go for it," Ernie said, nodding.

Genie put one foot forward, holding the shovel as if it were a baseball bat and he was about to attempt the worst bunt in history. He whipped the shovel forward, but not nearly hard enough. The poop plopped down only about a foot away. It was a pretty sad throw, and it was way too close to being a situation where poop was splattered all over Genie's Converses. Yeah, they were already covered in dust, but dust is one thing, even mud he could handle, but dog poop? There's no coming back from that.

"You gotta *fling* it, Genie. *Fling* it." Ernie demonstrated with a few ghost flings. "You see that tree over there?"

Genie looked out at all the trees in front of them and wondered which one Ernie was talking about. It was pretty much . . . a forest. Trees were everywhere. And Ernie wasn't really pointing at any one in particular. He just said *that tree over there* as if one of the trees had been marked with a sign that said THIS TREE, DUMMY. But Ernie was always on him about asking too many questions, so Genie just nodded.

"Watch and learn, young grasshoppa." Ernie held the shovel low, letting it hang behind him before hurling its contents into the woods. It splat against a tree. Perfect shot. It must've been the one Ernie was aiming for, because he threw his hands up in celebration again. "Bang, bang! Got it!" he howled. "Now, try again."

Genie picked up another clump, questions flying all over the place like those flies on the . . . poopidity. Why was there so much of it in the first place? Did nobody else care that there was mess all over the yard? When was the last time the yard had been poop-scooped? Genie tried to mimic Ernie's every move. He held the shovel low and let it drop back behind him a little so that he could get some good momentum. We're talking technique here. Sophisticated stuff.

"Aim for that old house back there," Ernie said, pointing into the woods. Genie focused and counted off. One, two, and on three, he swung his whole body, a kind of broke-down golf swing, the mess whipping from the shovel head. Genie definitely got some air on it this time! But he hadn't quite figured out how to aim it — Ernie left that part out. The poop zipped off behind him, slamming into a window in the back of the house. The *wrong* house. His grandparents' house.

"Genie!" Ernie shouted, his eyes bugging. And right after that came Grandma.

"Genie!" she called out. "Ernie! What in Sam Hill are y'all doin'?"

Grandma was the one who put Ernie and Genie on poop patrol in the first place, in case you were wondering. Neither one of them had ever had to shovel poop out of anybody's yard before, because first of all, in Brooklyn, most people don't have yards. And secondly, most Brooklyn folks just pick it up with plastic Baggies whenever a dog does his doo on the sidewalk. Not everybody, but the majority. But there were no sidewalks here in North Hill, Virginia. No brownstones with the cement stoops where you could watch the buses, ice cream trucks, and taxis ride by. Nope. North Hill, Virginia, was country. Like *country* country. And Genie and Ernie were staying there in a small white house on the top of a hill. Grandma and Grandpop's house. For a month. Like thirty *whole* days.

The boys had arrived two nights earlier after a long, cramped ride in the back of their dad's old Honda. Cramped at least for Genie, because Ernie, in a cheeseburger coma, had stretched out on the backseat as if it were his own personal couch, forcing Genie to be smushed against the window for most of the trip. Genie had thought about playing Pete and Repeat by mimicking Ernie's nasty snores, but then he realized it wouldn't matter because Ernie wasn't awake to get annoyed by it anyway. And that was the whole point of that game. So to take his mind off the discomfort of being trapped under Ernie's leg, stewing in the thick silence between his folks, who had managed to not talk to each other for the past four hours, Genie flipped through pages of his notebook — where he kept his best questions. Some had already been answered, and some were still mysteries. He landed on one that he had totally forgotten about — #389: Do honey badgers eat honey? — then tried telling his parents about how he'd read on the Internet that honey badgers actually *do* eat honey and how many of them have been stung to death by bees because they wanted honey from the hive so bad. The toughest, craziest animal ever.

"They're like weasels or somethin'. But tougher, know what I'm sayin'? Like, they're small, but they ain't scared to get busy, even on lions," Genie had rambled. The fact that his parents had neither asked him about honey badgers, or even knew why he cared about them in the first place, never stopped him from offering up random info at random times. That was sort of his thing. He was different from Ernie in that way. Genie was the kind of kid who kept a small jacked-up notebook and pen in his pocket just so that he could jot down interesting things whenever they came. The point was to keep a list — a numbered list — of all the things he needed to Google, because to Genie, the more questions you had, the more answers you could find. And the more answers you found, the more you knew. And the more you knew, the less you made mistakes. Genie wasn't about mistakes.

Ernie, on the other hand, was the kind of kid who wore sunglasses 24/7 just to make sure everybody knew he was cool, and to him, the biggest mistake anyone could make was not to be. That, and not being able to defend yourself. As a matter of fact, one of the only times Ernie didn't wear his shades was whenever he was doing karate, which he had been learning since he was seven. He was a brown belt, or as he put it, a "junior black belt." Genie loved to watch

15

Ernie's matches and tournaments, but not quite as much as he loved to watch *Jeopardy!* and *Wheel of Fortune*. Ernie, on the other hand, liked to watch girls. Genie liked to build model cars. Ernie . . . liked to watch girls.

"Boy, if you don't go to sleep, I'm a honey *your* badger," Ma had droned from the front seat after Genie finished telling her about the video he'd seen of a honey badger actually taking on a lion. She was staring out the window, and had been the entire time they'd been on the road. Genie sucked his teeth. That was when Dad adjusted the rearview mirror so that he could see Genie.

"Son, tell me something." He darted his exhausted-looking eyes from the rearview back to the road. "How much you know about sloths?"

"Sloths?" Genie thought for a moment. "Well, I know they're lazy, and they sleep all the time," he answered reluctantly, feeling the setup coming.

"Uh-huh," Dad said, flat. He glanced back in the mirror. "See where I'm goin' with this?"

Genie sucked his teeth again. He knew exactly where Dad was going with it. Straight to *Genie please be quiet and go to sleep* town.

But Genie didn't go straight to sleep, even though that was what his parents wanted. Instead, he stared out the window, like Ma, for about an hour, peering into the darkness, thinking about his girlfriend, Shelly, and his best friend, Aaron. He wondered if they were going to do all the things they always did in the summer, like play in the hydrant and buy rocket pops from the ice cream man, without him. If they were going to miss his rants and all his knowledge about random animals and insects, and if Shelly would be able to spot a bedbug like he had taught her. He wondered if Aaron would try to impress Shelly with his backflips (girls love dudes who can do backflips) and if she'd eventually fold to his flippin' charm and kiss him. Of course, if she did, it would be a loaner kiss, Genie decided. A kiss to make up for the fact that *he* wasn't there. Nothing real. Genie sat there thinking about all these things, annoyed by his brother's snoring, listening to his parents not say a word, totally unsure about what was going to happen when they finally got to Virginia. The only thing he did know for sure was *why* they were going to the country in the first place, why he and Ernie had to spend a whole month away from Brooklyn for the first time ever.

It all had to do with Jamaica. Well, really it all had to do with his parents "not saying a word." They were "having problems," which Genie knew was just parent-talk for maybe/possibly/probably divorcing. They said they needed some time to try to figure it all out. When his mother first told him about the "problems," all Genie could think about was what his friend Marshé Brown told him when her parents got divorced, and how she never saw her father again. When he asked his mother about whether he was going to have to choose which parent he wanted to live with, or if he and Ernie were going to have to split up too, all she said was, "No matter what, me and your daddy love you both. Always." But that didn't really answer the question, which made it clear in Genie's mind that "figuring it out" — which, by the way, was supposed to happen in Jamaica, the first vacation his parents were taking without him and Ernie — really meant figuring out which parent got which kid, which, of course, meant this would probably also be the *last* vacation his parents would be taking without them. And it got Genie thinking about who he'd want to live with, Ma or Dad, which led to him scribbling a list in the dark. Really, two lists.

Living with Dad

Pro: I'd be safe from fires and thieves.

Con: Dad works all the time and is never home.

Con: So I probably wouldn't be safe from fires and thieves.

Pro: I could watch scary movies.

Con: Dad can't cook.

Con: Dad stinks almost all the time, because of work.

Living with Ma

Pro: She can cook, real good.

Pro: She never ever stinks.

Con: She won't let me watch scary movies.

Con: I don't know if she can protect me from fire and thieves.

Con: Which means I'd have to protect her, and I don't know karate!

Eventually, after going back and forth in his mind about who he'd want to live with, and messily jotting his thoughts in the notebook, the smooth, dark road hypnotized Genie, finally coaxing him to sleep. He hadn't even realized he had drifted off until he was awakened by the sound of tree limbs scraping the sides of the car. The Honda was bumping its way up a hill, and the limbs looked like long fingers on big stick hands trying to get in and grab him. It was still dark, Dad had his window cracked, letting some air in, and he had changed the music from slow jams to nineties hip-hop.

"We here?" Genie muttered, wiping sleep from his eyes. He looked out the window but couldn't see anything except branches. The car dipped and bucked every few seconds as Dad kept slamming on the brakes to avoid potholes.

"Jesus! This road is a mess," he fumed, turning the radio off so he could concentrate. Genie quickly patted the space beside him on the seat, searching for his pen. Once he found it, he flipped to the next page of his notebook. #440: Does turning the radio off help you drive better? he scrawled as Ma turned to him and flashed a sleepy smile.

"Yes, honey, we're here." The skin on her face looked heavy, and Genie wondered if she had slept at all during the ride. Actually, the skin on her face had been looking heavy for a few months. Since her and Dad had the big blowup where she screamed, like *screamed* screamed, and told him that all his time went to work and the boys, but he could never seem to make time for her. Ernie and Genie had been outside having a snowball fight, and Down the Street Donnie, known for being a jerk, had covered a quarter in snow and zinged it at Genie. Zapped him straight in the eye. Ernie had run over to check on him and when he saw the coin, most of the snow knocked off, he commenced to karatisizing Down the Street Donnie, all the way . . . down the street. Meanwhile, Genie had run inside, his palm to his eye, and stepped right into Ma and Dad's crossfire over how she was feeling neglected. The swelling around Genie's eye eventually went away. But the heavy on Ma's face never did.

Anyway, the point was, Genie hoped Ma had gotten some sleep on the way to Virginia, because the one thing he thought he knew about Virginia, he was right about. It was *far*. Way too far to be awake the whole time.

Ernie, on the other hand, had slept the entire trip — was still asleep, his mouth hanging wide open in that way that made the bottom half of his face look like it was melting, his sunglasses lopsided, only covering one eye. Genie pushed Ernie's leg off him, but it snapped right back up to its place on Genie's lap as if it were spring-loaded.

"Ern, wake up," Genie said, jamming his

fingers into Ernie's thigh. "We here." Ernie didn't budge. "Ern!" Genie cried out, loud enough for Ma to hear. She turned around and slapped Ernie's leg. He snapped awake, confused, fixing his shades and wiping spit off his chin with the bottom of his T-shirt.

As the car approached the top of the hill, the sound of a dog barking came out of nowhere. Genie pressed his face against the window. Was that Grandma and Grandpop's dog? What was it doing outside? Did they know it had gotten loose? Was Grandpop up this time of the night walking it?

"Ernie, you remember Samantha?" Dad asked, cutting the engine a minute after cresting the hill.

Ernie craned his neck to see out the window, yawning. He had been to North Hill once before, a long time ago when he was four. Genie hadn't come with him because at the time he was still a baby. That was also the last time Dad had seen his father. It had been almost ten years. And Genie had no idea what *that* was about.

So this was Genie's first time to North Hill. As a matter of fact, this was his first time really going out of town at all. He had been to New Jersey, but that didn't really count. It took longer to get to his other grandparents' house, his mom's parents,

22

who lived in the Bronx, than it did to get to Jersey.

Genie had never met Dad's dad, his grandfather, but he had met his grandmother once. She had come to New York to visit when he was much younger, but he didn't remember too much about her except for the fact that she looked like Dad. An old lady version of him, minus the mustache and the beard. And she smelled like soap. Genie remembered that.

"Of course I remember Samantha," Ernie grumbled, his voice groggy from car sleep. He finally moved his leg and sat up. Genie could hear a dog chain dragging across the ground, then popping when the slack was up. He wasn't usually scared of dogs, and he wasn't *really* really scared of this one either, but it was definitely comforting — and weird — to know that this Samantha dog was chained up outside in the dark. Dogs left outside in Brooklyn ended up in the pound!

"We made it. Everybody out," Dad said, and by the time all the car doors had opened and Dad had popped the trunk, a light outside the house flickered on. The front door opened and a shapeless shadow filled the doorway like some kind of ghost. The dog, the trees, the little house all alone on the top of a hill — this, Genie thought, was definitely the makings of a scary movie.

A kinda scratchy but firm voice called out, "Sam! Stop all that dern yappin'!" It was the same kind of scratchy firm voice that Genie recognized from all those three-minute, twice-a-month phone calls that were always about how he was doing in school, and if he was taking care of his brother and his mother, which always confused him because he was the youngest person in the family. Grandma's voice. Now Grandma stepped onto the porch and closed the screen door behind her. It was a darker shade of dark outside than Genie was used to, but he could still make out the flowers on Grandma's long nightdress.

Dad nodded to Genie and Ernie to get moving, and led the way, lugging the family suitcase to the top step of the porch. He set it down and wrapped his arms around the old lady, tight. "Hey, Mama."

"Lord," she said, kissing him on the cheek, then reaching out for Ma. "Took y'all forever to get here."

"You know how your son is," Ma said, giving Grandma a quicker hug, then swinging around to make sure Genie and Ernie were right behind her. "Five miles over the speed limit is against the daggone law." Ma shook her head like she was annoyed at Dad, a look Genie saw all the time at home. But Genie didn't really understand it this time, because, well, five miles over the speed limit *was* against the law.

Genie let his mother take his hand as she pulled him forward. Ernie hung back.

"Well, you can blame me for that one, sugar. I'm the safe one in the family," Grandma said. "Now come on in, come on in. Let me look at y'all," she continued, excited, as she opened the door wide. "Right this way."

Inside the house was just as dark as outside until Grandma finally flipped a switch. A dim, yellowy light came on that made everything look like a smartphone picture with a vintage filter on it. They were in an old kitchen with peeling sea-green wallpaper, a school-bus-yellow fridge buzzing as loud as a Laundromat washer.

Grandma's face was slightly wrinkled but still looked like Dad's around the eyes. That was all Genie could see of her — her face — because everything else was covered up by the flowered gown that looked more like a bedsheet with a hole cut out for her head to go through than an actual nightdress.

"Line up and lemme see," Grandma directed as they shuffled around on the plasticky floor. "That city's beatin' on you, ain't it?" she said, sizing up Dad first.

"Mama, I been up since nine yesterday morning," he explained, sounding irritated and tired.

"I know, I know," she said, patting him on the belly. "At least you eatin' well up there." Then she turned to Ma. "Thank you for feedin' him, dear."

"My pleasure, Mama."

"And look at you. My sweet daughter-in-law," Grandma said with a little oomph in her voice while checking Ma out head to toe. "Two kids and still look like you in grade school." Ma bit down on her bottom lip for a second before letting herself smile. A little bit of attention goes a long way, Genie noticed. He also thought Grandma was a liar. He had known lots of girls in grade school, and most of them looked way better than Ma as far as he was concerned. Especially Shelly.

"And look at this cool guy," Grandma said, moving down the line to Ernie, who, of course, had his sunglasses on.

"Ernie!" Ma barked between clenched teeth. Ernie snatched the sunglasses off. Quick.

"Ohhh, it's okay. How are you, Ernie?"

26

Grandma said, giving him a kiss on the cheek.

"Fine," Ernie muttered, Ma's mad eyeballs all over him.

"And check out this one here, getting so big," Grandma finished up, putting her hand on Genie's head. "You 'member me, Genie?" She wrapped her arms around him. He could smell the soap. The same soap he remembered her by. The same kind his mother used.

After the lineup, Grandma herded them up a set of stairs, Ernie, Genie, Ma and Dad, all in one room with two big ol' beds. Ma and Dad conked out quick, no surprise since they had been driving all night. Ernie fell asleep right after them, because, well, he just never had a problem sleeping. It didn't matter if it was in a car or in a strange house, Ernie was going to find a way to catch zzzzs. But not Genie. He couldn't get comfortable. He wasn't in *his* bed. Or *his* house. Or even *his* city. He just lay still in the dark on a mattress that stank of sad old socks. A mattress so thin he could feel the springs in his back, like lying on a bed of fists. And to make it even weirder, it was crazy quiet! No police sirens, no loud music, no couples arguing outside his window on the street. No hungry cats, whose meows, for some reason, always sounded like babies crying. Only sound besides Ernie's snoring was about a million crickets, and a million frogs playing Pete and Repeat with the crickets. No way was he gonna ever get to sleep. No way . . .

When morning came, along with the brightest sunlight EVER, and the smell of eggs and bacon coming through the cracks in the wooden floor mixed with the smell of Ernie's big toe, which was way too close to Genie's nose, Genie woke up. So he must've fallen asleep after all. Ma was already up, the bed she and Dad had slept in already made as if they had never been in it, and the end of a colorful blanket was tightly trapped between Ma's chin and chest as she folded the bottom. She'd taught Genie how to fold like that at home. He still hadn't gotten it down, but she was a master.

"Good morning," she singsonged, making one more fold, then setting the blanket on the edge of the bed. A perfect rectangle. "Sleep okay?"

Genie, noticing the bags under his mother's eyes, wanted to ask her the same question, but instead just nodded and slipped out from under Ernie's leg. He thought Ernie was asleep, but then he felt his brother shaking from giggling.

"Hey, Genie, what my toe smell like?" Ernie busted out laughing from beneath the covers.

"Smell like your butt!"

"Genie!" Ma snapped.

He sat up just as Ernie tried to shove him off the bed with his knee.

"Stop!" Genie said, pushing back, trying not to fall.

"Ernie, cut it out. It's too early for this," Ma warned.

"What? I'm just playin' with him." Ernie reached for his sunglasses, which he had set carefully on the floor beside the bed the night before. Ma gave him the *Don't you dare!* look.

"Come on, Ma. It's stupid bright in here," he protested, sliding the shades on, cool. The windows didn't have curtains or blinds, so the sun just poured in. It bounced off the wood floor and the yellowy walls, making the entire room seem orange. Almost seemed like they were on the *inside* of the sun.

The room was crammed full with things. Old things, like posters of basketball players in crazy-looking wedgie shorts. A faded calendar on the wall from 1985 — *Back to the Future* themed. A dresser with navy-blue paint peeling off like the skin on someone's nose after they'd been in the sun too long. There were also some medals and ribbons there, a folded-up flag. And a small red truck — an old-school fire engine — on top of the dresser. Genie hopped off the bed for a better look.

"Watch for splinters, son," his mother warned as he walked over the gapped wooden slats to the dresser. The red truck, he realized, was a model, and the details, the ladder, the side mirrors . . . perfect. Even better than he could — dang! He'd left his models back home! And Ma had just bought him two new ones, specially for this trip. *Double dang!*

He'd just reached out to pick up the red truck when Grandma yelled from down-stairs, "Rise and shine, babies! Breakfast is ready!"

The boys and their mother followed the smell of food down the shaky wooden steps to the kitchen doorway. Grandma was standing over the stove, flipping bacon with a fork. The grease popped every time she poked the bacon, but she never flinched. An old man — Grandpop! — sat at the round kitchen table. He had on a white dress shirt with the sleeves rolled up, and, like Ernie, dark sunglasses. His face had that look old men get when they'd shaved the day before and the beard was just starting to grow back, white specks of dust all over his cheeks.

"Come in here and say hi to your grandfather," Grandma said, setting the fork on the counter and stirring something in a copper pot. She nodded to Genie, then at the empty chair to the right of the old man for Genie to sit in. Ernie sat in the one across from him. Ma sat next to Ernie, completing the circle.

Ernie spoke first. "Hi, Grandpop."

"Ernie. The almost-birthday boy." Grandpop grinned, holding out a huge hand. "Been a month of Sundays, son. Long time no see." Genie wasn't sure what "a month of Sundays" meant but figured Ernie must have known because he reached a hand out and gave Grandpop a five. That voice. Genie recognized it too, also from the phone calls. Grandpop was the one who would always ask if Genie was taking care of his father, which made it seem to Genie that his grandparents expected him to take care of *everybody.*

Ernie nudged Genie, urging him to speak.

"Hi," Genie said softly.

"Genie." Grandpop put his hand out again. "Nice to finally meet you."

Genie went to give him five, but Grandpop caught his hand, clamped down on it like a mousetrap on a mouse, and shook it hard and tight. Tight enough to make one of Genie's eyes close up. Tight enough to almost make him ask, *What's your problem?*

"The first one is always like this." Grandpop leaned in close enough for Genie to smell him — a mix of sweet and sweat — and lowered his voice to almost a whisper. "But now that we know each other, all the rest'll be fives." Then he grinned big. His teeth were like Dad's and Ernie's. Perfect, white. Speaking of Dad, Genie wondered where he was and when he was going to show up and maybe save him from this white-toothed crazyman. With Grandpop still clutching his hand, Genie peered around, looking for his father.

"Leave that boy alone, Brooke," Grandma said, slapping the old man on the shoulder, setting a plate full of breakfast food in front of him. Grandpop released his grip and Genie, happy to finally have his hand back, massaged his fingers. Grandma must've noticed Genie's nervousness, because she asked, "Who you lookin' for, your daddy? He outside. Be back in a second." She kissed Grandpop on the cheek, then dodged him as he swatted at her butt on her way back to the counter for another plate. Her silver hair was wound into a bun on top of her head, and her flowered nightdress was much prettier in the daytime. So was she.

The next plate was Genie's. Eggs, bacon, toast, and some globby white stuff that must've come from that pot Grandma had been stirring. Looked like movie prison food.

Grandma beamed. "Hope you boys like grits."

Ma laughed. "They don't know what grits are, Mama Harris, but they're gon' try some today."

Genie stuck his fork into the white slime and hoped it didn't taste like peas. Peas were the one thing he hated to eat more than anything. This stuff wasn't green, so that was a good sign. He let the gritty goo slip between the tines of the fork and plop back down onto his plate. He looked at his brother. Ernie seemed just as worried but lifted the fork straight to his mouth and tasted it anyway. Ernie was brave like that. He made a face like the white stuff — the grits — was good, so Genie tried it too.

"Taste like sand," Genie blurted, not quite wanting to spit it out, but not wanting to swallow it either. He just wanted to let it sit there in his mouth until it dissolved.

"Genie!" Ma hated when he said stuff like

that. At the same time, she was always after him to tell the truth. And the truth was, to him, the grits tasted like he was eating sand.

"Sand?" Grandpop said, looking amused. "Well, I got somethin' for that." He pushed his chair back just as Grandma finally sat down, and went over to the counter where there were three coffee cans. Popping the top off the middle one, he stuck his fingers in it, then closed it back up. He returned to the table and sprinkled something on top of Genie's grits.

"Try now."

"What was that?" Genie asked, worried.

"Magic dust." Grandpop grinned, a little less creepy this time, and sat back down. "Try it."

Genie picked his fork up and touched it to his tongue, just enough to taste. Sugar! And yeah, now the grits were *so* much better.

Grandma was looking intently at Genie, her head tilted like she was trying to figure something out. "You know who else didn't like grits unless they had sugar on 'em?" she asked.

"Uh-huh. Wood," Grandpop said. He'd been stabbing his eggs with his fork, but stopped suddenly, as if eating was getting in the way of thinking. "Wow. That's somethin', ain't it?"

"Uncle Wood?" Genie piped in.

"Eat your breakfast," his mother commanded. "Your grandfather got it all sugared up for you."

"Please don't have my son's teeth rotten by the end of the summer." A new voice in the room. Dad's. He appeared out of nowhere. Walking over to the table, he kissed Genie on the forehead, then Ernie. Then Grandma. He leaned in and just grazed Ma's cheek with his lips, awkwardly. It was friendly, but not . . . loving. But it was better than what Grandpop got, which was no kiss at all.

"Your plate's on the counter, but wash your hands before you eat," Grandma said, low, as if Dad was still a little boy. "Been out there foolin' with that dirty dog."

"What you talkin' 'bout, rotten teeth?" Grandpop said on top of Grandma telling Dad to wash up. "Please. You ate more sugar than any kid in history, and you still got pearly whites, don'tcha? Just one cavity your entire life." Dad didn't respond, just rinsed his hands in the kitchen sink. Grandpop started to pile his eggs on his toast, grits on top of that, topping it all with a slice of bacon. Ma glanced at Dad uneasily while taking in a spoonful of grits herself. Ernie,

35

after watching Grandpop construct his breakfast tower, did the same thing. Pete and Repeat! That made Genie wonder if maybe Ernie got the idea of wearing sunglasses in the house from Grandpop too.

Dad dried his hands on a towel hanging from the oven door and stayed standing. There weren't enough chairs at the small table, but it didn't seem like he wanted to sit anyway — when Grandpop offered Dad his seat, Dad refused and ate at the counter.

"So, Mama," he said, "why don't you let me put some money into fixin' up this place? The floor upstairs is all warped, and the planks must've shrunk; they're all spaced out — I can see straight through to the living room."

"Don't need no fixin' son," Grandpop answered before Grandma could get a word out. "My blood and sweat is in this house, built it with my own two hands. It's just gettin' old, just like me. But it's still standing, just like me." Grandpop lifted the breakfast tower to his mouth and smirked. "And . . . just like you."

Dad rolled his eyes and Grandma chimed in. "Ernest, um, that's sweet. But you save that money for these boys. And Jamaica, okay? You fly out in what, two weeks, right?"

"Yep. And I'm so grateful that you could

take the boys for so long — this was the only time we could get them down here, especially with Ernest having to pick up extra shifts so he could take off two whole weeks —" Ma was saying apologetically when Grandma waved her apology away, her eyes bright.

"Oh, baby, it's no problem. Happy to have 'em, she insisted.

Dad just bit down on his bottom lip and glared at his father before turning back to his food. Genie, however, was fixated on Grandpop — on his face, specifically his shades. Every few bites, Genie would look up and see his own reflection in the sunglasses. Then he would look back down at his plate, embarrassed for staring. But he just couldn't help it.

"What is it, Genie?" Grandpop asked at last, tower demolished, plate clean. He took a slurp of his coffee from a white mug that said in black letters, VIRGINIA IS FOR LOVERS, hearts replacing all the *V*s.

"Huh?"

"What is it? You keep staring at me. I told you, we know each other now, after that handshake, so that means you can tell me anything." He took another slurp, swallowed. "So spill."

Now everyone was staring at *Genie.* Except for Ernie, who was too busy trying to pile everything left on his plate on the last piece of toast. Ma nodded, which meant it was okay for Genie to say whatever it was he wanted to say.

"Um," he started, nervous. "Well, it's just that —" Genie looked at his mother one more time, just to make sure. She nodded again. "It's just that Ma always says you shouldn't wear sunglasses in the house. She says it makes your eyes go bad, plus it makes you look crazy."

His mother dropped her fork. His father snorted.

"Papa Harris, I'm —" she started immediately apologizing, but Grandpop cut her off.

"Well," he started, "your mom is a smart woman, but for me it's different." He wiped his mouth with a napkin, then balled it up and dropped it on the table. "Wanna know why?"

"Why?" Genie asked.

Grandpop leaned in close again, this time enough for Genie to get a whiff of the coffee on his breath. "Because I already can't see a thing, and I been crazy for years."

Two

#441: What made Grandpop blind? I bet it was the bright sun that almost blinded me and Ernie this morning. What does blindness feel like? And is it just blackness? Is it like being sleep, but awake, like sleepwalking? Is Grandpop just sleepwalking, and sleeptalking, and sleepeating? And if he's really awake, is he always sleepy? I heard if you put a blanket over a bird's cage, and they can't tell it's daytime anymore, they'll just go to sleep.

"Why you ain't tell me he couldn't see?!" Genie asked as his mother zipped closed the little pouch she kept her toothpaste, toothbrush, and lotion in. He had taken the red truck off the old blue dresser and was sitting on the floor, running his thumb over the wheels. Next to him, of course, was his handy notebook. He had lots of questions, but the most important one he had just asked. *Why you ain't tell me he couldn't see?!* And that was a question that needed to be asked out loud.

"Your grandpop is a tricky man, baby," Ma began to explain, but then she got hung up and didn't seem to know what else to say, so she looked at Dad. "Senior," she groused, snapping Dad out of his trance. Senior was what she called him because his name was Ernie too, and she wanted to make sure that whichever Ernie she was yelling at at any given moment would know she was yelling at him, and not the other.

"Yeah — um — yes," Dad stammered, still sort of zoned out.

"You all right?" she asked.

"Yeah, yeah, wassup?"

Ma cocked her head to the side. "Would you explain to our youngest son here why we didn't tell him about Grandpop?"

Dad looked at Genie and sighed. "Well, he's kind of a wild guy, Genie —"

"Not *wild,* Genie," Ma interrupted. "Just, um, interesting."

"Right," Dad agreed quickly. "We weren't trying to keep anything from you. . . . It's just that he made me promise a long time ago never to tell anyone he was blind. No one. Not even you two. It's something he likes to do himself after he's met the person.

That way they don't just come into his house thinking of him as, well, handicapped."

"Disabled," Ma corrected him.

"Yes, I mean disabled. That's the one thing he hates the most." Dad slid over to the corner of his bed, close to Genie. "Grandpop doesn't like for, y'know, people to help." Genie drew his knees up — his legs were starting to go numb — and Dad noticed the red truck in his hand.

"Be careful with that, son," he said, holding out his hand for the truck. "Wood made this, and it's the only thing from his childhood Grandma has left — it means the world to her." Dad peered at the truck as if he could see Uncle Wood sitting in the driver's seat. It clearly meant something to him as well. "Forgot Wood was a model guy. Just like you." He shook his head. "Crazy." He gave the truck back to Genie, who couldn't help but think about what other things he and Uncle Wood might've had in common. But Dad brought him back to the topic at hand. "Anyway, about your grandfather — Ernie got a heckuva surprise, too, when he visited the first time." Dad looked to Ernie, who lay sprawled on the other bed, clicking away on his phone. "What you doin', Ernie?"

"Tryna send this text, but it won't go through." Ernie stared at the screen in disgust. He had broken up with his girl-friend, Keisha, a few weeks before. Well, really, she broke up with him. Dumped him for a dude from Flatbush named Dante, but everybody called him Two Train. That was his rap name. And when Keisha told Ernie that Two Train wrote raps about her, Ernie started sending her a text message every day, crappy love poems, ridiculous attempts at rhyming that would put his whole "cool" thing at risk if anybody besides her, Genie, or his parents ever found out about them.

Dad laughed. "Text? Don't bother. No service out here, son."

"And no computer," Ma followed.

Ernie finally looked up, an insane expres-sion on his face. *No service? No computer?* This was bad news. BAD NEWS. And not just for Ernie, but for Genie, too. How was he gonna look stuff up now? He'd added at least sixteen new questions to his notebook since breakfast, mostly about being blind. *Now* what was he gonna do?

"So you might as well put that thing down and let her go," Ma advised. "She wasn't good enough for you anyway. Good luck with Two Train, sweetheart." Ma swatted the air, shooing the memory of Ernie's ex-girlfriend away. "What kind of rap name is Two Train anyway?"

Dad reeled the conversation back in again. "Not important. Ernie, tell your little brother about how it went down when you first met Grandpop." He grinned. "And his was way worse than yours, Genie."

Ernie tossed his phone onto the bed, looking ticked. "I don't even remember it. Y'all just say this is what happened."

"Because it did happen."

"But I was *four*."

"I know, I know." Dad was clearly getting annoyed by all of Ernie's back talk. "Forget it. I'll tell him. See, Genie, Ernie was actin' a fool, just like he is now" — Ernie sucked his teeth — "so I told him if he could just stay quiet —"

"Play the quiet game," Ma clarified.

"Be a sloth," Genie tossed in the pot.

"Right. If he could play the quiet game for twenty minutes, I would take him to Mc-Donald's." French fry bribery. That was how their parents always used to make deals with them. "So Ernie's on the floor, sloth silent, and I'm talking to your grandma. Grandpop was in the bathroom. Next thing I know, the old man came out to join us and tripped over your brother!"

"Grandpop fell right on his face," Ma

43

added, putting stacks of Genie's and Ernie's clothes — an entire *month's* worth — in the drawers of the blue dresser. Ernie's in the middle drawer. Genie's in the bottom. The top drawer was reserved for random items — handheld pencil sharpeners, school glue, masking tape, abnormally small screwdrivers, things like that.

"I thought we killed him!" she blurted.

"But nobody worried about me," Ernie added.

"Of course we did, Ernie, but you were okay. Nothing could damage *that* big head!" Dad said with a laugh, and threw a balled-up pair of socks at him. Ernie chopped them away. "You remember what Grandpop said after he fell?"

Ernie sat up. "Didn't he say something about me winning the McDonald's?"

"Yeah, he said that you deserve a week's worth of McDonald's because you were so quiet a blind man couldn't even hear you," Dad finished. "And that's how your grandfather told Ernie he was blind. Right there on the floor with a bloody lip. I know it sounds ridiculous, but that's how he likes to do it. It's just his way."

Genie glanced at Ernie with his toughest face, the one where he tightened his eyes. "And you didn't *tell* me?"

"It's your grandpop's rules," Dad reiterated. "And trust me, I learned from a young age not to break my daddy's rules. So we made Ernie promise not to tell you. Plus, we just didn't want you to be all worried about staying here."

Genie had to give it to his parents: They knew him well. He had worry issues.

"And y'all still owe me some nuggets or fries or somethin' for that, but I'll take ten bucks instead," Ernie said now. Dad shot him a look, then noticed all the *this ain't cool* on Genie's face. Because five minutes ago, Genie hadn't been worried about staying. But now . . .

"I promise, you're okay here, Genie. You really think me and your mom would leave you here if we didn't think you were gonna be fine?" Dad palmed his knees. "Plus, the old man ain't bad, for being blind. He can do just about *everything.*" He stood up and stretched his arms over his head, leaning to the left, then to the right, working the stiff out of his back.

"He can't drive a car," Genie said sharply, flipping the toy truck in his palm.

"Well —" Dad paused as he brought his arms down and waved a finger at Genie. "Careful with that. I'm serious."

"He can't drive a *car,*" Genie repeated,

setting the truck down gently on the floor. His father shoved his hands in his pockets.

"I guess you're right about that. He can't." Dad glanced at Ma, who just shrugged.

"So then he can't do everything."

Genie had proven his point.

When she finished unpacking their clothes, Ma told the boys to put the suitcase back in the car, which really meant leave grown folks to grown folks' business. As soon as they got outside, Samantha started barking like crazy. They both jumped a mile.

"Chill, Samantha," Ernie said, playing it off, trying to pretend like he didn't jump. Genie had seen him, but let him slide anyway. Ernie popped the trunk and threw the suitcase in with all the other junk their father kept back there. Spare tire, jumper cables, tools, a blanket — Dad's emergency kit that he never used because they never drove anywhere at home. Samantha kept on barking and jumping, the chain around her neck slapping dust into the air. She sounded like Dad's Honda whenever the engine froze up in the winter.

Ernie headed straight for the dog. Genie held back. There were tons of dogs in their neighborhood back home. Had to be at least ten just on their block, and we're not talking little cutesy-wutesy, yip-yap dogs. We're talking big dogs. Dogs that walk down the street like body builders. Thing was, Genie *knew* those dogs. He had grown up with them. But he and this dog, Samantha, were strangers.

She was all black except for the patch of white on her face and on each paw. But she had a pink nose. When Genie had asked Dad what kind of dog Samantha was, he just said she was a mutt. Grandma liked having her around so she'd know whenever someone was coming in the yard.

As Ernie got closer, Samantha stopped barking and just panted, her tongue dangling from her mouth like taffy, spit flying everywhere.

"Come on," Ernie called to Genie. "Her tail's waggin'. She don't wanna hurt us, man." He slowly stretched his arm out until the back of his hand was in front of Samantha's face. Samantha nosed it, sniffed, then settled down, leaving a wet streak across his knuckles.

"See?" he said, scratching behind Samantha's ears. "Just gotta let her smell you. Then she'll get comfortable. Bet she remembers me from last time I was here."

"From all the way back then?" Genie wondered if a dog's memory could be that good. Now elephants — *they* remember *all* their family members.

"Maybe." Samantha rolled over onto her back and Ernie began rubbing her pink, spotted belly.

"Yeah, but she ain't never met me before," Genie said. He took a step closer.

The screen door creaked open, and Ma and Dad came out, pausing to hug and kiss Grandma, who was promising that the boys would be fine, not to worry, and to really make the best of their time in Jamaica — Dad said they would, Ma didn't say anything — and to make sure to call as soon as they got back to Brooklyn.

"Boys, come give me my hugs," Ma said, heading toward them, arms out. Genie went first, wrapping himself around her tightly as she rubbed the back of his head.

"Everything'll be fine. You being here, me and your father . . . everything. Okay?"

Genie nodded. He wanted to believe her because she was pretty much always right. But this time, he wasn't so sure.

Then Ma called Ernie over. "You come give me some too, chump," she said. "I know you almost fourteen and everything, but you ain't too old to hug your mother." Genie let go, and Ernie came in for his hug. His wasn't as crazy as Genie's, but it was real. Ma hated fake hugs, or "pat-pats" as she called them. That's when you just reach your arm around the person and pat them on the back, but you don't squeeze. Real hugs squeeze. Then Ma grabbed Ernie by the face and kissed him on his forehead. He twisted his mouth into a frown. She smiled anyway. "Take care of your little brother, got me?"

"Of course," Ernie said. Ma knew him so well, she could tell he rolled his eyes even though he had on his shades.

"I'm serious, boy," she said with some bass in her voice.

Dad came over with his hand out. He gave Genie five, then pulled him close. Then he grabbed Ernie. "Y'all take care of each other. Remember, y'all are brothers. Understand?"

"Yeah," Ernie said.

"You too," Dad said, looking at Genie. "Got me?"

"Got you."

Dad explained that he and Ma would be calling to check in, even once they got to Jamaica. Then he told them that he loved them, then Ma said she did too, and then Grandma said she loved everybody as Dad and Ma got in the car. A straight-up love-fest. Samantha barked and barked as the car barked and barked until the engine finally turned over. Dad rolled the windows down and threw a hand up. Ma gazed at them, her eyes wet as the car pulled off.

The Honda turned toward the hill, Samantha still barking, trying to chase it but being snapped back by her chain, so Genie chased it for her. He ran behind the car for as long as he could, until it hit the slope and began bumping down to the bottom. The hill was so steep that from where Genie was standing, it looked like his parents had just driven off a cliff. He tipped to the edge and watched the brake lights blinking on and off until they disappeared.

THREE

The heat out there seemed so much hotter than what Genie and Ernie were used to in Brooklyn. Maybe it was that buildings in their neighborhood made shade, cooling down the streets, Genie thought. Here, even though there were trees everywhere, they just didn't do the trick when it came to blocking out the sun.

"I'm tellin' you, it's hotter here," Genie complained, kicking a stick toward Samantha, who sniffed it, then moved away.

"No, it's not," Ernie said. "It's all in your head."

"In my head?" Genie lifted his hand in the air. "Look. Look how much closer we are to the sun up on this hill. I feel like if I get a runnin' start, I can jump up and touch it. Shoot, I wish I could just slap it over there behind them trees."

Ernie ignored him and went on playing with Samantha, so Genie decided to escape the beating sun and go back inside.

Grandma and Grandpop were still in the kitchen. Grandma had just finished drying the breakfast dishes and was putting them back in the cupboard.

"I know it's been a long time, but eventually Ernest'll work through it. You can't make him forgive you," she was saying as Genie entered the room. Grandma and Grandpop's conversation — grown folks' business — ended right there. "Genie!" Grandma sang out. "Have a seat, and I'll fix you some iced tea." She headed for the fridge. "Y'all *do* drink tea up there in New York, right?" Genie nodded and sat in the same seat he'd sat in at breakfast, which he decided was *his* seat. Grandpop was still sitting exactly where they had left him, in *his* seat, his hands resting in his lap, listening to the radio. Fuzzy news.

"I'll get it," Grandpop said suddenly. "I'll get it," he repeated, this time softer, pushing away from the table.

Grandma stepped out of the way, cocking her head at Grandpop, confused-like. "Okay, well then, I'm gonna go make sure Samantha hasn't eaten Ernie."

"She hasn't," Genie assured her. "Matter fact, they already best friends." Grandma smiled and headed for the door anyway as

Grandpop made his way to the refrigerator. Then it hit him. How was Grandpop going to pour tea? He couldn't even *see* tea!

"I can get it," Genie quickly offered. And just like Grandpop had waved Grandma off, he did the same to Genie.

"*Boy* . . ." Grandpop raised his eyebrows well above the top of his sunglasses, letting Genie know he was serious about getting the tea himself. He turned to open the refrigerator door, and that's when Genie noticed something was sticking up from the back of his pants like a short tail. *Oh . . . my . . . G* — it was a pistol — the handle of a pistol! Genie had never actually seen a gun in real life, just on the cop shows Ma was always watching, or in movies — action flicks, sci-fi flicks, and even the scary flicks Genie and Ernie weren't supposed to be watching. Genie was as curious about that pistol as he was about the honey badger. And like always, it sparked questions, but he didn't have his notebook.

Questions to remember: *What's a blind man doing with a gun? Why would Grandpop have a gun, period?* Genie flat-out stared, but when Grandpop closed the fridge, a big jug of tea in his hand, Genie turned away fast, just in case the old man could somehow see him. It was ridiculous, Genie knew. And sure, he was *told* Grandpop was blind, but he wanted to play it safe — the whole blind thing might've been a bluff, a theory that seemed a lot less silly after what happened next.

Slices of lemon sloshed from side to side in the jug like little yellow lily pads in a brown lake as Grandpop reached into a cabinet and grabbed a glass jar, an empty one, first try. Running his hand along the mouth of the jar, he started pouring the tea in. Perfectly. Genie was back in staring mode as Grandpop lifted the jug higher and higher, a waterfall of tea all landing in the quickly filling jar. Just before it reached the very top, he stopped. He put the jug back in the refrigerator and set the jar in front of Genie. Without. Spilling. A. Single. Drop. Then he sat back down like it was no big deal. *Whoa.*

"Go on, then," Grandpop said, inching the jar closer. Genie leaned over and slurped from the top — it was so full he knew *he'd* spill some of it if he tried to pick it up. The ridges felt funny on his mouth, made him feel like he was drinking out of a mayonnaise container. And the tea was . . . *sweet.* Too sweet, even though on any day of the week, Genie could take down three or four rocket pops with no problem.

"Good?" Grandpop asked.

"Uh-huh," Genie said, choking the tea down. He didn't want to tell his grandfather that it tasted like liquid sugar. After embarrassing himself at breakfast, Genie had come to the conclusion that the truth could sometimes make things weird.

"Does it need more sugar?" Grandpop asked. "You like your grits sweet, like Wood used to, so you might like your tea like he liked his too — sweet." As if the tea wasn't already a spoonful of sugar away from being syrup!

"No, no," Genie eeked out, trying his best to swallow another mouthful. "This . . . this is . . . fine."

"Good," Grandpop said, leaning back into his chair again. Genie wondered if it was uncomfortable for Grandpop to sit with a gun tucked in the back of his waistband, or if he was ever scared about accidentally shooting himself in the butt. *OUCH!* But Grandpop didn't seem bothered by it at all. He turned the radio down. "So let's talk, Little Wood." He just threw that out there as if the nickname, Little Wood, was already a thing. Genie frowned but let that slide too. Old people got to pretty much call you whatever they wanted. It was the only awesome part about being old, Genie figured.

"Your mom said you're a little scared to be here with me," Grandpop now said.

Dang! Genie dipped his head fast, taking another slurp of the tea, wondering what the heck made his mother tell Grandpop that. He didn't want his grandfather to think anything bad about him, like he was a punk or something.

"And that's okay," Grandpop added, to Genie's surprise. "But you know the best way to get over fear? Confront it."

Genie kept slurping, big icky sweet slurps. If he just kept drinking, he wouldn't have to answer.

"So confront me."

Genie nearly spat the tea out. "What you mean, *confront?*"

"I don't know — ask me anything you wanna know. Anything. Once you get some answers, you might feel a little better about being here."

"Um . . . okay," Genie said, his mind, however, going completely blank. He wished his notebook weren't upstairs; he'd written so many questions for Grandpop. Questions like:

When did you get blind? and,

Did it hurt?

Plus there was the newest question that he'd just come up with, the one tick-tick-

ticking in his brain ready to explode out of his mouth — *What's a blind man doing with a gun?*

Asking questions usually wasn't a hard thing for Genie to do because he always had them. Always. Ma and Dad said it was a good thing, but it drove Ernie crazy. Ernie always said Genie asked too many questions. Ma said Ernie only said that because he never had enough answers. And now, here Genie was, with someone who *wanted* to hear all his questions, who was *asking* him for questions, and for some reason he was nervous. Nervous!

Grandpop was looking at Genie — toward him — expectantly.

"I can ask anything?" Genie stalled for time, lifting the jar and taking another sip, trying not to make a face even though he was pretty sure that Grandpop couldn't see his face. How much sugar was in this stuff? Ma, the sugar police, probably would've flipped if she tasted this!

"Shoot."

"Okay." Genie decided to just go for it. "When did you get blind?"

"Twenty years ago." And just like that, the question floodgate opened. Party time.

"How?"

"Glaucoma. It's a disease that destroys

your vision."

What? You can get a disease that can make you *blind*? Genie was horrified. Mental note: *Look up glaucoma.* But what he said was, "Oh. Did it, uh, hurt?"

"Going blind? Nah. It was like every day would get a little darker and a little darker until one day I woke up and everything was just . . . black."

"Were you . . . scared?"

"Not really."

"Why not? I would be."

"Don't do no good to be scared. I knew it was coming and I couldn't stop it, so I just had to deal with it and move on."

The glass had started to sweat and was now dripping on Genie's legs.

"So . . . you remember what Dad looks like?"

"Of course. He looks like his mother."

"You know what I look like?"

"Come here. I'll tell you." Grandpop reached out and palmed Genie's cheeks like Ma did tomatoes in the grocery store. He ran his fingers over Genie's eyes, nose, and mouth. "You look like your daddy."

Genie *did* look like Dad. Ernie looked like Ma but was lucky enough to have Dad's smile.

"How you know that?" Genie asked.

"Magic."

Please. I'm eleven, not six, Genie wanted to say, but instead just kept on with the questions.

"How you pour that tea?"

" 'Cause I know where the glass is."

"But how you know when to stop?"

"Because I can hear it. The closer it gets to the top, the deeper the sound."

"But how you know *when* to stop?"

Grandpop shrugged. "I just guessed."

"Dad says you can do a bunch of stuff."

"I hear you can too."

"But he tells me you can do stuff like, cook."

"Sure can."

"But . . . how? You not scared of burning yourself, or burning the whole house down?" Genie looked at the peeling walls. The sea-green color was broken up by segments of white where the paint had flaked off, shaped like continents on a map. Genie imagined the "wall world" burning.

"Nope. I just do it. I can feel the heat from the flame. I know where the food is. I know where the pots and pans are. No big deal."

"But, well, how you know where everything is?"

"Because it's been that way since me and your grandma been married. Pots been in the same place since your daddy was a little boy," Grandpop explained.

"But still, you don't never forget?" Genie went on.

"Nope."

"Never?"

"Never."

"But what if you do?"

"I won't." Grandpop reached in his shirt pocket and pulled out a white handkerchief that wasn't really all that white anymore and patted his forehead. It was definitely hot in the house. Almost as hot as it was outside. Almost as hot as it got in the kitchen at Genie and Ernie's house whenever Ma was cooking. But the tea was helping, and the little drip-drops from the glass on Genie's legs were helping even more.

"Next question."

"What did Grandma do before she had to take care of you?"

"She don't take care of me," Grandpop snapped, his voice jumping to a higher pitch.

Genie sat back fast. "Right. But, uh, what did she used to do before?"

"She was a nurse."

"Oh, good. So she can take care of you."

"She *don't* take care of me," Grandpop snapped again.

Suddenly the phone rang. Grandpop put

his hand up, making it clear that he wanted Genie to hold on. The phone started speaking in a robot voice, calling out the numbers of whoever was on the line. Genie could hear the voice in the kitchen, in Grandma and Grandpop's bedroom, and even in the bathroom. It was like they were surrounded by bots all shouting out numbers, which was both weird and cool.

"Who is it?" Grandma called through the screen door.

"Just the church," Grandpop said.

"Why didn't you answer it?" Genie asked. He figured people always answered the phone whenever the church was calling. Just seemed like the right thing to do. Maybe they were going to tell Grandpop about a miracle to fix his eyes.

" 'Cause you and me shootin' the breeze. Plus they just want to pray for the sick, and that's nice and all, but I ain't sick," Grandpop told him. And before Genie could even think on whether or not Grandpop being blind was, in fact, a sickness — especially since he said glaucoma was a *disease* — another question popped out.

"How did you know it was the church? You memorize phone numbers?"

"Yep."

"Even mine?"

"Even yours."

"I don't believe that."

"Why not?"

"Because you never call," Genie said. "Grandma does, but you don't."

Grandpop looked toward the window, which was kind of weird since he couldn't see out of it. He ran his tongue along the top of his teeth, then turned back toward Genie.

"Well, I know it, still."

"Then what is it?"

"Um . . . uh . . ." He tapped his forehead with his pointer finger. "I'm not sure. Shucks. I swear . . . this has never happened."

"See?" Genie knew Grandpop couldn't have known.

Grandpop poked him in the arm. How did he know his arm was even there, anyway? Then Grandpop said, "I'm joking. 646-555-8349. I can tell you your daddy's cell, your mama's cell, and their work numbers too, if you like, boss. *And* your address."

"What is it then? My address." Genie couldn't seem to stop testing him.

"It's 346 Mason Street, Brooklyn, New York, 11233."

The man on the radio was laughing about something, then said, *"It's just unbelievable,"* and even though the announcer was talking about news, it seemed like he was talking about Grandpop. Genie smiled and took another sip of tea.

"So what else you got?" Grandpop prompted.

"Okay . . ." Genie thought madly for a next question. Got it. "Why you wear those sunglasses if you can't see no sun?"

Grandpop laughed just like the man on the radio had. "Why do I wear them? Because they look cool. Why else?"

That was the same reason Ernie wore his all the time — total Pete and Repeat!

Genie looked at his reflection in Grandpop's shades. Then he held up a finger and moved it close to Grandpop's face. He just had to try it.

"Get your finger out my face and ask the next question," Grandpop demanded, not in a mean way, but definitely in a serious way. Genie yanked his hand back so fast he banged it on the table.

"Ah!" he hissed, flicking his hand around like it was on fire. Grandpop just grinned.

"Okay," Genie said, massaging his fingers. "Do you just sit here all day?"

"Do I what?! Of course not, that's no way to live. Plus, this seat is too hard on my old butt."

Genie wanted to follow with, *But you got a gun back there, so don't that hurt it?,* but for some reason he just couldn't bring himself to say it, so he asked, "How do you know where your room is, though? Or what if you gotta go to the bathroom?"

"I'm only blind, son. My junk still works." Grandpop's shoulders began to bounce up and down.

"Not like that!" Genie yelped, busting out laughing. "I mean, how?"

"I count."

"Count?" Genie raised one eyebrow. "Math? I hate math."

"I used to. But now I love it because I have to use it every day."

"What you mean?"

"Counting. From my room to the kitchen, thirteen steps. From my room to the bathroom, ten steps. From the kitchen to the bathroom, sixteen steps. From the kitchen to the front door, eleven steps. It's all counting."

"That's cool."

It *was* cool. And it was also cool that Grandpop was letting Genie ask all these questions without getting upset about it. Ernie would've punched him by now, and by the way, where was Ernie? Still out there with the dog? It'd been forever, plus Dad made it very clear that they were supposed to look out for each other. Plus, Genie was nosy. Plain and simple. So he asked Grandpop for a time-out while he went to check where Ernie was.

Out on the porch, Genie was surprised to discover that it was actually hotter *inside* the house than outside. A small bird hopped along one of the wooden floor planks. It had deep-blue feathers along its back all the way down to its tail, which seemed to split in two like a snake's tongue. The blue of the bird came up over its head and eyes like a hood, but under the beak and all along the chest the feathers turned reddish-orange. Genie had never seen a bird like it. He was used to pigeons, birds that matched the color of concrete. Nothing like this, a bird that matched the color of the sky and the country dirt. It pecked at something in between the cracks. Genie slowly squatted to get a better look without scaring it off. But of course that didn't go as planned. In one quick, fluid movement, the bird lifted its head, turned it all the way around, spied Genie, and flew away.

Genie jumped off the porch and headed around the side of the house to where Ernie was stroking the top of Samantha's head and whispering in her ear like a weirdo.

"What you doin'?" Genie asked.

"Teachin' her some stuff," Ernie said.

"By talkin' to her?"

"Yep. There's a whole TV show dedicated to this method," Ernie said, all confident; he had a way of saying stuff that made Genie believe it, even if it really didn't make much sense.

"If you say so." Then, looking around and not seeing Grandma, Genie asked where she was.

"I'ont know. Probably on the other side of the house," Ernie said, then began that whispering business with the dog again. Genie had only come out to see if Ernie was cool, and he was cool, so Genie was cool.

Back at the front door, Genie remembered what Grandpop said about counting his steps and decided to test it. It took him thirteen steps to get to the kitchen. Grandpop said it took him eleven, but Genie figured that was because his legs were longer. Grandpop was still at the table, turning the dial on his radio, trying to clear up the fuzz.

"So, has your brother been eaten?" he asked.

"Nope." Genie sat back down, feeling good about the fact that he had checked on

Ernie and was ready to dive back in with the questions.

"Good. Now, where were we in this inter-rogation?" Grandpop asked.

"Interrogation?"

"I mean, interview," Grandpop teased. Then he slipped in, "Detective."

Detective Genie Harris. Or maybe Detec-tive Little Wood. Either way, it was kinda cool.

"Okay . . . um . . . let's see." Genie put his hands together and tried to think. "Does Grandma pick out your clothes?"

"Why, you don't like 'em?"

"They're okay."

"Good, 'cause I pick 'em out myself." Grandpop made a fuss at brushing nothing off his shoulder.

"They all black and white?"

He laughed. "Ha! No way!"

"Then how do you match them up?" Genie asked.

"Funny you should ask, Detective. Touch right here." Grandpop unrolled his shirt sleeve and held the cuff out. "Right here. Feel that?"

Genie ran his finger over the fabric, hit-ting a cluster of little bumps, like the shirt had invisible goose pimples.

"What's that feel like?" Grandpop asked.

"I don't know," Genie answered, unsure.

"Close your eyes," Grandpop instructed.

Genie closed his eyes and rubbed his fingers over the same bumpy spot. He didn't know what he was supposed to be figuring out.

"What is it?"

Genie opened his eyes. He had nothing.

"It's a *W*. Stands for white. That's how I know this is a white shirt I got on," Grandpop explained.

Genie rubbed his fingers over the little knots one more time, and then it became clear. It was, in fact, a *W*.

"Your grandma started sewing initials into everything for me when we found out I was going blind. Fancy little stitches called french knots. A blue shirt has a *B*. A red shirt, an *R*. My trousers have the letters sewn into the waistband, and even my socks have them. So I never look crazy."

"But you *are* crazy, remember?" Genie reminded him.

Grandpop laughed again and put his hand on top of Genie's head. He did it with no hesitation, like he knew exactly where his head was! How'd he do that?

"Yeah, but the key is to never *look* crazy." Grandpop rolled his sleeve back up to his elbow. "Anything else?" he challenged.

The iced tea was almost gone, and it had actually started tasting pretty good. As a matter of fact, Genie wanted more. Thing was, Ma was big on not being too greedy when you're at other people's houses, so Genie didn't want to ask Grandpop for it. But dang, it was *so* hot and the tea was *so* cold.

"Yeah. What's your name?"

"Grandpop."

"No, your real name."

Grandpop looked at Genie, and for a second it seemed like he could actually see him. Like, he *looked* at him. "Brooke."

Genie had heard Grandma say the same thing, but he hadn't been sure he'd heard her right.

"Brooke? Like the girl's name?"

Grandpop flashed a thin smile. "Is it a girl's name if it's my name?"

Genie had never really thought about it that way. He had never heard of a man named Brooke but could relate to it being a girl's name because Genie was a girl's name too. There were some guys back home who teased him about it, that is, until Ernie came around. Then they quieted all that *Your mom wanted you to be a girl* and *Genie, Genie, the girl with a weenie* stuff down. But Grandpop had a girl's name as a guy's name and was cool with it, so maybe his name wasn't necessarily a girl's name after all. It was just . . . his.

"Guess not," Genie said at last. He took the final swig of the tea jar — it still felt weird to drink from a jar. "Wait — one last question?"

Grandpop whipped the cloth from his shirt pocket again, like a magician does before turning it into a bird. He wiped his neck with it, then his forehead, then stuffed it back into its place. "Last one."

"What was your job?"

Grandpop folded his arms and leaned back until the front legs of his chair rose up off the floor. "I was in the army. Fought in Vietnam. First Battalion, Sixth Infantry. My position was rifleman."

"Like, *rifle* rifles? Your job was to shoot rifles?"

"Pretty much."

Their dad had told him and Ernie stories about Grandpop teaching him how to shoot when he was younger, but he never said that it was because the old man was an expert, that it was pretty much his *job* to shoot. This, of course, set Genie off.

"Is that why you have a gun in your pants?" he asked with what seemed like perfect timing. But his excitement wouldn't let him wait for an answer. He just barreled on. "Wait . . . so can you teach me how to shoot?"

Grandpop froze. Then he *looked* looked at Genie again.

"Now, Little Wood —" Grandpop cleared his throat. "I'm afraid you done already asked your last question."

Four

Question time over, Genie went back outside, but this time his grandmother had something to say about it. She stopped him on the porch. "Now, listen here. You ain't gon' keep runnin' in and out of my house all day, hear me? You either gon' be in, or out, so which will it be?"

Genie squinted in the bright light to scope out Ernie, who was now shaking Samantha's paw, before responding.

"Out."

"Good. So stay out. I don't wanna be chasin' flies round the kitchen all afternoon."

As Grandma went in the house, Genie checked the porch for that sky/dirt bird again, but it wasn't there, so he headed out into the yard, farther and farther until he reached the spot where the cliff began. It was as if someone had snapped the land off, jagged and uneven like torn bread. The drop was steep. But what was even more fascinating than the cliff was the view. The sky seemed bigger than he had ever seen it, full of white clouds Genie pretended were in the shape of pistols — Grandpop still on his mind — until he snapped out of it and they turned back into big shapeless cotton balls. And there were so many trees, lush and green, peppered by only a few houses. A yellow one with black shutters. A white one like Grandma and Grandpop's, the roof caved in and half the house charred black. Two red houses side by side. Those were the ones that really caught Genie's eye. They were at the very bottom of the hill, across the narrow road that led to the entrance of his grandparents' property. There was someone on the porch of one of the houses, a person down on all fours, banging on something.

"Hey, Ernie," Genie called out. "Check this out."

"What?" Ernie said, jogging over. He looked down the hill. "Who's that?"

"You think *I* know?"

"Doesn't look like a grown-up," Ernie said, putting his hand to his brow to block the sun. "Is that a girl?"

"Looks like one," Genie said as they both stared at the girl and the red house as if they had never seen a girl, or a red house, before. A green car came up the road and turned into the yard of the second red house. The girl raised her head and waved at the driver, who tooted the horn, then bumped through the grass around to the back of the house.

"What's she doin'?" Ernie asked, now the one with all the questions.

Genie didn't answer, as he was trying to figure out the exact same thing. Judging by the constant banging, she was either fixing something or breaking something. Maybe a piece of wood from the porch had come loose and she was replacing it. There were a few cracked ones on Grandma and Grand-pop's porch that could use a little touch-up, so maybe that's what she was up to, Genie was thinking when Ernie slapped his arm.

"Come on." And he started down the hill. Genie scrambled after him, trying to step easy, but dang, that hill was steep. Too steep. Gravity yanked them both toward the bottom a lot faster than they had expected. They started to slide and *whoa, whoa, whoa,* doing everything they could to stay upright. Ernie had better balance — you had to have it to be any good at karate. I mean, he could stand on one leg for seventy-four seconds. Genie had counted. Genie, on the other hand, didn't have that talent, and after a few seconds of sliding down the hill, he slipped. And let me tell you, there's a big difference between a slip and a slide. A slide is an almost-slip. But a slip . . . now that's a problem.

A slip leads to a fall, but Genie didn't just *fall.* He fell, and *tumbled.* Feet over head, feet over head, feet over head, over and over again, grunting and thumping his way to the bottom, leaving a cloud of dust and burnt, dried-up grass trailing after him.

"Genie!" Ernie cried, cautiously sliding as quickly as he could to the bottom. Genie lay flat on his back, his arms spread out as if he was making a snow angel — a grass angel.

"Genie!" Ernie repeated, panicked, now standing over him. "You okay?"

Genie opened his eyes, his chest heaving. "Arrgh," he moaned, reaching out for Ernie's hand. "I'm okay, I'm okay. Stupid hill."

But once Ernie got him back to his feet and made sure that he wasn't broken all up, the fear turned into funny. At least to Ernie, who tried his best to fight his smile.

"It ain't funny!" Genie said, embarrassed. He examined his knees and elbows for scrapes and blood. "You better not laugh."

"Ain't nobody laughin', man," Ernie said,

a gumpy grin smeared across his face.

"Hey!" A voice cut right between them, reminding them why they'd come down the hill in the first place. Genie looked up. Across the road was a girl, the hammering girl. She glared at them, still on her porch but now holding the hammer up like a weapon. She was dressed in cutoffs and a T-shirt. No shoes, no socks. Her skin was as dark and shiny as a wet street, and so was her hair. She had it yanked back in a messy ponytail. "Who y'all?"

Genie and Ernie stood frozen like two statues, one dustier than the other.

Ernie got it together first. "Sorry," he said. "Sorry, sorry. Didn't mean to scare you." He put his hands up as though making sure she knew they had come in peace.

The girl, who looked about Ernie's age, wiped sweat from her forehead and squinted as if he and Genie weren't actually there, as if they were a mirage. She raised her hammer even higher when Ernie jumped a small ditch and walked across the road into her yard, Genie following, slapping grass and dirt off almost every part of his body.

Reaching the porch, undeterred by the hammer, Ernie introduced himself. "I'm Ernie, and this brilliant acrobat here is my brother, Genie." He waited for a smile. Got nothing. "Um . . . we visitin' our grandparents for the month." He pointed back up the hill.

"Who?" the girl said, lowering the hammer, but just by an inch. "Ma and Pop Harris?"

Genie nodded and wondered if the girl was somehow related, since she referred to Grandma and Grandpop as Ma and Pop.

"Yeah," Ernie said, nodding. "You know them?"

"Everybody know 'em," the girl said, now setting the hammer on the porch. "So y'all their kin, huh?"

"I . . ." Ernie looked at Genie. Genie shrugged. "Kin? What you mean?"

"Kin," she repeated. "Lord, y'all don't know what kin is?" She hopped up. "Means family. Related. Blood," she rattled off, flashing a *duh* face.

"Oh, yeah," Ernie said, trying to regain some cool. "We their kin."

"Well, y'all ain't from round here, obviously, so where y'all from?"

Genie spoke up. "Brooklyn."

"Brooklyn," Ernie confirmed, a step behind. There's something about calling out Brooklyn that makes you feel like you've grown a few inches, maybe sprouted some hairs on your chin, or an extra lump in your

77

bicep. And when you say it, your whole body goes into the word.

"Never heard of it," the girl said, her eyelids lowered to the *so what* level.

"*What?*" Ernie bawked.

"Nah, nah, of course I know where Brooklyn is. You city folk just always be thinkin' we country folk don't know nothin'. But we be knowin'." She smiled. "We be knowin'." Colorful rubber bands woven over metal braces covered her teeth. A rainbow in her mouth.

"I'm Tess, by the way." Now she jumped off the porch, landing a foot away from them. "So why y'all come down here?"

"To see our grandparents," Genie said, thinking Ernie had already made that clear when he said they were "kin."

"No, I mean, down *here*. What y'all want?"

"Well, we saw you bangin' from up there. And so we were just wonderin' what you were doin'." After Genie said it, he realized how creepy it sounded. Like maybe he and Ernie were stalkers.

"Fixin' somethin'?" Ernie added quick.

"Nah," Tess said, looking back at the red porch. "I ain't fixin' nothin'. I'm makin' some stuff."

She climbed back up to her workstation,

the boys cautiously following. On the porch were two coffee cans, a red cup, the hammer, a pair of wire cutters, and one nail.

"In this can" — Tess held one up — "are beer bottle caps."

She took a cap out and set it on one of the wooden porch planks. Then, without any kind of warning, she took the hammer and *BAM! BAM! BAM!* whacked the cap, over and over again until it was flat. Both Ernie and Genie jumped, then tried to recover quickly so Tess wouldn't notice. Especially Ernie. Ernie *really* didn't want her to notice, Genie could tell. Tess held the mashed cap up and looked proud, as if she had just dug up a piece of gold.

"Perfect," she declared, setting it back down.

Genie thought it looked like a coin from a different country. He had never seen any coins from anywhere else, but he wouldn't have been surprised if quarters in Mozambique looked like flattened beer caps.

"Then," Tess went on, "what I do is, I take this nail here, and put it right at the top of the cap, like this." She positioned the nail near the edge of the beer cap. "Then I make a hole." She tapped the nail lightly with the hammer, until it punctured the metal.

Now she reached into the red cup and

pulled out a little fishhook. "After that I take one of these and put it through the hole, but first ya gotta clip the ends or they might stick ya." Using the wire cutters, she snipped the pointy end of the hook, then stuck it into the hole she had just made in the bottle cap. "Then you twist it, like this, so it don't come out." She twisted the hook a few times, then dangled it up in front of Genie and Ernie. "Boom, you got a earring."

"A earring?" Ernie said, holding his hand out. Tess gave it to him.

"Yep." She held the other coffee can up. It was full of them. "I sell these bad boys down at the market. Y'all wanna try? I mean, I usually wouldn't offer 'cause, y'know, it's bad for business. But I doubt *y'all* finna cut into my profits. Plus, y'all kin to Ma and Pop Harris, so I'll make an exception."

Ernie jumped to it so fast that Genie knew Ernie's old girlfriend was about to be history. Too bad for Ernie, he had never actually used a hammer. He was pretty decent at smashing the cap flat, but when it came to hitting the nail, he definitely had some issues. As he dropped the hammer down, missing over and over again, Genie started firing off the questions that had been bouncing around in his head since Tess started this whole explanation.

"Where you get all these fishhooks from?" he asked first, hovering over Ernie, who kept bumping at Genie's leg, trying to get him to move back.

"Where I get 'em from? From a fisherman, where else?"

"Well, what does he use to fish with if you got all the hooks?" Genie persisted. Why would a fisherman give up all his fishing hooks? That was like a basketball player giving up his basketball. Just didn't make sense.

"Not just any fisherman. My daddy. And he don't fish no more. Roanoke River too far away, plus there ain't been no real bites in a long time."

"Well, where you get fish from then?" Genie now wanted to know.

Ernie shuddered, clearly frustrated with both Genie's questions and the nail he was struggling to hit.

"Uhhh, let me think, city boy. The store!" Tess teased. Ernie laughed at that, finally hitting the nail through the bottle cap. Genie cracked an awkward smile, embarrassed. But not so much that he couldn't ask another question.

"What about the bottle caps? You got a lot of 'em. Where you get 'em from?"

"I know you not gon' believe this, but I drank all those beers." Tess patted her belly.

This time Genie laughed, because he knew she was joking.

"Seriously," Ernie joined in. "Where *did* you get all these?"

Tess picked up the green bottle cap Ernie had just flattened and holed. She snipped a fish hook, slipped the hook in the hole, twist, twist, twist, then tossed it in the "finished" can.

"Come on. I'll show you."

She hopped off the side of the porch and headed around to the back of the second red house, the one right next to hers. Genie and Ernie trailed after her, exchanging *What the . . . ?* looks. There were a few cars parked back there in no particular order on what used to be grass, but was now mostly dirt, and tire tracks made it clear that there were usually a lot more than a few cars there. Tess led them up the back steps. A small sign with MARLON'S painted on it hung from a nail against a white door, which Tess now pushed open and walked through, Ernie and Genie at her heels. It only took half a second for them to realize that they hadn't walked into a house. They had walked into a bar.

"Hey, Jim," Tess said, heading for the counter as if it was no big deal that she was a kid . . . in a bar. The man, Jim, was skinny all over — arms, face, neck — but he had a big belly. Like a having-a-baby-in-a-few-days belly. There was another man there, sitting at the bar. He was old, had a gut as big as Jim's and a long gray beard. Black Santa. Tess walked past him and pulled out three stools. She hopped onto the middle one and patted the two on either side of her, a signal for Genie and Ernie to come sit.

"Tess the Mess!" the bartender greeted her. "Who ya friends?"

Ernie and Genie took their places on the stools.

"This here's Ernie and Genie, Ma and Pop Harris's grandkids. They from New York."

"Ohhhhhh," Jim said. "New York, huh? Well then, I gotta give you boys the North Hill Special."

"Oh that's okay, we good," Ernie said, confidently waving the man off.

"Come on, now. You boys cool with a little drank, yeah?"

"Make it three!" Tess said, slapping her hands on the bar, excited. Genie and Ernie exchanged another *What the . . . ?* How was it even possible for kids to order drinks at a bar? Maybe it was a country thing? Because in New York you couldn't even *sit* at a bar if you weren't twenty-one. One time when Genie and Ernie were hanging out with Dad, they popped into a restaurant for a quick bite. The place was packed, so Dad asked if they could sit at the bar, just for lunch. The answer — no.

"Three Specials comin' right up!"

"I don't —" Ernie, now less confident, started.

"Shhhhh," Tess quieted Ernie. "You ain't finna come down here to North Hill, sit your stank city butts at our bar, and not have a Special."

Ernie swallowed the rest of his words. Genie played Repeat and hoped he wouldn't get drunk on his first sip. He had seen the drunks in his neighborhood. They all looked so relaxed but talked so angry. Like, yelling, but not saying words. Just sounds.

Besides the oldies playing low on the radio, there was a buzzing coming from the door every few seconds. Genie looked over and noticed a lantern-looking thing glowing above the door frame. Tess caught him gazing.

"It's a zapper."

"A zapper?"

"Yeah. For flies. They love that blue light. Every time you hear that buzz, that's another fly going bye-bye, off to fly heaven."

Tess put her hand to her lips and blew a kiss at it. "Thank you, fly zapper." While Tess turned her attention back to the bartender, Genie stared at the glowing blue light. *Buzz.* Cringe.

A few moments later three Specials were sliding across the wooden bar. Black Santa took a few gulps from his own glass, the same kind of glass that now sat in front of Genie, Ernie, and Tess. The same color liquid, too — golden, bubbly. No straws. The man looked at Genie, then lifted his glass.

"Cheers, young buck."

Genie nodded awkwardly and looked over to Ernie, waiting for him to take the first sip. Ernie lifted the glass to his mouth. Tess flashed her rubber rainbow smile.

Ernie didn't say anything. He just raised an eyebrow and smirked, letting Genie know it was okay to take a sip.

Genie recognized the taste instantly.

"Ginger beer?" he asked, surprised. Whenever they ordered Jamaican food at home, Ma always got ginger beer with it. It was the perfect soda for a spicy food, and apparently, for tricking naive city boys like Genie and Ernie.

Tess and Jim burst into a howl.

"City boys," Jim scoffed, holding his hand up.

"City boys!" Tess repeated, completing the high five.

Genie flushed, embarrassed once more, but also super happy to have that ginger beer because the thirst was real.

Buzz went the zapper again.

"Listen, shorty," Jim now said to Tess, his laughter tapering off. "I've only got a few. You're early today." He reached behind the bar and pulled out a ziplock bag with a few bottle caps in it. "Tubs there needs to drink more beer," he added, loud enough for Black Santa to hear. The bearded man scowled at Jim and held his fist up.

"It's cool," Tess said. "I was just poppin' in to show these guys what was up." She took another chug of her soda, then hopped off the stool. She was a hopper, Genie thought. "My daddy here?"

Jim took her glass, tossed the leftover in the sink. "Yeah, he downstairs. Want me to get him?"

"Nah, it's cool. I'll see him later."

Ernie and Genie slid off their stools. "Thank you," Ernie said, taking a final swig.

"Yeah, thank you," from Genie, extra genuine because he *was* thankful — thankful and relieved. Relieved the Special wasn't beer. Well, not *real* beer, anyway. So relieved.

Jim reached out for a shake. "Anytime," he said. "Pleasure to meet you boys." His palms felt rough, like he had been smashing bottle caps flat too, but without a hammer. "And welcome to the country."

They had only been in the bar for fifteen minutes, but during that time, the big blue sky had become a big gray sky. The wind had picked up, and the smell of rain ghosted through the air like dinner cooking. As soon as they got outside, they heard Grandma, standing at the edge of the cliff, hollering their names. They said bye to Tess and as the rain began to sprinkle down, Ernie and Genie scrambled back up the hill.

FIVE

"Where were y'all?" Grandma asked as Ernie and Genie huffed their way to the top. The hill was definitely way harder to walk up than to walk down — or fall down — and Genie was surprised at how out of breath he was. There were no hills in Brooklyn. Not like this. At least not in Genie and Ernie's part.

"Down there, hangin' out with some girl named Tess," Genie told her, sucking in air as Grandma proceeded to march them back to the house. "You know her, 'cause she said she know you."

The screen door slapped the frame as Grandma closed the wooden door behind them.

"Yes, baby, I know her," she said, grabbing Ernie by the shoulder and steering him away from the kitchen. Without elaborating on Tess, she went on, "Ain't neither one of y'all 'bout to walk in *my* kitchen with all that outside on your hands. Hit the bathroom and wash up. Been out there with that dog and God knows what else." She said it the same way she had said it to Dad at breakfast.

Then *BOOM!* Thunder. Loud enough to shake the walls. Loud enough to scare the nails out of the floor and peel back the linoleum. Genie looked up at the bathroom ceiling as if he could see the clouds through it. As he scrubbed his hands clean, the thunder hit two more times, back to back, like the sky was literally cracking open.

"Your mama and daddy called. They made it back home safely. And it's a good thing they left early, missed this here storm," Grandma said when Genie and Ernie came into the kitchen. She looked up at the ceiling just as Genie had done a few moments before. "Lord, I hope it don't be too bad. Glad I started dinner early, 'cause ain't nothin' worse than bein' hungry in the dark."

"Got that right," Grandpop said, coming from a door just off from the living room — which was just off from the kitchen — glass in hand. It wasn't his bedroom door, or a closet door. It was a different door. One that Genie hadn't even noticed until that moment.

"What's in there?" Genie asked in his usual nosy way. Ernie didn't seem to care; he was poking around by the stove, seeing what was for dinner.

Grandpop pushed a key into the knob and turned it. Then he gave the knob a rattle to make sure the door was locked.

"Nunya bidness," Grandpop snarled, but playfully. He slipped the keys into his pocket and motioned for Genie to sit. Genie, of course, now wondered what was in that room. On top of that, he still wondered about that gun he had seen earlier, and reminded himself to tell Ernie about it. And on top of *both* of those, he wondered what was in Grandpop's cup. That vinegary smell sure wasn't sweet tea. As a matter of fact, he didn't really wonder what it was at all. He knew exactly what it was. That smell — the same smell Genie had just gotten more than a whiff of in MARLON'S — reminded him of Ms. Swanson, the drunk lady who hung out at the Laundromat back home.

Grandma shook a little bit of this and a little bit of that into the pots on the stove, shooing Ernie away, telling him to go sit down. While she cooked up the food — the aroma of onions, peppers, and garlic over-powering the stench of Grandpop's liquor — Grandpop cooked up a few stories.

Memories and jokes about how he used to be a better cook than Grandma, but how nowadays she had a leg up on him, or as he put it, "a two-eyed advantage." Unbelievable tales about being a child and watching his father slaughter and gut pigs from "the rooter to the tooter." But most of the stories had to do with all the craziness his sons — Dad and his brother, Wood, which Genie found out was short for Sherwood — got into when they were kids.

"Lemme tell y'all 'bout this boy," Grandpop began. "Gary Daniels, down the road there, who used to always pick on the younger kids after school. He was big for a child. Hell, he was big for a grown-up!" Grandpop took a sip from his glass, his face twisting up as he swallowed. "Anyway, this boy, Gary — everybody called him Cake — came up to your daddy one day. I think Ernest was in the third grade at the time, and Wood was in the sixth, and I think Cake was in the eighth or ninth but he looked like he was old enough to sign up for the military. Cake came up to Ernest and started pattin' his pockets, aimin' to take whatever Ernest had, which wasn't much because we ain't have much to give 'im. Now this here is what Ernest told me. He said Wood came out of nowhere and whopped Cake in the back of the head with a book as hard as he could."

"Oh man!" Ernie said, leaning forward.

"Probably knocked him slam out!" Genie added, hyped.

"Knock him out? Cake was *huge!*" Grandpop's voice went high. "All that did was tick him off! Wood came home with the blackest eye I've ever seen. *And* a busted lip. *And* he was limpin'."

"Dannnnng. Uncle Wood shoulda learned how to block!" Ernie threw his hands up and demonstrated a few of his favorite karate blocks, clearly forgetting for a moment that Grandpop couldn't see.

"What about Dad?" Genie asked.

Grandpop picked up his glass and swirled the liquid around. "Not a scratch. And you know what Wood said? He said, 'I'd rather Cake beat on me than on my little brother.'" Genie watched Grandpop sip his drink again, and thought about how proud Grandpop seemed to be of Dad and Uncle Wood. Which also made Genie think about how unproud Dad seemed to be of Grandpop earlier.

"Exactly," Ernie said, puffed up. "Except ain't nobody gonna beat on either one of *us.*" He slapped Genie lightly on the arm, then cracked his knuckles.

Genie felt a smile coming on account of Ernie's words, but he held it in and asked instead, "So nothing ever happened to Cake?"

Thunder boomed and Grandpop braced himself on the edge of the table. It was only for a second but Genie caught him.

"Oh, something happened, all right," Grandpop said, trying to regain his calm. "See, they all grew up. And Wood joined the army. And one day, when your daddy was in high school and Wood was home after basic training, they bumped into Cake at the fair. They had a few words, 'cause see, Wood could never let things go. He got that from me. So when he saw Cake, they said whatever they said, and then Wood gave him the blues."

"Beat him down?" Ernie asked.

"Blew his daggone candles out!" Grandpop cheesed and reached out for Ernie's hand.

"That's what I'm talkin' 'bout," Ernie said, slapping Grandpop's hand.

At that, Grandma turned all the knobs on the stove until they clicked, turning the flames off. "Okay, that's enough of this heathen talk. Dinner's ready." She pulled a stack of plates from the cabinet, then loaded each with baked chicken, mashed potatoes, and greens. But as soon as she'd set them all on the table and taken her seat . . . *BOOM!*

And the house went dark.

Grandma got right back up, grabbed a candle, lit it, and put it in the middle of the table, no big deal. Genie couldn't remember thunder being that loud in Brooklyn. He also didn't really remember the electricity ever going out either. But Grandma's response made it seem like she was used to it. She was already sitting back down and digging into the food. Dang! Country life! But after a few bites, Grandpop set his fork on the edge of his plate. "You boys wanna hear somethin'?"

"Lord," Grandma groaned.

"No, no. Not another story. Somethin' else."

"Sure," Ernie said, nibbling on the knobby part of a chicken leg.

"Sure," Genie Pete Repeated.

"Sweetheart?" Grandpop said charmingly. Genie knew Grandpop was batting his lashes behind his sunglasses.

Grandma shook her head and relented. "Okay . . . *sure.*"

"Well, since you insist . . ." Grandpop, lickety-split, dug into his pocket, and the first thing Genie thought was that Grandpop was going to whip out his gun. He definitely didn't want to *hear* that — they already had thunder — and didn't know why Grandpop would do this during a dark dinner. But Genie also didn't know why Grandpop did a lot of things, like . . . carry one in the first place. Turns out, Grandpop was reaching for a harmonica. He held it up, the silver glinting in the flicker of the candle flame.

"You know how to play the harmonica?" Genie asked, instantly intrigued.

Grandpop tapped it on the table a few times before bringing it up to his mouth. "I dibble and dabble," he said. Then he pressed the metallic bar to his lips and started blowing and sucking, moving the harmonica back and forth like a cartoon character eating corn on the cob.

The sound was like ghost music. Especially since they were in the middle of a thunderstorm in a room lit only by a candle. Grandpop played and played, his cheeks inflating and deflating, his head rocking side to side, the sound sometimes really, really quiet, and other times piercingly loud. There was one part where Grandpop even made it sound like a train, choo-chooing. A ghost train. Spooky. But cool, very cool, Genie thought. He completely forgot about eating. Ernie, too. Grandpop didn't stop until he was sweating and totally out of breath. Grandma leaned over and rubbed his back as he tried to get his wind. Genie and Ernie clapped like they just got a free concert or something. Grandpop just nodded — it was like he had blown out all his words.

Six

After Genie and Ernie remembered to start eating again, and finished with what they found out was Grandma's specialty dessert, banana pudding, there was nothing really left to do, because: (1) The storm. It was raining cats and dogs — more like bears and elephants, and (2) the entire house was dark. So they went upstairs, Grandma leading the way, holding the candle in one hand. After she took two steps, maybe three, into Genie and Ernie's room — *crunch.*

"What was that?" She set the candle on the blue dresser and started feeling around for a flashlight in the top drawer. She clicked it on, the bright white light beaming across the room for a second before she aimed it at the floor. "What in the world is this doin' down here?" she asked, bending down. It was the red truck. She picked it up, but one of the wheels stayed on the floor. In pieces. Cracked like hard candy.

Cracked, apparently like Grandma's heart. "Oh no," she cried. "Oh . . . *no,*" she repeated, her voice instantly dipping into sadness. Genie thought about whether or not this was one of those truths he should keep to himself. But he couldn't.

"Grandma, um, I left it there," he started to explain, then, realizing that that wasn't enough of an explanation, he decided to explain more. "I just left it there when Ma told us to put the suitcase in the car, and I thought we would come back up to the room, but then you said I couldn't go in and out, and so I stayed out, and I didn't know it was gonna rain and the lights would go out, 'cause the lights never go out in Brooklyn, right, Ernie? And I just didn't know they would go out here. If I knew all that stuff was gonna happen, I wouldn't have left it there. But it was an accident. I swear it was, Grandma, and I'm so sorry." Genie's voice became beggy. He got down on one knee to pick up the pieces of the wheel, dropping the larger half in his palm, pinching at the smaller piece with his fingers. And just when he had it clenched, the tiny bit of plastic slipped from his grip, hit the floor, bounced and rolled like a pebble, before — in what seemed like slow motion — falling through a crack. Genie immediately put his face to the floor, peering desperately between the wooden slats into the darkness downstairs. Then, with his heart in his throat, he looked up at Grandma. Her hand was over her mouth. "Grandma . . . I'm so, so, so —"

"Shhhh," Grandma interrupted, holding her hand out, the truck in her palm on its side. Genie dropped the bigger piece of wheel beside it. "It's, um . . . it's fine," she forced between her teeth. "Accidents happen." She set the three-wheeled model back on the dresser where it belonged and arranged the wheel chip next to it. She didn't say anything more. She didn't have to: Genie could feel her sadness. "You boys, uh . . . sleep tight," Grandma said softly. Setting the flashlight on the dresser next to the truck, she took the candle, gave Ernie a hug, kissed Genie on his forehead, and headed down the stairs. She still smelled like soap. And chicken. And now, disappointment as well.

Genie changed into his basketball shorts as the rain continued to come down hard. He sat on his bed with his notebook and imagined himself trapped in a staticky TV. A place where you couldn't see, or hear, or understand anything.

#442: Why am I so stupid?

Why did he have to leave the truck on the floor? Why? His first day at Grandma and Grandpop's house, and he had already messed up. The *first* day. He just couldn't believe it. He hated making mistakes. All he could think about was how he had to make it right. He had to fix it. But . . . how?

"Don't worry about it, Genie. It was an accident," Ernie said, pulling his shirt over his head. Genie wondered how Ernie always knew when he was beating himself up.

"An accident times two. *Accidents,*" Genie emphasized. "I just feel so bad."

"Yeah, but that ain't gon' fix it," Ernie said, straight. "You know that. So you might as well not even worry about it right now."

Genie nodded, shook his head, then nodded again, deciding he would figure it out, but not tonight. He needed a fresh mind to even begin to think about what to do about the truck. Not a mind full of his parents maybe divorcing and bottle caps and fishing hooks and fly electrocutions and thunderstorms and lights out and harmonicas and questions he still needed to write down about guns in old blind men's waistbands, and the flashlight was giving off just enough light for him to do so. *So:*

#443: Why would a blind man have a gun?

And then Genie realized he hadn't told Ernie yet.

"Yo, I meant to tell you . . . so you know earlier today when you were outside with the dog and I was sitting with Grandpop? Well when he got up from the table, he had a gun sticking out the back of his pants."

"What?" Ernie had been looking at his muscles in the mirror, and Genie figured the lack of light might've been making them look bigger. "You say somethin' about it?"

"Yeah, but he ain't answer. But what he did tell me was that he used to be a shooter, back when he could see. Like, that was his *job*," Genie added. "But he can't see now, so why would a blind man, of all people, need a gun?"

Ernie turned away from the mirror and leaned against the dresser. "Man, I'on't know, maybe he needs it for protection."

"Protection from what?"

"Protection from everything — from the world. I mean, think about how dark it is up here. Somebody could just come in this house and go all psycho on Grandma and Grandpop and no one would ever know." Ernie nodded, agreeing with himself. "You seen the movies, man. Grandpop's probably trying to make sure he don't get slashed."

"Ern, stop playin'."

Ernie chuckled. "Genie, don't worry." He jumped into fighting stance. "We safe and I don't need no gun. But seriously, maybe Grandpop just keeps it with him out of habit. Like, if I went blind, I would still wanna wear my shades every day. Even if I couldn't see myself in 'em I would still wanna wear 'em because they're a part of my life. I still would wanna be fly, even if I can't see how fly I am. Maybe that's how Grandpop feels about being a shooter. He's always gonna see himself as one, even if he can't actually *see* himself as one, y'know?" This sorta made sense, but Genie didn't respond with anything other than a *humph.* He turned back to the notebook and began writing like mad.

#444: Does Grandpop still see himself as a shooter? Is who we are only based on what we do? If so, are Ma and Dad just arguers? Will they become divorcers? And am I a model breaker? Or just a questioner? And if I become a rich and famous questioner, does that make me a questionnaire?

#445: What kind of test do you have to take to be a shooter? Do you get a grade? Can you still be a shooter if you get a C? Technically, you still pass.

#446: What or who did Grandpop shoot?

#447: What does it mean to shoot the breeze? I know one thing, ain't no breeze nowhere around here for Grandpop to shoot.

#448: What does a month of Sundays mean? Has there ever actually been a month of Sundays? Maybe the first month of Sundays was the January after Jesus was born.

#449: Is the sun hotter in the south? If so, then a month of sundaes makes more sense.

#450: The rooter to the tooter is stupid. Why not, the yapper to the crapper? Or the thinker to the stinker?

#451: How come thunder don't seem so loud in Brooklyn? And how come the lights never go out at home?

#452: Why am I so stupid?

#453: Why am I so stupid?

#454: Why am I so

"That was a crazy story about Dad and Uncle Wood, right?" Ernie asked out of the blue. Genie knew Ernie was trying to distract him, and he appreciated it because his questions started to tumble downhill just as he had done earlier. Ernie had dropped down to the floor and was doing push-ups. It was his nightly routine, fifty push-ups to keep his body in "fighting shape," as he put it. "Seven, eight, nine," he gasped out.

Genie closed his notebook for a moment, his finger stuck in to keep his place, and thought about what *he* would've done if *he* had been in that Cake situation. If he would've been able to take up for his brother like he knew Ernie would've taken up for him. If he would've been able to even take up for himself. He wasn't sure. He had been in a few small scuffles with kids at school over the girl-name thing, but nothing serious. A little shoving but no face hits. Nothing that required calling for backup. But still, what if? He didn't know anything about protecting himself except for the few moves he'd learned watching Ernie practice. Well, the few moves Ernie did on him. A leg sweep. And a roundhouse kick. Genie flipped the notebook open again.

#455: Would I fight for Ernie?

Then he scratched it out because he knew he would — of course he would — plus there was no Internet answer for this anyway. His brain continued surging with questions — lots of questions, from a long, long day.

#456: How come glaucoma isn't called eyecoma? Technically, Grandpop's eyes are 'sleep, right? Eye . . . coma. Makes more sense.

#457: Why would flies fly into shocker lights that kill them? Tess said they can't help it, they just love the light. Maybe it smells like dog poop.

So many questions. *So* many questions.

#458: Grits? What exactly are they? And I get that they're called grits because they're gritty, but who thought that name was a good idea? That's like naming peas green slime balls.

#459: If I put sugar on peas, will they taste better? Probably not. Stupid. Such a stupid thing to think. ~~Why am I so . . .~~

Then he thought of a question for Ernie. But Ernie asked one first.

"What you think about Tess?" Ernie was now doing sit-ups.

Genie's mind was *far* from Tess. But he tapped the pen to his lips and replied anyway. "She cool. What *you* think?"

"I think she cool too, but I mean, you think she like me?"

"Man, I'on't know. We just met her." Genie stuck the pen in his mouth like a cigar.

"Don't take long to know, little brother. Trust me, I knew Keisha liked me the day we met."

"But Keisha broke up with you."

Ernie stopped mid sit-up. "What's that s'posed to mean?"

"Nothin', man. I think Tess is cool. And anyway, it's nice to know we're not the only teenagers around here."

"*You* ain't no teenager," Ernie scoffed. He was ticked off about the Keisha comment, Genie could tell.

"Man, you barely one."

"Don't matter. I'm thir*teen*. Thir*teen*.

Almost four*teen*." Then he finished his sit-ups, double time.

Genie lay back and looked over his questions, ignoring the diss. Strangely, of all the questions Genie had, he didn't have any about the red fire truck. There were no questions to be asked about it, besides one, and Genie already knew the answer to it. Question: *Whose fault is it that it's broken?* Answer: *Genie's.* But Genie still had one question for Ernie. One that had been burning him up.

"Hey, Ern, what's the deal with Dad and Grandpop? Like, Dad didn't seem too happy to be around him, and I heard Grandma telling Grandpop that Dad would eventually forgive him, or something like that. But forgive him for what?" Now Ernie was practicing his front kicks. He paused, balancing on one leg.

"For making Uncle Wood join the army. That's my guess. Look, Dad told me that Uncle Wood wanted to be a firefighter, but Grandpop pressured him to go into the military, like he had. So Uncle Wood did. And then there was a war . . ."

"And he died in it," Genie filled in.

"Exactly," Ernie said. "And what I think is Dad blames that on Grandpop."

"Ahhh, and *that's* probably why Dad

became a fireman."

Ernie looked at him in surprise. "Yo, I never even thought of that. Dang. Probably so." He lowered his leg — most likely a world record — and took the flashlight from the dresser to set it on the floor between the two beds. He must've been finally done with his exercise routine, because he crawled into bed. Genie knew that it was only a matter of minutes before Ernie was out. He just couldn't stay up without a TV, and even if there was one, he'd still be dozing. It's just how he was. If Ernie was comfortable, he was snoozing. But Genie couldn't unwind that easy. The sounds of this night were different from last night's when all the nighttime critters had been out to play — couldn't hear the rain on the roof in Brooklyn. Not like this. And that made Genie think of the crickets.

"Yo, Ern, when it rains, where all the crickets go?"

"Huh?" Ernie grunted, already half-asleep.

"The crickets, where do they go when it rains?"

"I don't know, write it down, look it up," Ernie mumbled. Then he added, "Maybe they're out there, but you can't hear them because the rain is too loud."

"They don't drown? Seems like it would

be easy for crickets to just drown, raining this hard."

Ernie didn't respond.

"Ern?"

Ernie was already knocked out. It couldn't have been more than two minutes. That had to be a world record too.

Genie wasn't sure if it was the rain pouring down, or all that sweet tea Grandpop had let him drink, but as soon as he got comfortable and finally started drifting off to sleep, he had to pee. Of course. He thought about trying to hold it until morning, but he was scared that he would have that dream where he'd be going to the bathroom, except he'd actually be going to the bathroom in real life, and whiz all over the bed. And he was way too old for that. Plus he couldn't deal with another disappointed Grandma moment.

So he got up. There was only one toilet in the whole house, and it was all the way downstairs. Question to remember: *Why would a house with a room upstairs not have a bathroom upstairs?* Genie crept super slow down the dark steps, trailing his hand on the wall. The house was making noises, like knuckles cracking. *Quiet, house!* He didn't want to wake Grandma and Grandpop.

When he finally got to the bottom, he

heard a sound. Maybe a mouse. It was coming from the kitchen, clicking and clacking over the shushing sound of rain. Whatever it was, he didn't care, because he just had to get to the bathroom. He slid his feet on the floor instead of picking them up — quieter that way.

Click, clack, CLACK!

It was too loud to be a mouse. Genie peeked around the corner, and even though he couldn't see anything in the dark, he could tell there was somebody sitting at the table.

"Hello?" he whispered, nervous, slinking through the living room. He didn't want to just pop out and scare whoever it was.

"Genie?" It was Grandpop.

"Sorry, I just have to pee," Genie said, gliding through the kitchen and on to the bathroom. Sixteen steps. Seventeen and a half for Genie.

When he came out, he asked Grandpop why he was still up. Maybe Grandma snored loud too.

"Not really sleepy. The rain does that to me. Keeps me awake."

Genie could smell that liquor smell again. "Me too," he said, even though if it wasn't for him having to pee, he probably would've been asleep. "Too much thunder." Yes, that, and not enough Brooklyn. Oh, and a brain full of pistol and broken truck.

Grandpop kicked the chair out from the table so Genie could sit. It was dark, but after a few seconds Genie's eyes adjusted and he could see his grandfather. Not, like, *see him* see him, but see him enough to know he didn't have on a shirt, and that there was a glass, a bottle, and some kind of container in front of him on the table.

"Here, have some ice cream," Grandpop said, pushing the carton Genie's way. "It'll help you feel better about the truck. Plus it's gonna melt anyway." Grandpop wiped a spoon off with a napkin and held it out. Genie took it, more than a little nervous about Grandpop knowing about what had happened to Uncle Wood's fire engine model. Genie wanted to say something about it, but his nerves got the best of him.

Grandpop, who'd gone back to clicking whatever he was clicking, somehow realized Genie wasn't eating the ice cream yet. He stopped what he was doing. "Seriously, son. It was an accident. Grandma'll be fine. She's okay." Genie thought he saw Grandpop smirk. He wasn't sure. But he definitely heard it in his voice.

Then Grandpop got back to the *click-clack* business. So of course, as Genie finally dug the spoon into the carton, he asked, "What you doin'?"

Grandpop didn't answer. Now he was screwing something too. Was it his harmonica?

"Grandpop, what's that?" Genie asked, remixing the original question.

Grandpop sighed like he really didn't want to talk about it, which made Genie feel bad for asking. But then Grandpop took a sip from his glass and said, "A revolver. You know what that is?"

That wasn't at all what Genie was expecting him to say, and in that moment he was super happy Grandpop couldn't see, because Genie's eyes were bugging. "A revolver, like . . . a gun?" Genie wondered if it was the same pistol he had seen in Grandpop's waistband earlier in the day. He had never seen one whole, and he'd definitely never seen one all in pieces.

"Yep, the one you asked about earlier," Grandpop said, like it was no big deal. He screwed something else, then clicked and clacked it some more.

"Why you break it?" Genie asked, scooping out a fat frozen strawberry. Best part.

"It ain't broken," Grandpop explained. "It's called disassembling. It's somethin' we used to do all the time when I was workin'.

Not with this kind of gun, but same deal. I've taken it all apart, now I'm puttin' it back together."

Genie thought that was weird. He had never heard of anyone taking a gun apart. "Why you doin' that?"

A thunderclap rocked the house again. This time Genie barely jumped, but Grandpop jumped big-time.

"Thunder's gon' be the death of me," Grandpop muttered. He took a quick sip from his glass, then got back to the question. "I do it just to make sure I still can."

"Oh." Genie thought about what Ernie had said about him wearing shades. Just part of Grandpop's life. I mean, not Grandpop wearing shades. But Grandpop being a shooter. Genie thought about how he wouldn't mind it being part of *his* life too, so he asked, "Well, can I help?"

"No," Grandpop said, steely. Genie decided maybe he had asked *too* many questions this time. Grandpop clicked one last time, locking something in place. Then he twisted the skinny screwdriver a few more times. "There it is." He set the gun on the table in one piece. Genie thought about reaching out and touching it. After all, how would Grandpop know?

"Don't even think about it," Grandpop

said. He *knew.*

Dang.

The rain kept pouring, beating against the windows. Grandpop and Genie sat there for a few minutes, quiet. Genie was waiting — hoping — for Grandpop to calm down, and in the meantime (like, the *mean* time), Genie continued eating the ice cream, now melted into strawberry milk, which was just as good, until a low robotic voice cut through the silence with, *"The time is TEN TWIN-TEE-EIGHT PEE EM."*

"What's that?" Genie asked.

"Just the clock. Thankfully, it takes batteries." Grandpop's left hand was on the clock radio he'd been listening to earlier. "Just checkin' the time," he said, pressing the button again, his voice back to its regular gruff tone, not its annoyed gruff tone. A subtle difference, but a big deal.

After the clock repeated, *"TEN TWIN-TEE-EIGHT PEE EM,"* Genie asked another burning question.

"So remember today you were saying how there's a different number of steps to your room and to the bathroom and all that?"

"Yeah, I remember."

"Well, what about outside? You ever go out?"

Grandpop brushed his face with his hand.

It sounded like someone tearing paper. "Not really," he said. "I mean, I go from the door to the car, and from the car to the doctor's door, and back. That's pretty much it. Shoot, I'on't even remember the last time I played with Samantha."

"But why not?" Genie asked.

"Good question," Grandpop said. Genie didn't think it was that great of a question. Not nearly as good as, *Can I help?* But Grandpop blew a hard breath and went on. "I'm gon' tell you a secret, but you gotta promise to never tell nobody. Got it?"

He's going to tell me a secret? Nobody ever told Genie secrets. Seemed like people were always keeping secrets from him. At least his parents were. "Promise," Genie said. He was all ears.

"I'on't go outside because . . . well, I guess I'm a little . . . concerned."

"Concerned?" Genie repeated.

Grandpop cleared his throat. "See, inside I know where everything is. But outside, I'on't know where nothin' is. Things move on their own. Then there's that big ol' hill. If I lost my bearings and fell down that, it'd probably be my last fall. Too many surprises for an old man that lives in the dark, y'know what I mean?"

That led Genie to figure that "concerned"

was grown-up code for "scared."

"Yeah, but you never, like, I'on't know, just walk around your yard? Not all the way to the edge, but just a little bit? 'Cause if I had a big yard like this back home, I would be in it all the time. Even if I *was* blind," Genie said.

Grandpop cocked his head. "Is that so?"

Genie wiped his mouth with the back of his hand. "Yep."

"Well, I guess I gotta figure out how to get as brave as you, Little Wood."

Genie didn't know what to say to that, so he just sat there wondering what it must be like to be trapped in a house. Never even get to play with your own dog. Grandpop sat there quiet too, until Genie started to get a little sleepy. But he didn't want to go back to bed just yet. Not until Grandpop was ready.

"The rain always gets me," Grandpop said out of nowhere. He rubbed his hand up and down over his face just like Dad did whenever he was tired after an overnight shift at the firehouse but had to stay awake while Ma caught him up on all the stuff Genie and Ernie had been up to.

"Senior, I know you tired, but let me tell you about your youngest son," she'd say, while Dad wiped his face with his hand,

116

from top to bottom, over and over again.

"What you mean?" Genie now asked Grandpop. "The rain gets you, how?"

"It just always makes me think about Wood. He was born on a rainy day, and even though it was ugly out, it was the happiest day of my life." Grandpop lifted his glass, and then put it right back down. Genie could tell by the way it sounded when it hit the table that it was empty. Huh. That must be what it's like to be blind. You see things by the way they sound. Grandpop continued. "And he was buried on a rainy day. I remember every drop feelin' like a bomb fallin' down on me." He sighed, grabbed his bottle, and poured himself another glass. "It's been twenty-five years, but every time it rains I think about my boy."

"What war was he in?" Genie's dad made them all have a long moment of silence every Memorial Day, but Genie couldn't remember him ever going into particulars.

Grandpop sipped, swallowed. "Desert Storm. We only lost round a hunnid-fifty men. That's it. And *my* boy . . . *my* son was . . ." The words became clay in Grandpop's throat. And before Genie could pick up where Grandpop left off and ask anything else, or maybe even get into Grandpop and Dad's strange and strained relationship after Wood's death, Grandpop reached over and hit whatever button on the clock radio triggered the robot voice.

"The time is TEN FIF-TEE-FOUR PEE EM." Grandpop put his hand on Genie's shoulder — which was still such a surprise to Genie, that Grandpop could know where it was — as the old clock repeated itself.

"TEN FIF-TEE-FOUR PEE EM."

"I, uh, think the rain is starting to let up. You should head on back to bed now, Little Wood," Grandpop suggested. Genie could tell the conversation was over.

But the rain wasn't letting up at all.

SEVEN

As the rain eventually tapered off, Genie fell asleep to the thought of this new secret he had to keep about Grandpop's fear, along with the sound of Grandpop breaking apart his gun and putting it together again faintly slipping up through the floorboards. It seemed like he had just closed his eyes when morning came and he and Ernie were jolted awake by Grandma banging on a pot from the bottom of the steps. What the . . . ?

"What time is it?" Ernie asked as he and Genie zombied into the kitchen. Genie had done a quick scan of the living room floor for the piece of wheel. Didn't see it. No Grandpop either, but he couldn't have still been asleep after all that banging.

Grandma pointed to the kitchen chairs. "Have a seat. Now, boys, so we're all on the same page, there are some rules y'all gon' need to follow, okay?" Grandma began pacing back and forth like a teacher at the board. Genie studied her face to see if any sadness about the fire truck still lingered. But he couldn't get a good read. "Rule number one," Grandma started, and Genie imagined how she'd finish. *No leaving precious toys that mean the world to me on the floor.* "We're up at seven thirty every morning."

"Seven thirty!" Ernie yelped.

"Yes, seven thirty. And that's late. Lettin' you boys sleep in. I rise with the sun every day. Round six forty-five."

"But why *we* gotta be up early?" Again, from Ernie.

"To do chores."

"Every day? At six forty-five? But — but — it's summer break! We gotta do chores every day?"

"Yes, Ernest. Every day."

"But at home Ma only makes us do them on Saturdays. And our house is always pretty clean," Genie told her, fearing this might be some kind of punishment. Grandma ignored that and put two fingers in the air.

"Rule number two." Genie's brain kicked in again: *Don't touch nothing red in this house. Nothing. Not an apple or a fire extinguisher, and definitely not the model fire engine that my sweet son made!* "We go to church on Sunday. I'on't know what y'all do up there in the Big Apple" — Grandma emphasized *Big Apple* like it was a disease — "but down here, we go to church. I'on't wanna hear no whinin' 'bout it. Got it?"

"Got it," Genie said, thinking about how much he could use a miracle. Church didn't really bother him, anyway — unless it was going to be a month of Sundays — even though it wasn't really something they did at home. At least not often. They went on Christmas and Easter for the long services with their grandparents in the Bronx. But that was about it.

Grandma gave Ernie the stink eye, clearly waiting for him to agree too. "Yes," Ernie finally mumbled.

"And rule number three." Three fingers up. *Genie, you have to sleep in the doghouse with Samantha.* Genie told his brain *Stop it!* "And this is because of your adventure yesterday. You are free to roam around outside. This ain't the city where kids are confined to the block. Here, you can go down the hill, or back in them woods, and play fightin', or football, or whatever y'all do. But" — Grandma popped her lips on the hard *B* — "if I call for you, you better come. I'm a give you five hollers. That means you gotta be close enough to hear me. If you ain't lookin' in my face by the end of the fifth, well, you gon' wish you woulda been. Understand?"

Ernie and Genie both agreed — fast, this time — but Genie could tell Ernie was already annoyed, even though they were only on rule number three. Even though they had way more rules at home.

It was that first one, the one about the chores, that led them to slinging poop in the yard for the first time. That's what led to Ernie catapulting dog doo deep into the woods, and Genie somehow launching his behind him, where it splattered against a window in the back of the house at the exact time a car pulled into the yard.

The dog was going wild. Then came the screech and pop of the screen door. Grandma.

"Genie! Ernie! What in Sam Hill are y'all doin'?" she yelled.

"Nothin'," they said in unison, dropping the shovels. They hightailed it back to the front of the house. Grandma was already in the yard, looking from grandson to grandson, completely ignoring the fact that someone had just arrived in the most beat-up car Genie had ever seen.

"Got up all the poop, Grandma," Ernie announced. Grandma fixed him a look, frowning like she knew he and Genie were up to something.

The motor of the car shut down, and the man in it got out. He was tall and lanky, and looked around Dad's age. When he walked, he rocked up on his toes, as if he was trying to fly but couldn't get off the ground. In his hand were two brown paper bags.

"Mary," he said to Grandma, a short, unlit cigar that looked like a bitten-off finger in his mouth. He put his hand up to the brim of his filthy hat, tipped it. Grandma finally looked in his direction.

"Crab." The way she said it made Genie think that maybe Grandma didn't like him too much.

"Who these boys here?" the man called Crab asked. He pulled the cigar from his mouth and spat on the ground.

"My grandbabies," Grandma said, waving them closer to her. "Ernie, Genie, this is your father's friend — well, now, I guess more your grandfather's friend, Mr. Crab-tree." Now "Crab" made sense.

"These Ernie's boys? So this one here's a junior, huh?"

Ernie nodded.

"Uh-huh. Then you must be the one my daughter been hemmin' and hawin' 'bout."

"Who?" Ernie asked, startled.

"*Who?* You done forgot her already?"

"Shut up, Crab." Grandma jumped to Ernie's rescue. "Ernie, baby, this is Tess's daddy."

"Yeah, I'm Tess's daddy." Crab looked Ernie up and down, scowling the whole time. Then he loosened his face up and mumbled, "I think she like you." Ernie smiled, closed-mouthed. He tried not to, but Genie knew he couldn't help it. "But don't try nothin' mannish or I'll flatten your cap, just like she do them beer tops." Crab hammered one fist into the other palm for emphasis. Then he turned to Genie. "And Genie? Genie, right?" Crab held his hand out for Genie to shake. Genie gripped the big paw tight, shook it hard, and nodded.

Crab spat again, then stuck the cigar back into his mouth. "What lamp you come from?" he said, cracking a smile. Each tooth on his top row was longer than the tooth beside it. Like upside-down steps.

"I'm from Brooklyn." Genie didn't smile at all. Brooklyn style.

Crab looked at Grandma, but she didn't smile either. Genie wasn't sure what it was, but he wasn't getting a good feeling from this guy.

"The old man in there?" Crab asked.

"Where else he gon' be?" Grandma replied, glowering at him.

Crab headed for the house, bouncing on his toes like a crooked-tooth ballerina. Samantha finally stopped barking.

"That's really Tess's dad?" Ernie asked.

"Unfortunately, baby," Grandma said like she was sad for Ernie, and even sadder for Tess. "He comes by here once a week and hunts back there in them woods."

"Does he ever shoot anything?" Genie asked.

"Sometimes. A squirrel here, a rabbit there."

"Squirrels and rabbits don't bother nobody. Why would he shoot *them*?" Genie, again.

Grandma widened her eyes. "So he can eat 'em."

"*Eat* them?" Ernie squealed. "Don't nobody eat no squirrels!"

Grandma shrugged. "He do."

As weirded out as Genie was about this Crab guy shooting furry animals and, according to Grandma, eating them, he was also really impressed by the fact that he was a good enough shot to actually hit a squirrel. Squirrels were *fast.* And small!

"So he must be a good shooter then, huh?"

Grandma nodded. "He better be. Your fool granddaddy taught him." Then she harrumphed and went over to the water hose, which was tangled up like a dead snake on the side of the house — right next to where Ernie and Genie had dropped the poop slingers.

"Only one dern spigot out here and it's on the wrong side of the house," she groused, twisting the knob that turned the water on. Then she sprayed a quick squirt at Samantha, who almost hurt herself trying to scramble inside her doghouse. Grandma laughed. "Dog bark all the time, but run from a little water. She a girl, but she sure act more like a boy in that way." Grandma filled the dog's water bowl to the top, which was a good thing, because it was already hot out there. *So* hot. Then Grandma dragged the hose toward Ernie and Genie. "Ernie, here, take this," she said, handing him the hose. Her forehead was already shiny with sweat. "We finna tend to the peas."

"Peas," Genie repeated.

"Half a garden full. Folks round here love my peas — just wait'll you taste 'em."

She was joking, right? Everyone knew Genie hated peas. Hated, hated, hated them. He would *not* be tasting any peas. But sure enough, Grandma had a bona fide pea patch (pea patch?) on the other side of the house. Genie had never seen an actual pea patch — a pea garden — before. It looked like a miniature forest except for the little fence-looking things in the middle that the vines were wrapped around. The weird part was that Genie didn't see any peas. Maybe because they were green and the vines were green too, so everything just blended in. Or maybe the pea growing wasn't going too well.

"Okay, so first we check to see if they need water. We got all that rain last night, so my babies should be good, but it can't hurt to check," Grandma said. She squatted and pushed her fingers deep into the soil, then pulled them out and stuck them back into a different place in the dirt. Back out again. "Nope, we'on't need none, so you can drop the hose, baby," she told Ernie. She wiped her fingers on her thigh, leaving a brown smear. "So we're just gon' pick the ripe ones today."

But Genie *still* couldn't see any actual peas. They must've been invisible or something. So of course, he asked.

"Look here." Grandma motioned for the boys to get down in the dirt with her. And if there's one thing about city boys, as Tess had dubbed them, it's that they don't do dirt. Especially wet dirt. "You gotta get right up on the vine to find the pods," Grandma said, reaching into the tangle of green. "See?"

"Pods?" Genie asked, squatting timidly. Gnats buzzed around his head.

"Yep, that's what they're called. Pea pods."

Well, that was a stupid name. Reminded Genie of pee pads, those things little dogs who live in the house — not like Samantha — pee on.

Grandma was rambling on, pea-this, pea-that, interrupted only by the sound of the screen door, then the slam of a trunk. Genie guessed Crab was headed out hunting, and wanted to pop up to see if he could catch a glimpse of him with his rifle, but decided that Grandma wouldn't like that. So he stayed low and listened on.

"Now if you snap it in half, you can see the peas in there." Grandma handed the pod to Ernie, who bent it until it broke open, and showed Genie. Inside the pod, these things that looked like little green pills were hiding out. Genie couldn't believe it.

"Now, the way you tell if the peas are ready is just by squeezing the pod. *Before* you pick it! If they feel empty, like you don't feel full peas in there" — Grandma took the broken pod from Ernie and squeezed it, showing the boys that the peas were just the right size — "then they not ready. *Don't* pick those! Put the good ones in that basket over there."

"We eating all these peas?" Ernie asked, slapping a mosquito on his neck. Genie wanted to say, *I'm not eating no peas,* but he already knew Grandma wouldn't want to be hearing *that.*

"No, child. I told you, folks round here love 'em. I go to the market and sell 'em. I'm goin' next week, and since y'all here, and you so strong, I might need you both to come with me."

"Oh, okay," Ernie replied, a sense of triumph in his voice.

"If you need anything, just holler. I'm gon' be over there dealin' with the weeds. And y'all might as well get used to the mosquitoes and flies, 'cause ain't nothin' you can do to stop them suckas. Y'all must got sweet blood. Got that from me," Grandma said, wandering away, slapping her own arm.

Genie wondered why Grandma didn't just get one of those fly zappers they had in Marlon's as he and Ernie squeezed and snapped peas off the vine, tossing them into the basket. They worked as fast as they could, yanking pods off sometimes two at a time because they didn't want to be out there all day. Not with the heat, not with the wet soil, and definitely not with the mosquitoes.

Every couple of minutes they would hear gunshots. Crab. Genie flinched each time, but he couldn't stop thinking about how cool it would be to be out there shooting at stuff.

"You think that man really eat squirrels?" Ernie asked, pinching a pod, then leaving it hanging on the stalk.

"I'on't know," Genie said, now giving in and falling down on his knees in the moist earth to get at the ripe pods growing down low. Some of them had grown so big they had busted open. Grandma hadn't said what to do with those, so Genie figured he'd better leave them.

"Man, I'on't think so." Ernie answered his own question. "Don't nobody eat squirrels. That's just nasty. I think Grandma was just playin' with us."

Another shot rang out.

"Yeah, except Grandma don't really seem like she play too much," Genie replied.

When they finished picking all the ripe peas, Ernie took the water hose, squirted their hands clean, then sprayed a mist into the air. The water came sprinkling down on them like snow, making their skin tingle. It felt amazing, but before Genie could ask Ernie to do it again, Ernie dropped the hose and jogged over to the edge of the hill, craning his neck as if listening to something in the distance.

"Thought I heard somethin'," he said when Genie caught up to him.

"I didn't," Genie said, flat. He knew what his brother was doing. He was doing what he always did whenever there were girls in any situation — getting all crazy, or as Ma would say, he'd start smelling himself, which meant his nose was open, which meant . . . girls.

"I did. I mean, I think I did," Ernie said, geeking out. "I'm a go check."

Before Genie could even respond, Ernie started down the hill. He told Genie that he could come too, but the way he said it — like a no-look pass too fast to catch — was in the way that really meant, *please don't come.* So Genie went back over to the pea patch, grabbed the basket of winners he and Ernie had picked, and headed back toward the house.

He figured he could take this time to look for the piece of wheel. It had to be somewhere in the living room, and if he found it, he could just glue it all back together. But Grandpop had other plans.

"Who's that comin' inside bringin' all that outside with 'em?" Grandpop was standing at the counter, using a spoon to smear peanut butter on the side of an apple.

"It's me, Genie." He left the peas on the porch, took his muddy Converses off at the front door, and left the bathroom door open as he washed the rest of the grit and soil-sludge off his fingers.

"Tell me, son, how does a small boy like you have a smell comin' off him so big?" Grandpop tugged the tip of his nose as Genie came back into the kitchen.

Genie lifted his arms. Sniffed. Didn't smell anything.

Grandpop was wearing a white V-neck T-shirt tucked into a pair of navy-blue slacks. A black belt. No gun, Genie noticed immediately. He had a tiny piece of tissue stuck to his chin. Must've cut himself shaving, Genie thought. Dad did the same thing all the time.

Genie sat at the table. Grandpop poured a glass of water.

"If you sittin' out here, you'll be sittin' alone," Grandpop said, setting the water in front of Genie.

"Where you goin'?" Genie asked.

Grandpop poured himself a glass of . . . not-water, from the bagged bottle Crab had brought. He held the glass in one hand, but before picking up the peanut-buttered apple, he set a smaller paper bag — the one that wasn't covering a bottle — in front of Genie.

"Little Wood, the real question is, are you comin'?" Then he walked out of the kitchen.

What did *that* mean? But Genie took a swig of water, grabbed the bag, and followed. They didn't go far. Maybe eight or nine steps into the living room before reaching that door. The *nunya bidness* door. Genie inspected the floor quickly, his eyes landing on every knot in the wood, thinking it could be the other half of the wheel. Where could it have gone? Maybe it hit the floor and rolled into *another* crack — a crack in the living room floor — which would make Genie the unluckiest kid in the world. Or at least in North Hill.

"Grandson, reach in my pocket and grab the keys in there," Grandpop said, interrupting Genie's frantic forage. Genie slipped his hand into Grandpop's pants pocket and pulled out a set of keys on a key ring. What in the world would Grandpop need so many keys for? It wasn't like he was going anywhere without Grandma. "It's the square one." Genie pushed the key in, turned it, then turned the knob. The door didn't budge. "Gotta push it hard, son," Grandpop advised.

So Genie pushed for all he was worth, and as the door flew open, he stumbled forward into . . . into . . . what the heck? Genie gawked, trying to look in every direction at once. He glanced back at the door. Where was he? Did Grandpop have some weird portal in his house? Was North Hill some kind of country version of Narnia, or something? Sure did seem that way. Behind him, he could still see the part of the house he was used to. The peeling sea-green walls. The linoleum floor of the kitchen. The television in the living room. It was all still there, so he was still "there."

But inside the room — the nunya bidness room — was . . . weird. *Weird.* First of all, sunlight filled every cranny, because the entire ceiling was glass. Like, a giant sunroof. Then, there were plants everywhere. E-v-e-r-y-w-h-e-r-e! Six-foot-high trees growing out of pots, about twenty of them! Vines crawling all along the walls, and plants with crazy-colored leaves, some the size of paper plates. Then there was the floor. The floor was covered in thick fake grass — grass! — vibrant green. It was some kind of miniature golf course carpet or something.

Once his eyes (and brain) finished adjusting, Genie realized it was also crazy noisy. Bird sounds every which way! Tweets and chirps and loud singing all happening at once. Whaaa? Genie took one hesitant step forward, then another, until he saw, tucked between all the foliage, five birdcages all made of wood and wire and set up like small castles. Some were entangled in the plants, leaves growing between the skinny bars. Genie glanced warily at his grandfather, then went from cage to cage. Wow. Just . . . wow. He recognized the birds — one in each cage — they were the same kind as the one he'd seen pecking around on the front porch, the one wearing blue feathers like a cape and mask. They flitted around, their wings flapping against the wiry walls, cheeping their blue heads off.

There was one window facing the yard. It had a brown smear on it. Genie figured that was the window he'd hit with the poop. Oops! He was glad Grandpop wasn't in there when that happened. Might've scared the old guy to death.

In the middle of this indoor forest, smack in the center of it all, were two rocking chairs and a small table between them with a small cassette player on it. Grandpop moved slowly through the foliage, not stopping until he bumped one of the chairs with his hip. He tapped the table lightly before setting his glass down. Then he went back the way he came, pausing to make a *chit-chit-chit* sound at one of the cages he passed, and closed the door. Then he was back, apple still in one hand, easing himself into one of the seats.

"Sit," he said, pushing the arm of the other chair so that it rocked slightly.

"Wha . . ." Genie looked over. He'd been feeling the weird grass carpet — it was soft as . . . grass. "What . . . is this place?"

Grandpop took a huge bite of the apple, chewed, chewed, chewed, swallowed, then said, "This room here . . . is my outside. Had it added on to the house right before my ol' blinkers went black."

He bit down on the apple again, this time just to hold it in place so he could pick up the cassette player. He ran his fingers along the face of it, the knobs like eyes, the row of buttons — play, stop, rewind, pause, fast-forward, eject — like teeth. Grandpop could've easily asked Genie to do some of these things, to help, but he wouldn't. He hit play. But the music wasn't music. It was just sounds. Breeze blowing. Outside noise.

Genie, still holding the paper bag, sat down uneasily in the other chair, trying not to freak out. Especially since they were sitting in front of five birdcages, which, Genie realized, if you looked past the entwining vines and leaves, were arranged in a semicircle.

"But . . . we're still *inside*!" Genie exclaimed, now starting to see all the things he knew Grandpop hadn't. Like the fact that there was bird poop all over the place, and that some of the vines were so thick they could be hiding pythons or boa constrictors or something! And some of the plants were dead. Brown-as-dirt dead.

Grandpop pulled the apple from his mouth, taking another juicy chunk out of it, pushed back in his chair, then let it rock forward like a little kid on a swing.

"Little Wood, my boy, you're way too young not to have an imagination," he said between chewing. He stopped the chair suddenly, leaned toward Genie, and sniffed.

"What?"

"Nothin'." Grandpop pulled back. "It's just, you smell like your daddy and your uncle used to smell. Oh, hand me that bag."

Genie gave Grandpop the bag, then took another whiff of his armpit. Still nothing. "They picked peas too?"

Grandpop set the half-eaten apple on the table and opened the bag. "They sure did. They picked peas, cut grass, washed cars, and a whole bunch of other stuff. And I used to be right out there with 'em. Your grandma don't play. I'm kinda happy I'on't gotta look at peas no more." He gave a small laugh, but it didn't quite sound happy. "Under the table is a can. Hand it to me, would ya?" Genie reached down for the blue coffee can, and set it in Grandpop's lap. "I'm also happy this room is completely soundproof. Can't hear nothin' in here out there, and nothin' out there in here. Don't even have to hear her yappin' 'bout my babies." Grandma called her peas "babies," and Grandpop called his birds "babies," and all Genie could think about was whether this was what happened to parents when their kids grew up. When he and Ernie left home, was Ma going to start calling popcorn her babies? Dad, the remote control — his baby?

"Grandma don't like birds?" Genie asked.

"Ha!" Grandpop whooped. "She HATES birds! Can't stand 'em. They always munchin' up her crops. She won't even set foot in this room, and these babies are in cages! Matter fact, she told me she's so happy you here, so she'on't have to feel bad about it no more. At least for a month. That's one month, guilt free." Grandpop took the apple and stuffed the rest of it in his mouth, core and all. Then he peeled the top off the coffee can and poured whatever was in the bag into the can. "To be honest with you" — slurp, chew, slurp — "I'm glad she don't come in here. This is . . . my private space, y'know?" Genie had never seen anyone eat a whole apple before. Like, the *whole* thing. As Grandpop crunched and chomped, he pressed the top back on the can and handed it back to Genie. Then he stretched his legs out in front of him. His pants rode up, exposing a nasty scar on his right ankle. It was thick and raised, wrapping around the bottom of his leg like an ugly bracelet. What the heck was that? And what the heck was in the can? Genie was about to ask when there was a muted thump on the door.

"Brooke?" The voice was muffled, but Genie could still make it out. It was that guy, Crab.

"Come on in!" Grandpop hollered. He felt under the table for something else, a small cup Genie hadn't even noticed, right next to the mystery coffee can. Grandpop spit all the apple seeds into the cup and spit the stem into his hand the way kids back home in Brooklyn did sunflower-seed shells. "Seed cup. Just because Mary don't come in here don't mean I gotta be messy," he said with a grin. For sure, Grandpop had no idea how messy this room was. Like, a bird-sty. He put the cup back under the table, then he used the stem to pick his teeth. The sound of an airplane flying overhead came from the cassette player just as Crab forced the door open and walked in, dripping with sweat, rifle in his left hand.

"Hit anything?" Grandpop called out, now using the other end of the stem to dig under his fingernails. The guy was resourceful.

"Nah. Suckers ate their Wheaties this mornin'," Crab said, leaning the gun against the wall, moving through the room like it was a familiar space. He and Grandpop started jawing about how deer season was in a few months, and who knew what else because Genie wasn't paying much attention — he was too busy staring at the rifle. It was ten or eleven feet away from him! Boy, was it long. Then Grandpop said his name, which of course always brought Genie back to any conversation. Even the ones that were none of his business.

". . . and Genie are here for 'bout a month. Ernie got a birthday comin' up in a couple weeks. Fourth of July. He'll be the big one-four."

"Y'know that's the one my little girl's spinnin' over, right?" Crab said. Grandpop smiled. Cocky. Proud. Crab didn't smile at all. Annoyed. Worried. "I would ask you if you gon' make him a man like how we used to do back in the day, but I guess —"

"Uh-uh-uh." Grandpop put his hand up to stop Crab from saying anything else about Ernie being made a man. Then he sniffed again and grimaced. "You smell like dog crap." Genie was relieved it wasn't *his* stink again.

Crab looked at Grandpop weird, but then brushed it off. "Yeah, well . . . I know. It was so strange. Mess was everywhere out there."

Poopidity.

Crab and Grandpop went on talking while Genie snuck peeks at the rifle, how the smooth wood contrasted with the gray steel. Then Crab pulled a wad of money out of his front pocket. Genie definitely noticed *that.*

"A'ight, well, lemme square up witcha and get outta here, old man," Crab said, peeling off four bills and rolling them tight like a cigarette. "Heading over to the junkyard, see if I can find a bumper for the Oldsmobile." Now Genie understood why Crab's

141

car was so wild-looking, and why he'd never seen any models like it before. Grandpop held out his hand, and Crab put the bills in his palm. "Twenty bucks. Four fives, like usual."

"Sounds good," Grandpop said, tucking the money in his pocket. Then he added, "And remember, not a word to Mary."

"She still don't know about rent-a-forest, after all this time?"

"Nah, man, she think you payin' me in bottles of your daddy's basement hooch and bags of dead flies."

"Them flies are one thing, 'cause that's the zapper doin' the work. But that hooch is *mine,* not my daddy's," Crab clarified, prickly. Wait . . . *flies?* Genie wanted to know what in the world they were talking about. *Flies? Zapper?* Like, flies from the . . .

"Boy, please. Marlon taught you that recipe. And I been drinkin' it since I saved his butt in Vietnam. Since before you was even born."

"Yeah, yeah, yeah," Crab said, rolling his eyes. "And now you drink it for free. And I know, I know, crazy fool even left it in his will. Don't need to remind me."

"For all eternity." Grandpop chuckled, but then he tilted his head back as if letting the memory of his friend wash over him. He nodded, and after a moment or two, snapped out of it. "That's loyalty. And I 'preciate you honorin' his word. And for the flies. My babies are grateful. Now, as for this scratch you payin' me for the privilege of shootin' up my backyard, this here's private money." Hold up, did Grandpop just pour *dead flies* in that coffee can? Was *that* what those birds ate? Also, Grandpop had a private room, private money? Genie wondered if his father had secrets like this. Or if he would need these things when he got old too. Pets that could only eat nasty bugs, and secret treasures hidden in his own house.

"Private money for what?" Crab asked.

"In case some miracle happens and I can see again, I'll be able to afford one of those intelligent phones everybody been talkin' 'bout," Grandpop joked. "I'm foolin', man. It's just, I'on't know, my rainy day stash. Me and Mary got ours, which is really hers, and I got mine." Grandpop rocked forward, this time with enough momentum to propel him to his feet.

Crab nodded. "I hear ya. That Tess is gon' bleed me dry, even though she sells her jewelry and whatnot. She a teenager and she need stuff. Them braces alone damn near broke the bank. And don't even get me started on Karen. Ev'ry week I gotta pick up a new 'scription for a new problem. Don't know if I told you — they cut my hours back at the plant, and that old bar brings in diddly. So I definitely understand needin' a secret stash. But come to think of it, that's probably why Mary don't like me. She think I'm just usin' you." Crab headed for the door, grabbing his rifle along the way.

"Or maybe she don't like you 'cause you come in her house smellin' like the backside of a mutt," Grandpop razzed. Genie snorted. Couldn't hold it in, especially since he knew where the dog poop came from.

Crab shot Genie a look but then turned it into a funny face, like Genie was a six-year-old. Then he came back over and shook Grandpop's hand before leaving, closing the door behind him.

At that moment, one of the birds began chirping like crazy. That got the other four of them squawking. And in that perfect half circle of birdcages, the rocking chairs set right in the center of the arch, it struck Genie that it was almost as if Grandpop was the conductor of his own bird orchestra.

"Grandpop, um, question. You feed these birds . . . dead flies?" Genie asked.

"Well, yeah, 'cause that's what they eat,"

Grandpop said. "To tell you the truth, every time I feed 'em, it's another one of those moments I'm happy I can't see."

I bet, Genie thought, but followed with, "What kinda birds are these, anyway?" He had to know what birds ate dead flies and not birdseed.

"They're all barn swallows, except for one. One is a parrot," Grandpop answered, easing back down into his chair. Genie looked from cage to cage, confused. There was no parrot. He had never heard of barn swallows before, but he had definitely heard of parrots, and no parrots were present.

"Um, Grandpop, ain't no parrot in here."

"What?" Grandpop's voice was full of surprise. He gripped the armrests of his chair as if he was about to stand right back up. "Somebody done stole my parrot? Well, I guess that means I'm just gon' have to talk to *you* now." He reached out for Genie's hand and squeezed it for a second before going back for his drink. "So, Little Wood," Grandpop said after taking a long sip, his voice low. "Lemme ask you somethin', and maybe I shoulda asked you this earlier. How good are you at keepin' secrets?"

"Pretty good. I'm still keepin' the one you told me last night," Genie said. "Matter fact, I only told one my whole life, and that was because Ma made me." That was the time Ernie was practicing his roundhouse kicks and knocked a picture off the wall. Glass from the picture frame was everywhere. Ma cut her foot, and *I don't know who did it* just wasn't working.

"Okay, well, how 'bout you meet me in the kitchen at twenty-two hundred hours."

"Meet you in *twenty-two hundred* hours?" Genie wasn't a math whiz, but he knew that twenty-two hundred hours was a lot of time. Like a hundred days.

"No, *at* twenty-two hundred hours. That's military time for ten o'clock p.m."

So why the heck wouldn't he just say ten o'clock?

Military time.

Old people.

EIGHT

Just before lunch, the Grandma "Five Call Warning" started up. Genie worried that Ernie wouldn't make it all the way back from Tess's, but luckily, he was up the hill before the fifth call. And before Genie could even tell him about Grandpop's inside-outside room, Ernie steamrolled him and proceeded to spend the next seven jillion hours going on and on, yapping about how cool Tess was.

"Genie, I'm telling you, man. She's different. She's tough, but sweet, y'know? And she's creative and about her business. And she got that cute accent.

"Genie, she took me back to the bar and we had more ginger beer, but this time in those skinny champagne glasses.

"Genie, she said she likes my sunglasses. I let her wear them for a little while, and you know I don't never let *nobody* touch my shades.

"Genie, she kept telling me to smile, said she liked it. You know I don't really just be smilin' to be smilin'. But she likes it, so whatever.

"Genie, she thinks I look a little bit like a movie star, but she couldn't remember which one. But still.

"Genie, I made like a hundred earrings with her. She taught me how to hit the nail better. She hits the nail so good, she could be in construction. It's kind of amazing.

"Genie, she gave me her phone number, man. Wrote it on a paper towel and told me not to lose it, but it don't matter if I lose it, because I already memorized it."

Genie, Genie, Genie.

Most of it Genie let go in one ear and out the other, only because if there was one thing he knew about Ernie, it was that he was a sucker for girls. Always had been. There was Keisha, who left him for the rapper. But before Keisha, there was Jessica, a girl in his karate class who he fell out of love with after she hip-tossed him once. Hard. Slammed him right on the mat. Before Jessica, there was Dominique, who moved from Brooklyn to Queens, which to a Brooklynite is like moving to another country. And each time Ernie fell for a new girl, Genie's cool, confident brother would become a goofy, googly-eyed fool. Genie knew how it always ended — with text-message raps and extra-hard karate "practice" chops to Genie's arms.

Blah, blah, blah, was all Genie heard, the rest of the day, through dinner, and even through the after-dinner talk where Grandma called Tess "a cutie-patootie sweetie pie," and Grandpa called Ernie "a brick off the old pile." At least nobody was talking about red trucks, one of which Genie was thinking about as much as Ernie was thinking about Tess. *Blah, blah, blah,* up the steps. *Blah, blah, blah,* in the room. *Blah, blah, blah,* as Genie stared at the broken piece of wheel, wondering what happened to the other half. *Blah, blah, blah,* during Ernie's push-ups and sit-ups, which he did for twice as long just because he was sure Tess would like muscles. *Blah, blah, blah,* as Ernie stared at himself in the mirror, examining (and super-weird, kissing) his golf-ball biceps. Genie even wrote in his notebook, #461: Blah, blah, blah. Blah, blah, black sheep. Black sheep. Black sheep? Do black sheep exist? Ernie went on and on "Tessing" the room up, and Genie continued to ignore him, that is, until Ernie said, "Oh, and guess what else, man? She got Wi-Fi in her house."

Record scratch.

"What?"

"Yep," Ernie said, slapping his hands together over his head in a jumping jack. "The Internet."

To Genie's ears, Ernie's voice suddenly sounded slow and low, like, *In-ter-netttt.* Like this was a dream. Genie had *so* many questions he needed answers to — he was getting nervous about the question backup — and his dear friend Google was apparently not a friend of his grandparents. But Tess. Ah yes, Tess.

"I love Tess," Genie said, cheesing. "I love her, and I totally understand why you're so into her. She's so much better than all the other girls. Especially Keisha."

"You think so?" Ernie asked, happily. Genie just smiled and nodded, chortling to himself, *In-ter-netttt.*

Eventually, thankfully, Ernie yapped himself out and fell asleep, snoring so loud he drowned out the crickets and the frogs. But Genie had to stay awake for his twenty-two-hundred-hour mission. He glanced at the old digital clock on the dresser every few minutes, waiting for ten o'clock. Moonlight made shadows from the things on the dresser, including the handicapped red truck. If he could only find the other half of it, he could repair it. He could glue it back together. Sure Grandma might not have any hobby adhesive, or cement glue, or any of the other kinds of fancy glues that Genie would normally use on a model, but good ol' plain white glue would work. He'd just have to hold the wheel together for, like . . . half a day, then hold the wheel to the truck for the other half, but still. At least it'd be fixed. But that couldn't happen without the other half. The other good thing about this new discovery of Tess's Internet was that maybe he could figure something else out. Maybe he could find someone online in North Hill giving away models, and he could just do some surgery — take a wheel from something else and attach it to the red truck. And because of this — the Internet — he felt a flush of Tess love. Was that how Ernie felt?

When what had to be the world's slowest-moving clock finally arranged its glowing red robot dashes to ten o'clock, Genie rolled off the bed and creep-walked down to the kitchen. Grandpop was already there. "Right on time," he said, voice low. His clock had just finished saying *"PEE EM."* Genie could also hear Grandma's snores coming from her and Grandpop's bedroom. Whoa! She *was* as loud as Ernie.

As soon as Genie was sitting, Grandpop dove right in, his voice dropping even lower. "So remember last night when we were talkin' —"

"About the gun?" Genie cut him off.

"No. About how I haven't been outside — like, really been outside — in years?"

"Oh. Yep. You said you were . . . concerned," Genie said, keeping his voice as soft as Grandpop's.

Grandpop shifted in his seat. "Is that what I said?"

"Yep."

"Well, I want you to take me out there. Help me practice."

"Practice what? When?" Genie asked.

"Practice, well, being outside. Like, really outside. Now."

Genie glanced to his left and to his right. Just felt like someone else had to be listening. At least he hoped someone else was listening, so that he would know he wasn't the only person hearing how crazy Grandpop was sounding. "Outside?"

"Outside."

"But . . . it's dark."

"Don't matter to me. Matter to you?"

"Guess not. But I'on't have no shoes on."

"Got on socks?"

"No." Genie should've had on socks,

especially since his mother had warned him about the splinters in the floor upstairs, but he just couldn't sleep in them. He unstuck his feet from the warm linoleum and wiggled his toes.

Grandpop kicked off his slippers. "Me either. So you gon' take me out there or not?"

Back home, Genie's mom would never let him or Ernie be outside that time of night. Only wild kids were out after dark, she said. But up there on that hill, Genie and Grandpop were the only wild ones, so Genie figured they'd be fine. Maybe. Probably. Plus Samantha, the guard dog, would be out there, right? So . . .

"Um . . . okay," he reluctantly agreed.

Grandpop put his hands together in a single silent clap. "Great. C'mon." He made his way silently to the front door. Genie knew Grandma would not be cool with this. He wasn't even really sure if he was all the way cool with it, because if he broke her husband like he broke her red truck, she might never forgive him. But it was happening anyway. What he couldn't help but wonder was why Grandpop chose now to do this. Why all of a sudden he wanted to go exploring after so many years. And why do it with Genie, his eleven-year-old grandson from Brooklyn, who knew nothing about the country outside in the nighttime?

"Grandpop," Genie whispered as he was unlocking the door. "Wouldn't it be better to do this during the day?"

"Because I . . ." Grandpop started, but caught his words and began again. "Because I don't need nobody thinkin' I gotta be babysat or somethin'. Like I can't do for myself. Even though I can't see people, I know they can see me, and I'on't like that." Genie could understand that, especially after what Dad explained about Grandpop.

"So why don't you just ask Grandma to take you, then?" Genie asked. "Especially since she already takes care of you."

Grandpop's voice went cold. "You got one more time to say she takes care of me. I'm not gon' tell you again. She doesn't."

"No, I know. I'm sorry, I just meant —"

Grandpop had unlocked and opened the door. "Listen, I'll tell you why I can't ask her when we get out there," he said, rolling over the question. He grabbed at Genie's shoulder the second they stepped out onto the porch. Whoa. He really *was* nervous. Genie also realized that it was dark and light at the same time. It was dark because it was night, but the moon looked as close as the sun did during the day. Genie remembered how Ma used to call it God's nightlight when he was little, and for a second he wondered what his parents were doing at that very moment. He hoped that they were doing something nice, like maybe walking home from dinner someplace, maybe even looking up at the same moon. Not, he hoped, at home arguing.

It was still pretty warm outside. The crickets and the frogs were in full swing with a loud game of Pete and Repeat. They hadn't drowned the night before and Genie felt unexpectedly relieved, like he wanted to make a *ribbit* or a . . . or a . . . whatever sound crickets make, himself.

"Take it slow, son," Grandpop said, positioning Genie in front of him and placing a hand on each of Genie's shoulders. "There're steps comin' up. I'm used to those from going to the car for my doctors' appointments. But still, take it slow." Genie didn't need to be told that. He was just as nervous as Grandpop.

"Okay, here's the first step," Genie warned softly, easing down to it. Grandpop squeezed his shoulders. "Step." They both took a step down. Then another. Genie was now on the grass, but Grandpop had one more step to go. Again, Genie said, "Step." Grandpop took the final step off the porch, still clinging tight to Genie. The dew-covered grass tickled Genie's feet and he instantly started walking up on his toes just like the man, Crab, did. He had never felt wet grass on his feet before, and he decided he didn't really like it.

"Um . . . so, where you wanna go?" Genie asked, taking another step forward. With Grandpop holding on to Genie's shoulders for dear life, Genie felt like he was wearing a human-size backpack. One that could talk.

"Take me to the middle of the yard," was Grandpop's order, but Genie could hear the shake in his voice.

Genie tiptoed as slowly as he could, Grandpop counting under his breath the whole time until they got to where Genie guessed was the middle of the yard.

"Seventeen," Grandpop said, finally letting go of Genie's shoulders. He breathed deeply like he was trying to suck in all the breeze, or maybe smell the night. What outside really smelled like. What was odd was that Samantha didn't bark. As a matter of fact, he didn't hear her chain move at all. Maybe she was sleeping too. Grandpop was turning his head every which way, listening to the bugs and the critters, who were so loud it was no wonder Samantha didn't hear him and Grandpop.

"It's been a while." Grandpop said it like he was talking to the outside. As if outside was a person. He rocked back and forth on his toes, then bent down to roll his pant legs up to the middle of his shins. "I never could stand wet cuffs," he muttered.

And there was that scar again, the smooth of it gleaming in the moonlight. "Grandpop, I been meanin' to ask you, what happened to your ankle? I saw it earlier today."

Grandpop began to march in place, just a few steps, as if to stretch his legs. "Ah. Detective Little Wood finds another clue," he said. "Tell me somethin'. You this nosy with everybody, or just old blind men?"

Genie didn't answer, because if he did he would've had to say *everybody.* He didn't know any other old blind men.

"Okay." Grandpop sighed. "It has to do with why your grandma ain't my . . . uh . . . let's just say, first choice for this expedition." Grandpop stopped marching. "When I first went blind, I used to walk around out here all the time. I just didn't want my life to change — I didn't want things to be different." He tilted his head way back, as if looking at the stars he couldn't see. "Don't get me wrong, I didn't go far — just a few steps off the porch, a little to the left, a little to the right. Nothin' crazy, and most of the time, it was just me sittin' on the porch, playin' my harmonica while Mary would be out in the garden shooing away the birds and whatnot."

Genie thought that sounded kinda cool — Grandma out there picking peas and Grandpop sitting on the porch with his shades on, playing some kind of pea-picking sound-track.

"One day we were out here and I stepped off the porch," Grandpop went on. "I took six steps — was it six? It might've been seven — to the left when I heard it, the loud hiss, like all the air being let out of a big tire."

"What was it?"

"What *was* it?" Grandpop snorted. "It was a damn copperhead, is what it was. I was headed right at it, and by the time I realized it was a snake, it was too late. It bit me. Clamped right down on my ankle. Hurt like I'on't know what. I fell down screamin', and Mary came runnin' over. By the time she got there, at least the snake had let go. We rushed to the hospital and they took care of it, but my skin had a weird reaction to the bite, and that's how it healed up — with that scar."

A copperhead! Genie knew exactly what a copperhead was. It was part of an extensive

Google search he had conducted: CAN (blank) DEFEAT A HONEY BADGER? Turned out, no, copperheads can't beat honey badgers. But they *can* beat humans. Genie tried to imagine what it must've been like to not be able to see the thing that was biting you. To hear it coming, but to not be able to get away. Oh man!

"I mean, had it been something more poisonous, it coulda took me out," Grandpop went on. "I woulda hated to leave your grandma like that. So, that was it. Mary was all messed up by it, and so was I. I ain't been out here since."

Now, this was the perfect time to be quiet. To just let the story end there and move on. But Genie's brain started adding things up, running the story over and back. A few steps from the porch. *They* were seventeen steps. Way more than a few. This was the same yard. A yard that once had a copperhead. Which meant there could be more copperheads. And despite the glowing moon, it was still dark enough for Genie to have a hard time seeing things in the grass, especially something moving as fast as a snake.

"Uh . . . Grandpop?"

Grandpop grunted.

"You think there might be snakes out here now?"

"Probably," Grandpop said with a shrug. "But don't worry, this time of year they usually sleep at night."

That made Genie feel a little better, but he definitely kept his eyes aimed at the ground and listened — listened hard — for that hissing sound. All he could hear, though, was the Pete and Repeat, and . . . a sniffle? Sniffling? Genie looked up. The moon shone on Grandpop like a spotlight, and he was slipping a finger behind his sunglasses and wiping his eyes. Was he crying? Why was he crying? Wasn't this what he wanted?

"What's wrong?" Genie asked, panic rising.

"Nothin'," Grandpop said, toughening his voice. "Nothin'," he repeated, now a little softer.

But then he took his glasses off, used his thumb and pointer finger to pinch the tears away.

"Tell me somethin'," he said, putting the shades back on. "Are there any stars out tonight?"

Genie looked toward the moon — no stars there — it was probably too bright. But in the opposite direction, there they were. Thousands — no, millions! Genie had never seen anything like it.

"Yep," Genie said, staring. "A whole lot of 'em."

Grandpop nodded and gave a small, sad smile. Genie watched him, wondering what thoughts Grandpop must've been thinking, what memories must've been swirling around his head about being outside. Then Genie turned his eyes back to the stars and thought about how terrible it would be to never be able to see them again.

NINE

#462: Where is Sam Hill? I thought we were in North Hill.

#463: Is the moon brighter in the South? Maybe if the sun is hotter, then that would mean it's probably brighter. And if almost every star is a sun, basically there's just a bunch of suns in the sky. Maybe the sun is the sun only to Earth, but to all the other planets, it's just a star. Like how Dad is only Dad to me and Ernie. To Ma, he's a husband. And to Grandpop and Grandma, he's a son. But to the people he saves in fires, he's a star.

Day Three started with a phone call from Ma.
Ma: Hi, Genie!
Genie: Hi, Ma!
Ernie: Hi, Ma.

Ma: Ernie? What, y'all got me on speaker-phone?

Ernie: Yeah.

Ma: Well, give me the verdict. How's it been?

Genie: Ernie met a girl.

Ernie: Genie!

Ma: A girl? Already?

Ernie: She lives down the hill. Her name's Tess.

Ma: (Sigh) Well, I'm glad y'all have somebody else there to hang out with besides Grandma, Grandpop, and that dog.

Genie: How's Shelly?

Ma: Haven't seen her. But I'm sure she's fine.

Genie: How's Dad?

Ma: Your father's good, Genie. Sleepin' right now. He's been putting in that overtime — so he has to work tonight. You sure sound pretty comfortable, son. Grandpop's not so bad, huh?

Genie: No, he's pretty cool. And Grandma, too.

Ernie: She made us pick peas.

Ma: Peas! (Laughter) You boys are gettin' a real taste of the country life.

Genie: But what about you and Dad?

Ma: I told you, baby . . . he's sleepin'.

■ ■ ■ ■

After talking to their parents, Genie and Ernie did their early morning grandson duties, which on Day Three were exactly like Day One, just add in some pea-patch watering, which now had the twist of Genie looking every which way for snakes. Genie wanted to tell Ernie about the snake thing, but he was scared that Ernie would start asking questions and then Genie would let Grandpop's secret slip. So he just looked out for snakes for the both of them.

After the peas, Genie and Ernie went down to Tess's. Genie pretty much became invisible to Ernie because Tess was there, obviously, and that was okay because Ernie became invisible to Genie because, well, Google was there. *In-ter-netttt.*

"Tess, can Genie use your computer?" Ernie had asked as soon as they reached Tess's front porch, where she stood as if waiting for the brothers from New York — the city boys — to come barreling down the hill. At least Genie didn't wipe out this time.

Tess smirked. "What you wanna do on the Internet?" she'd asked, blocking the front door as if Genie might just rush past her and barge inside.

"Well." Genie slipped his hand in his back pocket and yanked out his notebook. "I got some research I need to do."

"*Research?* What kind of *research?* We ain't in school, boy. It's summertime," she poked.

"Exactly," Ernie said, shaking his head as if just as disappointed in Genie's lack of summer protocol.

"Yeah, but I need to find out stuff, like, I don't know . . . stuff like if there are actually black sheep in real life."

Tess studied Genie's face, waiting for the punch line that, after a moment, she realized wasn't coming. "Is he serious?" she asked Ernie.

"Unfortunately."

"Well, in that case, *of course* there are," Tess told Genie. She tried to keep a straight face as she continued, "Black sheep are the ones black people count when they tryna get to sleep." She stared at Genie, dead serious. Then her face leaked a grin. Genie sucked his teeth.

"I'm just jokin'," Tess said. "I ain't never seen no black sheep, but that don't mean they don't exist. I ain't never seen no New York boys either, and here y'all are, standin' on my porch, lookin' at me, wantin' my Internet."

"You lookin' at *us*," Ernie cracked back, slick.

"Ain't nobody lookin' at you!"

"Nobody but you," he quipped.

Tess stared him down and sized him up in that way that meant she either wanted to punch him or kiss him. Either way, Genie didn't care. He just wanted to use the computer.

"So," Genie said, trying to steer the conversation back to what was important. "The Internet."

"Dang, you on a mission," Tess said. "A'ight, hold on." She swung the screen door open and dashed into the house. It slammed shut behind her. A few mangled bottle caps lay scattered by the porch railing, and Genie wondered if they were Ernie's bads. An old car pulled into the yard next door. A '71 Mustang! Genie had built a model just like it once. Sweet car. But this one's cherry paint was being overtaken by rust.

Tess's house wasn't much different from their house back in Brooklyn, except for the furniture — the couches and chairs were covered in thick plastic. *All* of them. Maybe the furniture was new, and Tess's parents just hadn't had the time to take the plastic off yet? They hadn't met Tess's mother, but Crab didn't seem like the kind of guy who would care about stuff like that.

And there were containers of wet wipes all over the place. Genie was about to ask who the neat freak was as a joke when Tess pointed to the corner. "There's the computer." It was set on one of those specially made desks with the drawers and the slide-out keyboard tray, and a designated compartment for the printer. Genie felt a surge of happy, as if he were reuniting with a long-lost friend. He was over there in a blink, setting his notebook down, tapping the space bar on the keyboard to wake the monitor up.

Ernie and Tess sat on the couch, the plastic farting as they tried to get comfortable so they could have, what seemed to Genie, uncomfortable small talk. Ernie asked Tess if she had ever eaten squirrel. She told him that she had and that it tasted just like chicken, but you had to be careful because the buckshots from the shotgun shells would sometimes be stuck in the meat and could crack your tooth if you didn't catch it. Ernie pretended he wasn't grossed out while Tess followed up with her own question about whether Ernie had ever seen any stars, and after he replied that he had seen tons of stars, especially since he'd been in Virginia, Tess slapped him on the arm and said that she meant *stars* stars. Like Beyoncé stars. And while they gabbed on, Genie focused his attention on the monitor, typing:

Is there really such a thing as black sheep?

Then he deleted that question and started with something a little more important.

Where to find model car wheels

Genie scrolled through, looking for answers, but couldn't find anything helpful. Everything was pretty much saying, *Buy a whole new model, ya big dummy!* But Genie couldn't do that, so he'd have to figure out another way, and in this moment, Google wasn't being particularly helpful, so he pushed the red truck to the back of his brain and started flipping through his notebook pages, moving on to other pressing questions, like:

Where do crickets go when it rains?

And:

What's so good about barn swallows?

While Genie clicked through the answers, reading about how crickets typically protect themselves by going underground, which led him to a new question — didn't water *sink* underground? — there was the sound of a door opening down the hall. Tess stopped talking. So did Ernie. But Genie continued to scroll and read about how swallows are supposed to be symbols of hope and life and should never be harmed, because they represent young people who have died, as well as brotherhood. Well, that was super fascinating, especially since Grandpop knew a young person who died — Uncle Wood. Maybe that was why he had all those swallows! As Genie was about to start searching the next question, his Googling was cut short.

"Tess, who these boys?" came a voice from the other side of the room. Genie glanced up.

"I just told you, Mama, these are Ma and Pop Harris's grandsons," Tess said, sounding annoyed. "They visiting for a while." She turned to Ernie and Genie. "Y'all, this my mother."

Tess's mom didn't look anything like anybody's mom Genie had ever seen. It might've been the face mask and the plastic gloves that threw him off.

"Oh, that's right," the woman said, popping herself in the head with an open hand. "I'm guessing you the one my Tessy been goin' on about," she said, looking at Ernie.

"Ma!" Tess yelped.

"Girl, hush," her mother said, adjusting the mask's elastic around her ears. She looked like a ninja from the neck up. "Nice to meet y'all. Sorry 'bout the mask, but I'm a little sick and I don't want y'all to catch nothin' and take it back up the hill. I been knowin' your grandfolks for a long time, and I would hate to make 'em ill." She went to the window and, using one of her gloved fingers to bend a shade, peered at the bar next door.

"Ma grew up with Pop Harris," Tess explained.

"I ain't grow up *with* him," Tess's mother clarified. "He way older than me. Matter of fact, I barely saw him because he had already been drafted into the army. But his *mama* used to babysit me when I was a little girl." She released her finger from the blind. It snapped back into place. "And his daddy taught me how to make birdcages, which is where I think Tessy got her craftiness from."

Genie perked up. "Birdcages?"

170

Tess's mother left the window and leaned back into the corner, as if three kids were poisonous and she was afraid to come too close.

"Yep, birdcages," she confirmed, "back when the Harrises lived in a different house, way back in them woods." The yellow house! The one Genie had noticed when he and Ernie were poop slinging for the first time. *Aim for that old house back there.* That'd been Grandpop's childhood home?

"Now, Pop Harris's mother, Millie, she was the sweetest woman on earth. Took care of everything and everybody, includin' me. But Old Man Harris — that's your great-granddaddy — he was topsy-turvy," Tess's mother went on. Genie and Ernie glanced at each other.

"What you mean, topsy-turvy?" Ernie asked.

"It means . . . I'on't know how to explain it . . . like, he had two personalities in himself he was strugglin' with." Tess's mom popped each plastic glove at the wrist, then folded her arms across her chest. "He was in World War II, and some days you could really tell he was still dealin' with it, because he'd lock himself in the bedroom all day. And then other days, he'd be so nice. So gentle." She inched a few steps closer and

171

sat on the arm of the chair next to the couch. "Matter fact, that's how the whole birdcage thing happened. They had this window in their house. Great big one." She spread her arms to show how wide. "And sometimes, when I would be playing in the front room, there would be like a thump against the glass. Then we'd find a little bird on the porch. Stupid things would be flying around, and see their reflection in that big ol' window, and attack, full speed, headfirst. *WHAM!*" She clapped her hands together, the gloves muting the normal pop. "Your great-granddaddy, if he was in a good mood, would come out there and see the little hurt birdies, and he'd scoop them up and put them in these wood-and-wire cages he'd made, so that they could hopefully heal up in peace, and not be eaten by the family dog. What was her name? Shoot, I can't even remember now. Anyway, they didn't want the birds to be eaten by the dog, or worse, by a snake." Out of the blue, Tess's mother stood up. Checked her mask. Checked the wrists of her gloves. Cleared her throat. Then she sat again. "And so he taught me how to make the rescue cages. For when he wasn't around. I mean, he wasn't even that old, but I guessed he figured, just in case."

"And now you all know the history of North Hill, Virginia, where the people save birds who get hurt trying to fight themselves," Tess said, witty.

"Don't be smart, Tess," her mother snapped. "Anyway, nice meetin' y'all. Tell your grandfolks I say hello." Then, turning to Tess, she said low, "Tess, you know what to do."

Once Tess's mother disappeared down the hallway and they heard her door close, Ernie whispered, "What did she mean, 'you know what to do'?"

Tess sighed. "Sorry, boys, but now I gotta kill y'all." She made the *stab, stab, stab* movement at Ernie, then laughed. But her laughter trailed off quickly as she began explaining what was really going on. "Nah, it's just that I gotta wipe down everything when y'all leave. Especially the computer." She rubbed her cheeks hard. "She's crazy, my ma," Tess said, blunt. Then she turned to Ernie and repeated it, this time looking straight in his eyes. "She's *crazy*. Seriously. She's out of her mind. She wears that mask because she thinks she's sick and everything around her is sick. Every week it's a new thing. Last week she thought she had tuberculosis. Week before that, asthma. Yesterday she told me that she's pretty sure she's coming down with cerebral palsy, but then this morning she said it's cystic fibrosis, and just before I let y'all in, she said she thinks it might be Alzheimer's, but she can't remember."

"I'on't know what *any* of that stuff is, except asthma," Ernie admitted. "None of it."

"Well, I didn't either, but she looks each thing up on the Internet and tells me every daggone detail. She hasn't left the house in like a month. Some days she won't even leave her room."

"But is she really sick?" Genie asked, wondering if maybe he should've written down all these disease names.

"Did you drink beer the other day at the bar?" Tess asked.

"No. Ginger beer," Genie said, confused. Tess pulled a wet wipe from a small container set on the end table beside the couch. Stepping over Ernie's legs, she came over to the computer and began wiping down the keyboard. Well, that explained all the wet wipes.

"Exactly," Tess said, running the white cloth over each key, spreading the strange scent of cooked flowers. "Looked like beer, but it was just ginger beer. The Special."

"Right. The Special."

"Well, let's just say my mom's another version of the Special."

"*Or,* we could say that your mom's a hypochondriac," Genie said.

Tess cocked her head. "I don't know how y'all do up in New York, but down here, we don't just go callin' people's mamas names."

"I'm not," Genie backpedaled. "I'm just sayin' that's what's wrong with her."

"And how you know that? You a genius?"

"No. He's a nerd," Ernie said. Genie shot him a look, but nothing too cold. It wasn't that big of a deal. He'd been called a nerd before.

"Saw it on the Internet," Genie said with a shrug.

"So you mean to tell me, you know what a hyper cognac is but —"

"Hypochondriac."

"Whatever. You know what that is, but you don't know whether there's such a thing as a black sheep?"

Genie's cheeks started to burn. "Well, that's different." But what wasn't different were the new questions coming to Genie, which he frantically scribbled into his notepad before leaving Tess's wet-wiped house.

#464: Why are swallows called swallows? Did people used to eat them? Maybe

Great-Grandpop? Gross.

#465: How do hurt birds heal themselves? Do they have to be in safe spaces like cages? Wouldn't they feel trapped? Can you be trapped and safe at the same time?

And that was how it went for the rest of the week, Genie catching up on his questions either at night or in the morning, after dinner or before chores. And as soon as Grandma's litany of duties were done, Genie and Ernie headed down to Tess's. Genie sitting at the computer, typing away, reading about all the things that no one else seemed to care about, including the unfortunate fact that there was no way he could find a replacement wheel for the red truck — turned out nobody in North Hill was giving any away. And he'd looked all over the living room floor for the other half of the broken one, but apparently the floor had eaten it or something. So, yeah. Bummer.

As for Ernie and Tess, they'd sit on the couch each day, scooting closer and closer to each other. Ernie would be trying to prove how tough he was by letting Tess pinch him or punch him as hard as she could. Tess's mom would yell something from the back, like, "Tess, go tell your father

I need medicine for athlete's foot. Chronic athlete's foot! I'm pretty sure I have it!" Tess would roll her eyes, which would be Ernie and Genie's cue that it was time for her to wipe down the living room, and for them all to go back outside. So they'd help Tess make earrings, or sometimes just throw bottle caps at each other, or sometimes even walk around the yard in search of anthills to poke holes in, then watch the fire ants pour out the top like lava with legs. Then they'd usually hit the bar for a cold ginger beer and stale peanuts that were disgusting to eat, but perfect for trying to see who could catch the most in their mouths.

And Genie and Ernie finally began settling into country life. They had even been to church with Grandma, which was nothing short of a snoozer. An old building, with old people, singing old songs. Genie and Ernie slept through most of it, which Grandma didn't mind because they were sitting in the back anyway, since they didn't have any dress clothes, and Grandma said she wasn't about to be embarrassed. She said God could still get inside them even if they were asleep. Ernie wondered out loud why they couldn't have just stayed home if that was the case. And Genie wondered if that was why Grandpop didn't have to come.

Back at the house, the sweet tea had finally started to taste good. Genie and Grandpop spent a little time each day in the inside-outside room, where Grandpop would have his drink and his apple, always spitting the seeds in the small cup he kept under the table. Genie had taken to apples too and was getting pretty good at seed spitting as well. More importantly, he got a new chore, one he picked all on his own — cleaning up that crazy room. He was starting to really like those birds, especially after learning what the barn swallows symbolized. He decided they needed names, and since there were five of them, he named them after the Jackson Five. Then he decided that he'd make sure they were getting fed. He cleaned the poop out of their cages, Grandpop showing him how. It was so crazy that Grandpop had been doing it himself all this time, which explained the mess on the fake grass floor. Grandpop gave Genie a toothbrush that he'd attached a long wooden stick to so that it could slide in between the bars to scrub the white-gunked cage bottoms. It wasn't perfect — at first Genie worried that he'd poke one of the birds while he was scrubbing, but they always hopped out of the way — and it was pretty gross, but it was better than the mess Grandpop had going on.

Genie also felt bad about those poor thirsty plants, so he started watering them, and plucking off the leaves that had died — tricks he'd learned from Grandma in the pea garden. Ernie was invited to come into the room with them as well, and he did sometimes, but it kind of freaked him out, Genie could tell. All the cages and plants and birds — it was, yeah, a little freaky. Plus Ernie was way more interested in Tess. *She* was his new chore. She would sometimes come up the hill to visit, and she'd sit with Ernie out on the porch like old people and talk, or fool around with Samantha until the sun disappeared behind the trees, and the sky became layered with colors they *never* saw in Brooklyn, and the red houses at the bottom of the hill darkened. Then, on Day Eight, the humdrum routine that Genie and Ernie were actually starting to like was broken.

TEN

Apparently, North Hill had a town to it. Who knew? And that was where Grandma told Ernie and Genie they were going, right after they both finished picking peas, scooping poop. Y'know, the usual. Destination: the flea market. Genie felt a flush of excitement to be going somewhere, anywhere, other than church or Tess's. Before they left, Genie and Ernie washed their hands and changed their shirts — Grandma's rules — and Genie took the red truck from the dresser and slid it gingerly into his pocket.

"What you takin' that for?" Ernie asked.

"Because maybe somebody might be sellin' model car parts at the market. Might need to match it up."

"Man, Grandma sellin' peas, so it's probably just gon' be people sellin' food. Ain't nobody gon' be sellin' no toy parts."

"It's a model," Genie corrected Ernie. "And so what if people sell food there? You got them sunglasses from the bodega at the end of our block, and they sell food too. Plus, Tess sells her earrings, and can't nobody *eat* earrings, Ern." Genie had proven his point.

Downstairs, as Ernie ran ahead toward the front door, Genie told him he would be right there, but he had one more quick thing to do. Feed the birds.

He pushed the inside-outside room door open. Grandpop had started leaving it unlocked because, Genie could tell, YES!, that he trusted him, and knew that Genie was hell-bent on making sure everything — the birds and the plants — was being properly taken care of in there. Grandpop wasn't there, which was fine because Genie didn't need him to be there to do what he came to do. He reached under the small table and grabbed the can that held the . . . dead flies. They still grossed Genie out, but every day he got more used to it by shaking the flies into his hand with one eye closed and pretending they were seeds. Seeds, with wings. The can had gotten low, but Genie figured he could divvy out the flies fairly, four or five apiece, and each of the Jackson Five would get enough. But he calculated wrong. By the time he got to the last swallow, Michael, Genie was down to one fly.

Michael was the smallest of all the birds, and he didn't need a lot to eat, but he had to have more than one fly. Plus, that fly was all mooshed. No way was Genie touching that. First he considered the plants. They were everywhere, but he wasn't actually sure that birds ate plants. Grandpop said they ate Grandma's crops, but eating peas and eating Grandpop's weird inside-outside plants might've been two entirely different meals. Genie had never seen the birds in Brooklyn pecking at plants, but that was probably because he never really saw plants in Brooklyn. Then he thought, maybe he could give Michael Jackson bread. He always saw people back home feeding pigeons bread in the park, but pigeons might have stronger stomachs than these country birds. The Jackson Five might not be used to stale city rolls. They might only eat farm-raised. Organic. Couldn't get much more organic than flies. He looked in the can at the last fly left. It looked just like . . . And that was when it hit him. *Duh.* Seeds! As in, apple seeds!

Genie slid the empty coffee can back under the table and grabbed the cup Grandpop used to spit his apple seeds in. His "seed cup." Seeds, flies, same size, same thing, Genie decided as he tapped a few apple seeds out of the cup into his palm. He put the cup back, then dropped the seeds one at a time into Michael Jackson's cage. Michael seemed immediately interested and hopped from his perch to the cage bottom, and Genie left the room relieved. No birds would go hungry on *his* watch.

"Sorry, had to feed the birds," Genie said as he climbed into the car, the engine already running, Grandma behind the wheel, ready to go. He wiggled the truck out of his pocket and tucked it in the pouch behind Grandma's seat, so she couldn't see it, and so it wouldn't get further damaged by Genie being squished up in the backseat with exactly 627 pea pods in a basket, a bunch of school-lunch-size bags, and a scale. Ernie rode shotgun.

"Had to feed them stinky birds, got it. Now, buckle up." Grandma turned the knob on the radio. That's right, Grandma's car radio was controlled by a *knob.* Not a button. A knob. But even though her car was old, it wasn't old and ugly like Crab's car, at least. The radio went from news, to jazz, to rap. When she landed on the rhythm and bass of hip-hop, Genie livened up and started nodding his head. Then Grandma changed the station again.

"*Here* we go," she said, setting the radio on a church music station. She pulled the visor down to block the sun and slowly turned the wheel to head down the hill. When they got to the bottom, she turned the music up loud. Neither Ernie nor Genie minded listening to loud music, but when it was loud church music, and your grandmother was singing at the top of her lungs like she was actually *in* church, it got kinda strange. Ernie just kept looking out the window, trying not to laugh. And Genie tried to come up with a question to ask to get Grandma to turn the music down.

"Grandma," he said, finding one, pushing the pea basket pressing into his hip over a little. She didn't respond. "Grandma," he repeated, but she was in the middle of singing to Jesus. She kept putting her right hand in the air and waving it in front of her face like she was fanning away a stinky burp. "Grandma!" Genie shouted. She finally turned the radio down and looked at him through the rearview mirror.

"Yes, baby."

"Can I ask you somethin'?"

"You just did."

"Oh." Huh. "Well, can I ask somethin' else?"

"Boy, ask me!" She looked back at the road.

"Does anybody at the flea market actually sell fleas?"

Ernie groaned.

"What?" Genie moaned.

"Stupid question, man," Ernie scoffed.

"No, it's not," Grandma replied, taking her eyes off the road again, this time to glare at Ernie. Then she refocused, straight ahead. "No baby, they don't sell fleas. At least I don't think they do. I ain't never seen no flea sellers there, but if you spot any, make sure you let me know. I'll pick up a few as a gift for my ol' buddy, Crab." Then she doubled back. "Oh wait, I better not. Ernie might have a mad *girlfriend* on his hands, and we don't want that, now do we?" She looked at Genie through the mirror again and winked. Ernie just shook his head, crushing his smile between his cheeks.

The flea market was one bizarre, amazing place. It was like a circus and a carnival mixed together, except with no animals and no rides, though you could definitely buy light-up swords and cotton candy. You could also buy tires. And doorknobs. And pretty much anything else. Genie hadn't known what to expect. He'd never been to a flea market before, and they both figured it would be a bunch of geezers like Grandma, talking trash, singing church songs, selling a bunch of fruit and vegetables they'd grown in their yards and forced their grandkids to get up at six in the morning to pick so they'd be fresh off the vine. And there were some people there like that, but a lot of people were just selling . . . stuff. Like, anything. Which gave Genie hope that he might be able to find a replacement wheel for the red truck. It wasn't impossible, since there were people selling things like old black-and-white photos of random people, rusty screws, paintings and drawings — some were cool and some were lame.

This one lady just had a table full of white socks. That was it. She just sold white socks, which seemed crazy, but once Genie thought about all the times he'd heard Ma going off about how filthy their socks got, and how they always had holes in them, white sock lady seemed more like a genius. She probably would've been Ma's new best friend if Ma lived here.

"Just set the basket right there," Grandma said after she covered her table with a blue bedsheet. "Put the scale and the bags next to it. When somebody comes, they'll scoop as many as they want into a bag. Ernie, you'll take the bag and weigh it." She pushed down on the scale — the red arrow moved from zero to one then snapped back to zero. "Genie, you holler out the number that red hand lands on. And I'll tell 'em how much they owe. Got it?"

"Got it," Genie said. Ernie just nodded, playing cool as usual, a thin layer of dust building up on his sunglasses.

"Now stand back and let me show you how to call," Grandma said, moving to the front of the table. Then, taking a deep breath, letting the air swell her chest, she belted out, "Sweet pea, sweet pea, sweeeeeeet pea!" as if "sweet pea" was somebody far away she was hollering at. Also, as if peas were actually sweet, which Genie knew was not the case. Talk about embarrassing!

"Sweeeeeeeeet!" Grandma sang out again as people started looking over at the table and smiling. Genie was thinking he could maybe hide under that blue sheet, and he could tell that Ernie probably wanted to do the same. He was just thinking about how lucky he was that at least no one knew him in North Hill or his life would've been ruined, when Grandma nudged him. "Help me out here, son. No one will be able to resist that cute little face of yours. Go on, yell it out just like I did."

Really? *Really!?!* Genie shot Ernie a *Help me out here, bro* look, but Ernie took off his sunglasses and pretended he was cleaning them, like that was more important than bailing his brother out. Grandma nudged Genie again, this time with less patience. So Genie cupped his hands around his mouth and just got it over with. "Sweet pea!" he yelled, and Grandma shrieked "Sweet pea" herself, and then Genie did it again, but this time louder and longer. Ernie just stood there, in mid-clean. Shocked. Then Grandma nudged him too and cracked a joke about him being too cool. Then she went back to her call, this time adding a rhyme. "Not in the store, not on the street, you ain't *nev-ah* seen a pea this sweet!" And then again, "Sweeeeeeet!"

The next shocker was the crowd. Why would anyone rush to a table to buy peas? But that silly call totally worked! So many people. So many peas! Bagging and weighing, pound after pound, dollar after dollar, for what Genie considered to be the nastiest food on the planet. Amazing. After everybody bought up most of the pods, and the crowd died down, Grandma taped a sign to the front of the table that said, SORRY, PEA-PLE, WE'RE SOLD OUT. Then she paid Genie and Ernie ten dollars apiece! Triple shocker! They'd been working for her, sure, but they hadn't thought she was going to actually *pay* them for it. They figured it was just more grandson labor.

"Now, let's go have a look around," Grandma suggested. "Might be somethin' here y'all want."

Genie ran his hand over the lump in his pocket. He knew exactly what he was looking for, and now he even had the money to pay for it. Vintage model car kits or even model cars already put together that he could take apart. Anything that had a wheel he could use to replace the one on Uncle Wood's truck. There had to be someone at the flea market selling them. At least Genie hoped there was. But he couldn't tell Grandma. Well, he could've, but he didn't even want to get her mind going.

Dust kicked up around them as they wandered up and down the rows of tables, each one selling something different. One man sold 3-D glasses. He was wearing a pair. It was weird. Another guy was selling old magazines. There were a bunch of people around his table holding up faded covers of Martin Luther King Jr. or the Beatles. There was a lady selling board games. Genie saw *Jeopardy!* and got excited at first, before figuring *Jeopardy!* was best played on TV. With Alex Trebek. No Alex, no fun. And then there was the woman selling video game controllers. She had them organized in crates by what systems they were for, some going back to the really, really old games. It was like stumbling upon a bunch of broken pieces to a spaceship. A few tables down from the video-game lady there was also a little kid selling shoestrings. Just . . . shoestrings. And for some reason, this was the table Grandma stopped at.

"So, young man," Grandma said to the boy. He stood with his hands behind his back, real proper. Like he was some kind of big-time businessman. Even had on a shirt and tie. "I'm sure my grandsons here are dyin' to know. Do these laces come with the sneakers, or are those sold separately?"

The boy started laughing, straightening up the laces on the table. Genie and Ernie recognized the metal tips on the ends of the shoelaces. They were the ones that came with Jordans, not that either of the Harris boys had ever had a pair of Jordans. Their father refused to spend that kind of money on sneakers. But Genie's best friend, Aaron, had some. And Shelly. And theirs had those silver tips on them.

"No, no, ma'am," the boy said in his best sell-y voice. "These *were* shoelaces. But they're not anymore." He took one of the laces and wrapped it around his wrist a few times, and the metal points stuck together. "I use magnets on the tips. Now they're bracelets. Or necklaces." He circled another one around his neck. *Ta-freakin'-da.*

"Oh . . . wow." Grandma was obviously impressed. Genie wasn't. Maybe it was because he'd seen Tess make something way better out of bottle caps. Or maybe it was because he knew that shoestrings as jewelry would never fly back home in Brooklyn. "That's cool, right, boys?"

"Right," Ernie said, slowly inching away. And Genie was inching right along with him.

They checked out a few more tables, some really cool, like the one with all the gold chains (even though Grandma said they were fake), and some not so cool, like the one with the dude who was selling his paintings. But he only painted cows. And they didn't even look like cows.

But what Genie was looking for he still hadn't found. Ernie, on the other hand, didn't seem to be looking for anything, but when he came across this lady who was making these weird dolls — at least they looked like dolls — he stopped.

"Howdy," the lady said, but not in the real

way. It was a fake, funny *howdy.*

"What are these things?" Ernie asked. Grandma picked one up and examined it. Genie looked at the sellers to the left and right. Picture frames and belt buckles. Still no model cars.

"I call them Bite Buddies. They're for dogs. I make them out of rubber. They're virtually indestructible, and they've got a little squeaky thing in them," the lady said, pinching the head of one of the dolls.

Genie didn't think the dolls were really that cool. They were better than the brace-lace-lets — the shoestring jewelry — but not by much. Apparently, Ernie felt differently. The sign on the table said BITE BUDDIES: SIX BUCKS. Genie knew Ernie had to have seen it too, but Ernie still tried to hit the lady with the okeydoke.

"How much?" he asked, like some kind of wheeler and dealer.

"Where you from?" the Howdy lady asked.

"Brooklyn," Ernie replied, puffed up as usual.

"Okay, so for you . . ." She put her hand to her chin like she was considering cutting Ernie a deal. "I'll give it to you for . . . say . . . six bucks."

Ernie's face got so tight it looked like it was going to suck into itself. Grandma did an air-spit and burst into laughter. Howdy lady was slick. Ernie didn't laugh, but he did fork over that ten-dollar bill Grandma had just given him and purchased for himself, well, purchased for Samantha, her very first Bite Buddy.

Just as Genie was thinking he wouldn't mind a bite as well — a bite of lunch — Grandma said, all excited, "Ooh, I want y'all to try somethin'." She made a beeline through the food section of the market — past the corn dog stand, the guy selling turkey legs. "Something I *know* y'all can't get in the big city," she added, moving faster than they'd ever seen her.

They stopped in front of a blue trailer that had the longest line of all, everybody rocking back and forth, fanning themselves, waiting for whatever sandwich the old guy inside was handing out through the small window on the side.

"What is that?" Ernie asked, looking at a young boy biting into the mystery sandwich, his eyes closed in delight.

"It's soft-shell crab," Grandma said, inching forward as the line did.

Now Ernie was the one with all the questions. "Like a crab cake?"

"Just wait and see."

Ten minutes later they were at the window

and Grandma was slapping a twenty-dollar bill down, telling the old man she wanted three, laughing about somebody named Russell trying to sell paper-clip necklaces for fifteen bucks a pop, introducing Genie and Ernie to the old man — Mr. Murphy — and then finally getting their sandwiches and stepping to the side.

So here's the thing about the sandwich. It was really a crab. Like, a whole crab with legs and pincher claws, all fried up, wedged between two pieces of white bread. Genie and Ernie looked at each other like, *I ain't eating this,* but before they could say anything, they heard the crunch of Grandma biting into hers.

"Eat, boys," she encouraged, smushing a paper napkin against her lips. "Just go for it."

Ernie shrugged. Then, upholding his big-brother responsibilities as "first taster," he nibbled on one of the claws hanging out from between the bread. Then he took a bite. Genie watched Ernie's face, waiting for the signal. Ernie nodded, then took a bigger bite — a chomp — which meant that now Genie had to do it too. So he did. And it was weird at first, especially since the inside of the fried crab looked like scrambled eggs. But it was good. Real good.

On the way back to their table, Grandma stopped once more, this time to talk to the wildest-looking man ever. He had white hair only on half of his head. His skin was pale like he was dusted with powder. He wore a dingy tank top and jeans cut into booty shorts, with kneesocks and sandals. Dude looked crazy.

"Binks, where you been?" Grandma said, giving him a hug.

"Not selling today. Figured I'd just come out and bop around a little bit. See what bait is getting the bite, you know?" he replied.

"I hear ya," Grandma said. Genie's head was still on the swivel, scouting the scene for model sellers, when Grandma touched his shoulder. "Let me introduce y'all to my friend here," she said. "Boys, this is Mr. Binks. He usually sits at the table next to mine, but today he deserted me. Binks, this is Genie, my youngest grandbaby, and Ernie, my oldest one."

"Ernie," he said, shaking Ernie's hand. "And Genie, right?"

"Yes." Genie waited for him to crack some stupid joke, like Crab did. Like everyone did.

But Mr. Binks simply said, "Great, nice to meet you." He shook Genie's hand, and

Genie squeezed as hard as he could.

"After this one, the rest will be fives," Genie said seriously. Mr. Binks smiled wide, flashing the whitest teeth Genie had ever seen. Whiter than Ernie's. Even whiter than Grandpop's.

"So what you lookin' for out here, Binks? Peas?" Grandma asked.

Mr. Binks chuckled and said, "Nah, not peas. Roller skates."

"Roller skates?"

"Yep," he said, flicking a fly off his shoulder.

"For who?"

He pointed at himself. "Me."

He didn't seem like the type of guy who would roller-skate. Then again, he kinda did.

"But we don't have no roller rinks round here, Binks. So it don't make much sense to get skates."

"I don't need a rink. I plan on skating to work. On the road."

Ernie almost snotted on himself trying to hold in his laugh. But Genie thought it sounded pretty awesome. Weird, but awesome. Binks reminded Genie of those people he saw performing on the A train, the people who just didn't care about what anybody thought, just doing their thing no matter what. There was something really cool about that.

They left Mr. Binks after he got caught up at the white socks table buying twenty pairs of socks, Genie guessed for when he got his skates. They took a quick peek at the movie table — Ernie was always hunting for old karate movies, but the seller only had old VHS tapes, so Genie and Ernie didn't look long. Afterward, Grandma led them back to their table to start shutting everything down for the day.

"You boys have fun?" Grandma asked, folding the blue sheet the same way Ma folded blankets. Ernie grabbed the empty basket.

"I did," Genie said. He was disappointed that he hadn't found anything to fix Uncle Wood's truck, but the market was random and weirdly awesome, and he was definitely glad he came.

"Ernie?" Grandma prompted.

"It was cool," he said, turning the basket upside down. A few loose peas fell to the ground.

"Good," Grandma said.

"Grandma? What does Mr. Binks sell when he's out here with you?" Genie asked, because he figured a man who could dress like that, and buy roller skates and twenty pairs of white socks, might also be a guy who sold vintage model car parts. Never know.

Ernie laughed. "He's probably that guy Russell who makes the paper-clip necklaces!"

"No, no. He's not Russell," Grandma said, heading for the parking lot. "Binks is selling what everybody wants."

"And what's that?" Genie asked.

"Good luck."

Eleven

Good luck? Good luck? Maybe Genie needed to buy an extra-large order of whatever Mr. Binks was selling, because he discovered shortly after he got home that his luck was bad. *Way* bad. First the thing with the truck. And now . . . Michael. As in Michael Jackson, swallow number five.

As soon as they pulled up in the yard, Ernie bolted over to Samantha with the new Bite Buddy, and Genie ran into the house to put the truck safely back on the dresser upstairs. Grandpop was on the kitchen floor doing sit-ups. Genie froze in his tracks. Grandpop — exercising?

"What's the matter, son, you never seen an old blind man work on his abdominoes?" Grandpop grunted.

"No. I mean, not really," Genie replied, aching to correct Grandpop. *Abdominals. It's abdominals.*

"Yeah, well, now you have. Care to join?

Only if you think you can keep up."

"Hmm, that's more of an Ernie thing."

"Hey, they your ab-dominoes. Do what you want with 'em," Grandpop said. "Oh, Crab stopped by. Brought some food for my babies. Bag's on the table."

"Perfect. I gotta put something away and then I'll fill the can."

"Always business with you, Little Wood. I love that," Grandpop said, starting his next set of crunches.

Genie put the truck back upstairs, then grabbed the paper bag and headed for the inside-outside room, where he poured the bag of flies into the empty coffee can. Then, starting with Jackie, he went from cage to cage, checking on the cheeping birds. Tito, fine. Jermaine, good. Marlon, fine. And then got to the fifth cage. Michael's. No cheeping. Or chirping. Or even chittering. Michael was on his side. On the bottom of his cage. Stiff.

No. No, no, no. This can't be happening! Genie gave the cage a gentle rock. "Michael," he whispered. "Michael, wake up." He grabbed the long-handled toothbrush and poked the bird. It didn't move. He poked again. "Come on, Michael. Come on." But nothing. No response. Not even a wing-flitter. But Michael was definitely alive when Genie had left that morning after he fed him that . . . *"No."*

"No, what?" Grandpop asked, standing in the doorway, rubbing his stomach. His *abdominoes.*

"Nothin'," Genie shot back, quick. Then adjusting his tone, he repeated, "Nothin'. Just talkin' to my buddies in here." He cut his eyes to Michael. Dead Michael.

"If only they could talk back like my parrot used to, huh?"

Genie faked an awkward laugh. "Right."

Wrong. If they could talk back, they'd be snitching on Genie, squawking, *Murderer! Murderer!* This was *so* wrong. First the truck, now a bird. And what was he going to tell Grandpop? What *could* he tell him? *Sorry, Grandpop, I think I killed Michael Jackson.* In a panic, Genie pushed past the old man and headed outside to tell the only person he thought could help. Ernie.

Ernie was teasing Samantha with the toy. He'd squeeze the head of the Bite Buddy, and Samantha'd go nuts. She was jumping and tossing her head, her tail whipping back and forth like a windshield wiper.

"Ernie," Genie called out frantically.

"Genie, look, man! She loves it!" Ernie held tight to the chew toy as Samantha tried to wrestle it away from him.

"Ernie, I need to talk to you, man. It's important," Genie said, trying to keep his voice down.

"Hold on, man. You gotta see this other thing I taught her just a minute ago." Ernie ripped the toy from Samantha, then dropped down to his knees, cooing at the dog as if it were a baby.

"Ernie!" Genie snapped. Ernie looked up and must have realized that Genie was serious and something was wrong. *Really* wrong, because he hopped back up.

"I need to tell you somethin'," Genie said, low.

"What's goin' on?"

"I killed Michael Jackson."

"You did *what*?"

"I killed . . . Michael Jackson. One of Grandpop's birds, man. I killed him."

"Wait . . . what? Why? How?"

Samantha was jumping around like a mad dog until Ernie finally dropped the Bite Buddy.

"I didn't mean to. It was an accident. I fed it apple seeds."

"And you think that's what killed him?"

"He's the only one I fed apple seeds and he's the only one dead." Genie's eyes welled up. "Grandpop's gon' kill me, man. And then after he kills me, Ma gon' dig me up,

202

bring me back to life, and kill me again."

"Genie, calm down. Chill, chill," Ernie said, putting a hand on Genie's shoulder.

"I can't!" Genie cried out, then he quickly dropped his voice back down into secret zone. "I can't calm down. Michael Jackson is *dead*."

"But you don't even know if you're the reason he died. Mighta just been his time to go." Ernie shrugged. "Look, why don't we go down to Tess's, see if you can look up if apple seeds kill birds. Don't seem like they would. You might find out this ain't got nothin' to do with you, and then it'll be all good."

Genie sized Ernie up just to make sure this wasn't Ernie looking for another excuse to go visit Tess. But Ernie looked, yeah, *earnest*. And for the first time since Genie'd found Michael, his stomach unknotted, just a tiny bit, but still. Ernie was looking out for him. And that helped.

They got down the hill in record time. Tess wasn't outside, so they took the porch steps two at a time and rang the doorbell.

Genie rocked back and forth nervously. Tess had to be home. She *had* to be home.

At last Tess came to the door. She lit up when she saw Ernie; then, seeing Genie, dimmed.

"What's wrong with him?" she asked Ernie through the screen, skipping the formalities.

"Can I use your Internet?" Genie asked, blunt.

"Nope. Not till you tell me what's goin' on."

Genie looked at Ernie, then Ernie looked back at Tess. "No snitchin'," Ernie said.

"Do I seem like a snitch to you?" Tess retorted.

Ernie nodded at Genie. "Go 'head and tell her, man."

Genie's mouth shot off in a million different directions about how there were birds in cages in a room in the house that he was responsible for feeding that he thought represented Uncle Wood or something like that but Michael Jackson was so small like the runt of the bird family and so he needed to eat something but it didn't have to be a lot and so he gave him apple seeds and dead, dead, dead.

"Whoa, whoa, whoa," Tess said, now coming outside. "Wait. Michael Jackson? What?"

"I'll translate," Ernie said. "There's a big problem. Genie fed one of our grandfather's pet birds, who he calls —"

"Michael Jackson?"

"Right. Genie fed Michael Jackson apple

seeds. And now the bird is dead. So he needs to use your Internet to check and make sure it wasn't the apple seeds that did it."

"Got it," Tess said. But before she let Genie in, she warned, "Listen, my mom is 'sleep, so . . ." She held the screen door open and Genie made a break, tippy-toe quiet, for the computer. He'd never typed so fast.

Can you feed a bird apple seeds? Enter.

The first link: Top ten common foods that can poison your bird.

Uh-oh. Genie swallowed, then moved the mouse over the link and clicked.

chocolate
apple seeds
doesn't matter because . . . apple seeds.

Genie's eyes began to well up again. That settled it. It was his fault. He'd poisoned Grandpop's bird. He x-ed out of Google, then sank back into the chair, his head in his hands.

"Psst." Tess was peering through the screen door. "You done?" she whispered. Genie nodded and slowly got up. Tess held the door for him as he stepped back out onto the porch.

"So what's the verdict?" Ernie asked. Genie's face said it all. "Dang."

"Yeah, I could tell it was bad news," Tess said.

Ernie drew air through clenched teeth, as if to say *yikes*. But what came out was, "We'll figure it out, man."

Genie pounded on the porch railing and cried, "I'on't even know how that's possible." He was halfway talking about how a bird could die from eating apple seeds, halfway talking about how he and Ernie were going to "figure it out."

"First of all, we have to do somethin' about the bird," Ernie said, looking to Tess for agreement.

Tess jumped in. "Wait, is it still in the house?" she asked.

"Yeah. I didn't know what to do, so I . . . kinda . . . panicked and came to get Ernie," Genie explained, flat. He sank onto the porch floor, drew his knees to his chest.

Tess squatted beside Genie. "So, you just left a dead bird in there? What if your grandma finds it?"

"She won't." Genie dug his chin into his knee miserably. "She hates birds — won't set foot in that room."

"You better hope she don't start today." Tess had a point. It would've been right in

206

line with Genie's luck for Grandma to decide to go into the inside-outside room.

"We need to get it out of there," Ernie agreed, lowering himself down until he was sitting cross-legged. "Plus, it's gonna start stinkin'."

"I'on't know how much you city boys know about dead animals, but when they get to rottin' . . ." Tess stuck her tongue out and faked a gag.

"Yeah, okay, fine. I'll get it out of there, but then what?" Now Genie beat his chin against his knee, harder and harder.

"Then . . ." Tess hopped up happily. "You replace the bird. *Duh.*"

"And where do you suggest we get a bird?" Ernie looked up at Tess. "You think it's that easy to just catch one?"

Instead of answering, Tess looked out toward the horizon. Birds swung and swooped in the distance. Then she snapped her fingers and turned back to them.

"You remember my ma talkin' about that old house in the woods that your grand-daddy grew up in?" she began excitedly. "Well, my daddy goes back there all the time, y'know, to hunt. And he always talks about how that house is full of birds. *Full* of 'em. Just livin' in there. Creepville, if you ask me. *But.* That would probably be your best bet. Better than y'all just runnin' round the yard chasin' after 'em with a butterfly net or somethin', which, don't ask 'cause I'on't have one."

Genie wasn't sure if Tess was telling the truth. Actually, that wasn't true. He figured Tess was probably telling the truth, but it was the truth her daddy had told her, and Genie didn't trust Crab to tell truths. He seemed like a liar. So, even though Tess, up until this point, had proven to have great ideas, Genie wasn't so sure about this one. But Ernie . . . well, that was a different story.

"Genie, what other option do we have?" was how Ernie told Genie, *I love Tess and I think everything she says is right.* And Genie, desperate as he'd ever been, agreed.

TWELVE

#466 Stupid. Stupid. Stupid. Stupid. Stupid. Maybe the real reason Adam and Eve weren't supposed to bite the apple is because then all the birds would've had access to the seeds, and the Garden of Eden would've become the Garden of dead . . . doves? Doves were the only birds back then, I think. Stupid stupid. Stupid!

#467 Why are flea markets called flea markets?

#468 Do crabs feel pain when their whole bodies get fried? Does the shell protect them from feeling it? Why does the shell get soft? Did dying an apple seed death hurt Michael Jackson? Apparently the seeds are poisonous, but Grandpop eats them every day, which means by now he's probably had at least a million, and seems fine . . . minus the whole glaucoma thing.

#469 Am I now technically a model-breaker questionnaire bird murderer? Stupid question. YES. I AM.

#470 So STUPID!

That night Genie and Ernie devised a plan, because that was what detectives and criminals did, Genie figured — devised plans — and since Genie and his brother were going to attempt to replace a dead bird with a stolen one, they were technically, sort of, kind of, criminals. Not real criminals, but still.

"We gotta get rid of Michael first thing in the morning," Genie was saying, giving the red truck up in their bedroom a poke. Even though he had basically given up on searching for the other half of the wheel and still hadn't found a way to replace it, the truck problem was small potatoes compared to this new one.

"Grandma'll be up and all over us," Ernie said, jumping up from push-up position. "She's like the first person in the entire world to get up."

"Then we gotta be *first* first," Genie decided. Ernie started doing jumping jacks.

"How early we talkin'?"

"I'on't know. Maybe like five. Gotta be before the sun even comes up, because Grandma says she wakes with the sun, remember?"

"Man, that's early." Jumping jack, jumping jack, jumping jack. "Also, how you gon' get the dead bird out the cage?" Now Genie laser-stared at Ernie, not blinking, as Ernie jumped and jacked, until finally Ernie, catching on to what was happening, stopped mid-jump. "Genie. No."

"Come on, Ern! I can't touch that thing. It's . . . dead!"

"But *you* killed it!"

Genie's face melted instantly, and he threw himself back onto the bed like a toddler. He knew he was too old to act that way, but he also knew he needed Ernie to help fix this bird situation for him. Ernie lowered his arms and let out a defeated sigh. "Fine."

Early the next morning, before daylight, Genie and Ernie got up. Actually, Genie got up and woke Ernie up. Genie hadn't slept a wink. Instead he spent the night thinking of all the things that could go wrong just trying to get the dead bird out of the house. What if the bird wasn't even really dead, just really *really* asleep (maybe apple seeds did to Michael Jackson what cheeseburgers did to Ernie), and what if the moment Ernie grabbed it, it woke up and flew out of the cage? Then they'd have a new problem on their hands. What if when Ernie reached in to get it, maggots came out of it? Genie had seen that in a movie once. And *that* was nasty. What if, what if, what if . . . and then it was five a.m.

"It's time," Genie whispered, now all creepy.

Ernie moaned, pulled the covers over his head, then yanked them back down to his neck in frustration. He slapped his hands over his face and sat up.

When it comes to devising plans, well, that's for detectives and criminals. But when it comes to executing plans, well, that's for ninjas.

Genie and Ernie crept down the steps, like ninjas. Slithered through the living room and to the nunya bidness door, like ninjas. Opened it and slipped into the inside-outside room, closing the door behind them, like ninjas. But it was only when they were at the cage that they realized they hadn't thought the whole plan through. There was one key factor they hadn't considered: how Ernie was going to get this dead bird out of the cage without having to touch it. Genie hadn't thought about it because he just figured Ernie would use his hands. But once Ernie unlatched Michael Jackson's cage door and saw the bird — a stiff hunk of feathers — he decided that his skin couldn't touch a corpse.

"I can't," Ernie said, backing away.

"What you mean? Just pick it up."

"If you think it's that easy, then *you* just pick it up," Ernie whispered back.

"You can talk regular. This place is sound-proof."

"Oh, right," he said, his voice back to normal. "Well, I need somethin' to cover my hands with. Anything."

Genie looked around the room. There was nothing to use except for the big leaves of some of the plants, and Genie had spent so much time taking care of them that he couldn't even think about snapping a healthy leaf off. So that was out. But there was nothing else in the room they could use. Genie thought for a moment.

"Toilet paper!" He ninja'd back out the door. When he returned — the trip to the bathroom and back was nothing short of ninja brilliance — he was holding a roll. "Hands up."

Ernie held his hands out like surgeons on TV do before the nurses put the gloves on them. Genie started wrapping them with the toilet paper until the whole roll was gone and Ernie was left with two big mummified mitts. "How 'bout now?"

Ernie turned one hand to the left, the other to the right, a bemused expression on his face. "I think I can do it," he finally declared. "Get the cage door."

Genie held the door open, trying not to look too hard at the dead swallow, just in case there were maggots. He knew he would lose last night's dinner if he saw little white worms crawling out of . . . anywhere. Ernie, his toilet-papered hands out in front of him like a zombie, came closer, slid his hands into the cage, then sort of clapped them around the bird — he had to do it a few times to get a good grip, but once he did, he lifted it like a construction crane. With the swallow pinched between the mess of toilet paper, Ernie walk-ran toward the door, and with perfect timing, Genie yanked it open. Then, like ninjas, they moved through the house to the front door and ran outside, Genie first making sure the door didn't slam behind them. Once they got to the side of the house, Ernie dropped Michael Jackson in the dirt.

"Why you drop it?" Genie asked, low.

"I couldn't hold it no more," Ernie said.

"It's just gross."

Genie got it. It was a dead thing, and a dead thing — a dead anything — is nasty to be touching on. But it couldn't just stay there at the side of the house like that. "What we gon' do with it now?" he asked.

"I'on't know," Ernie said, trying his best to unravel the toilet paper from his hands. Samantha came out of her doghouse, happy and wagging. Even at five-something in the morning. Ernie looked at Genie, one eyebrow raised.

"No, no, no, man," Genie groaned, picking up on what Ernie was thinking. He reached over to help his brother get the toilet paper off, which was tricky because he didn't want to be touching toilet paper that had been touching dead stuff either.

"Why not? She's a dog. And it would get rid of the evidence," Ernie said.

"Because what if dogs can't eat birds? Just like birds can't eat apple seeds? How would we explain a dead dog?" Genie could see it now, Day Nine, Disaster #3: Dead Dog. Now Ernie had one hand free and was using it to unwrap the other. Genie was holding the ribbons of paper as if they were toxic.

"This dog eats chicken all the time. Chickens are birds."

"Not the same thing, Ern."

"Fine." Ernie sighed, then looked up at the sky. There was the first hint of bright on the horizon. "Well, we don't have time to bury Michael Jackson. But . . ." He looked over to where the shovels were leaning against the house, snatched one up, and brought it over to Genie. "Here ya go."

"But you just said we don't . . . so what am I supposed to . . ." Then it hit him. "Oh. Wait . . ."

"It's your best bet," Ernie said, a crafty smile on his face. "*Your* turn." Then Ernie grabbed all the paper from Genie's hand and replaced it with the shovel. "I'm gonna take care of this." And off Ernie went back into the house with the toilet paper, leaving Genie and Michael Jackson alone. With a shovel. The sun was steadily on the rise and the living birds were beginning to chirp in the distance. Genie was running out of time.

"I'm sorry, Michael Jackson," he uttered. Then he took the shovel, stood over the bird, swallowed hard, and scooped it up. Once he got to the edge of the yard, he lowered the shovel back behind him, counted to three, and flung as hard as he could, watching the swallow take its last flight.

Phase One: Complete.

Now for Phase Two. Operation Birdnap.

Ernie made it back just after Genie had "done the deed," and just in time, because Grandma came out onto the porch. She really did rise with the sun.

"What you boys doin' up so early?" Grandma asked suspiciously, sleep still in her throat.

"Just gettin' a jump on our chores," Genie said, trying not to be weird. He pushed the shovel under a conveniently positioned pile of poop and looked at Samantha, who was now lying on her belly. She was the only witness. *No snitching, Samantha.*

"Yep," Ernie followed up. "Just wanted to knock it out before it gets too hot."

Grandma looked at them for a few moments. Just looked at them. And Genie, afraid she'd see the lie, continued to focus on the business of scooping poop.

"I see you boys are finally growin' your country legs. It don't take long to smarten up, does it?" Grandma said, finally seeming impressed.

Genie had no idea what she was talking about. Country legs? And he was already pretty smart before he got to North Hill. As a matter of fact, before he got to the country, Genie had never broken a model or killed a bird before, so maybe North Hill was actually *messing* his smartness up.

"Well go 'head on. Breakfast'll be ready in ten minutes." And she headed back into the house.

After poop flinging, scarfing down breakfast, and watering peas (no picking!), it was time to go steal a bird. Genie sure hoped Tess was right about the old house, because it was his butt on the line.

"Goin' explorin' out back!" Ernie shouted to Grandma as he and Genie headed for the woods, leading the way like he always did. As they trekked through the brush, Ernie swatted limbs to the side. The ground, covered in what had to be a million years' worth of dried leaves (and one dead swallow), crunched under their feet. Genie looked out for snakes, and every time he heard a rustle, he tried to figure out where it was coming from. If there *were* snakes out there, hopefully they would eat something else, like maybe Michael Jackson, before they got Genie. Usually the swishing sounds were only squirrels, but to be safe, Genie broke a limb off a tree and swiped the leaves off it to make it into a weapon. Just in case.

"Ugh." Ernie stopped short, pinching madly at the skin on his forehead.

"What's wrong?" Genie asked, stick ready.

"Nothin'. Just a stupid spiderweb." He led on, pinching and pulling the nearly invisible thread away, looking like he was doing some kind of weird sign language. Genie was just hoping the spider who spun that web hadn't been home when Ernie came crashing through. And were there *poisonous* spiders in the woods too? Great. Something *else* to worry about.

Every so often, Genie turned around to see a) if there were any copperheads creeping up behind them, and b) how far they'd come. Their destination was farther away than it looked from the yard. But finally, there it was. An old yellow house. An old yellow house WITH A TREE GROWING UP THE CENTER OF IT. Holy moly — that tree had to be fifty feet high!

"Look at this place," Genie exclaimed, stepping out of the woods and into a crazy overgrown yard. Ernie snatched his sunglasses off.

"Yo, this is nuts."

"Nuts, man," Genie seconded, staring. How did a tree just . . . *how*? And how was this house still standing? The brush was wild but the grass was dead. Some of the windows were busted out, others still intact, but painted over with what looked like white paint. A raggedy old swinging chair covered in bird droppings hung from a porch rafter. On another beam, a bird's nest. On the porch, a shaky-looking wooden table, its paint shedding like snake skin.

"Come on," Ernie said, motioning for Genie to give him the stick, pressing a finger to his lips.

A huge hole right beside the front door gaped all the way through to the inside of the house. They tried to peek through the few clear spots in the windows but couldn't see much, so Ernie, instead of just climbing through the hole, tried the front door. He put his hand underneath his shirt so only the fabric would touch the doorknob. Then slowly, slowly, in full ninja-mode, he pushed the door open. Genie wasn't sure what he was expecting to see once they got inside, but . . . Tess was right. *Real* right. A million times over right. Birds! Lots of them. Hundreds! They were *everywhere*! Some looked like pigeons and others were big and black, strutting around like tough dudes, pecking at the dead bodies of other birds, which was the nastiest thing ever. And, oh man, the paint on the window . . . wasn't paint. It was bird mess. And the stink of the place was . . . *ugh.* Killer. They both pulled the necks of their T-shirts over their noses at exactly the same time. It wasn't funky.

We're talking *FOWNKY.*

Even though they had come to pull off a bird-napping, they couldn't help but look around first. The house itself, as far as Genie and Ernie could tell, was empty . . . of people, at least. There was no furniture, no pictures, no things. Just black-and-white dung-speckled wood. And that tree, really, made *no* sense. How could a tree just grow through a house? How could it be strong enough to push through the floor, and then through the roof? Was the house built on top of it first, trapping it underneath? And Grandpop grew up here? Did the tree chase him and his parents out? Or maybe the birds?

Ernie was holding the stick up like a sword, positioning himself in front of Genie. They moved across the room stealthily and saw that it wasn't *entirely* void of human-ness. In one corner lay a couple dozen beer cans and stubby, burned-down cigars. Someone else had definitely been there. Most likely Crab.

One of the huge black birds flitted around, lifting off the ground for a few seconds at a time. Another tried to push his brother — maybe they were brothers — out of the way so that he could have a bite of a dead bird that they were both competing with a hundred flies for. That was beyond disgusting, so Genie began creeping toward the other side of the house.

When he got to the back window, he stopped short. "Ernie!" Ernie hustled over and *he* stopped short.

Out in the backyard were birdcages. Birdcages made of wood and wire. Birdcages exactly like Grandpop's. Positioned in a half circle.

"It's just like Grandpop's room," Genie whispered. "Crazy, right?"

"Real crazy."

The crescent of weather-beaten bird cages, the rusted chairs left on the back porch, the sound of birds cawing and flapping around — it was all kinda freaking Genie out. But when he told Ernie this, his brother, in typical Ernie fashion, just got on with the task at hand. He dug in his pocket and pulled out a plastic grocery bag. "We gotta catch a bird 'fore we can leave."

As Ernie shook the bag open, Genie grabbed his wrist, shaking his head no. "These birds ain't like the birds in Grandpop's room. These all look like the birds we got in Brooklyn."

Ernie scowled. "What difference does it make if they Brooklyn birds? *Grandpop* can't see them."

"But he can *hear* them. These birds don't sound nothin' like the ones in Grandpop's room. Swallows tweet. Like . . . chirp. These birds shout."

"What the . . . seriously?"

In that moment, Genie had a quick flash of the honey badger who got stung to death by bees because he wanted the honey so bad. This was *not* a good idea.

"I'on't know, man. I just know they different. And if it ain't the right bird, then . . ."

Ernie shook his head and crammed the bag back in his pocket. "If you say so."

What a bust.

"Yeah, so let's get outta here," Genie said, both discouraged and relieved. He and Ernie, returning to ninja form, tiptoed back toward the porch — Genie didn't think it was a good idea to startle that many birds. One of the movies he had sneak-watched once was a movie about killer birds, and now he was regretting ever checking it out.

"I got a cool idea," Ernie whispered from the doorway. "But you gotta get out to the grass first."

"What?"

"Over there. Just go over there. We came all the way out here, might as well have some fun." Ernie had a scheming look on his face. "Trust me, this is gonna be sweet."

Genie wasn't sure what his brother was up to, but he was so glad to be out of that creepy house that he jogged out into the middle of the yard. Ernie stayed by the doorway, looking into that weird world of wings. Then, to Genie's amazement, a barn swallow landed not two feet away from him. It was the perfect shades of blue and orange! Genie wanted to call to Ernie but didn't want to scare the bird. But Ernie had the bag. Could Genie catch it beforehand? It was *two feet away.* The swallow pecked at something on the ground as Genie laser-eyed it like he was trying to will it over to him. He inched forward, best stealth ninja ever. A foot and a half away. He reached out his arm, slowly, slowly . . . a foot away . . . but his will must've gotten crossed up in the tall grass, because instead of the bird coming his way, it took flight. Genie took off after it — maybe the bird would land somewhere, leading him to a nest. Then he heard Ernie snapping his fingers to get his attention. Genie paused. Ernie put one hand in the air. Countdown. Five. Four. Three. Two. Just the pinkie left. One. And with all his might, Ernie slammed the door.

Wham! Birds burst from every broken window in the house like dark smoke, others tornadoed up through the roof. First they were all separated, exploding into different directions, but then they swooped back toward each other, like family, and became one big black wave, twisting and sweeping up through the trees around them. The sound of wings, like a giant deck of cards being shuffled, filled the air.

Ernie came running over to Genie to catch as much of the show as he could. Just as the last bird had disappeared beyond the treetops, they heard Grandma's voice calling for them. Uh. Oh. The five-call rule, and they were way the heck deep in the woods.

So Genie gave a last glance in the direction the swallow had flown, and then he and Ernie dashed through the woods. Ernie swiped stuff — the spiderwebs and the annoying branches — out of their path with Genie's stick as they ran. Four calls left. Then one of the branches that Ernie brushed aside snapped back and came flying at Genie, whacking him in the eye. Bad. Friggin'. Luck.

Three calls left.

"Argh!" Genie pressed his hand over his eye, but he kept pumping — two calls — hurdling over the fallen trees, the bottom of his feet pulsing in his flimsy Converses. Grandma's voice was getting louder, and not only because they were getting closer. Then she was on her last call. They charged out of the woods into the yard and there she was, hands firmly on hips.

"You boys *just* made it," she said, a mad-bull look on her face.

Genie bent over, trying to catch his breath, his chest burning. Ernie had straightened up and locked his hands on top of his head. That was when he saw Genie had his hand over his eye.

"What happened?" he asked, followed by, "Let me see." It was a rerun of when Down the Street Donnie hit Genie in the eye with the snow-covered quarter, except this time, who was Ernie gonna beat up, the trees? Ernie pulled Genie's hand down and examined the skin at the corner of his eye. "It's just a welt. You okay?"

"Yeah." But Genie winced when Ernie touched the sore part. "One of those branches snapped back on me."

"What happened to your brother?" Grandma said, coming closer.

"Nothin', nothin'. A branch hit him, that's all," Ernie said.

"What were y'all doing out there anyway?" Grandma asked, even more suspiciously. Now she examined Genie's eye.

"We were just exploring that old house

back there. The yellow one, with the big tree going through it," Genie explained.

"What the heck were y'all doin' at that house?" she asked, but thankfully, instead of waiting for an answer, she just continued, "That there house was your great-granddaddy's. All this was his land, which eventually ended up being your grandfather's land. And lemme tell you, this land was one of the only good things that old-timer ever did for Grandpop."

"Why you say that?" Ernie asked.

"Yeah, if his father left him all this land, he couldn't have been so bad, right?" Genie added. "Plus, didn't he teach Grandpop to make birdcages, like he did Tess's mom?"

Grandma kissed Genie on the welt, like parents do boo-boos for babies. And even though Genie wasn't a baby, he couldn't deny that the welt felt a little better after the kiss. "I see Karen's been runnin' her mouth. What else did she say?" She steered the boys toward the house.

"Just that Grandpop's dad was topsy-turvy," Genie blurted, and as soon as he said it, he immediately regretted it because what if Grandma got upset with Tess's mom, which could possibly lead to her being upset with Tess, which meant Tess wouldn't want to hang with Ernie, which,

227

for Genie, meant no Internet, and some karate chops. Lots and lots of karate chops.

"Well, she's right about that one," Grandma said, letting Genie off the hook. "It was like he was trapped in his own memories. Sometimes he would get scared someone was tryna attack him, or tryna hurt him. He was so paranoid that he'd lock himself in his bedroom for hours — sometimes days at a time — while Grandpop's mother, your great-grandma, Millie, would have to take care of the house and everything else. The old man just lost his grip. Then one day — your grandfather and I had just gotten married, and he was building this here house for us — your great-grandfather got in his car and drove off. Never came back."

"Tess's mom said it was the war that made him act like that," Ernie said.

"Tess's mom don't know everything."

"So he just left? Where did he go?" Genie asked, gingerly touching the corner of his eye.

"He said he was gonna grab more wood and wire for his birdcages. But they found his car a few hours up the road. He had jumped in the James River," Grandma said, flat. As they approached the porch, she stopped. "Your grandpop's mother was never the same. And neither was that house. And once she died, that tree grew right through the floor. Don't know how or why. All I know is that old house might as well have been one big birdcage — the biggest of them all — and your great-grandfather was like a bird with a broken wing that just couldn't heal. Just couldn't save himself from all the things in his mind. Like fear and guilt." She brushed a spiderweb out of Genie's hair. "That make sense?"

Ernie nodded.

"I think so," Genie said, trying to work it all out — man, it was crazy. *Great Grandpop killed himself?* Genie's brain started throbbing as much as the welt over his eye. And . . . whoa — *Grandpop* locked himself in a room too. With birdcages! There wasn't any tree pushing through the floor, thankfully, but Grandpop *did* lock himself inside. And he was scared to go *outside.* Genie felt like his brain was exploding; Grandpop was literally the king of Pete and Repeat. Way better than him and Ernie. Maybe even way better than everyone! But Genie hoped Grandpop didn't Pete Repeat the whole James River thing. That would not be cool.

"Okay, now listen here," Grandma warned. "Don't be mentioning that house, or Old Man Harris, or any of this to your grandfather. It's a bit of a sore spot." Then she switched gears. "At any rate, it's been a long time since I've been out there. Anything going on I need to know about?"

"Other than all the birds?" Genie asked.

Grandma made a throw-up face. "I know all about those birds. Anything else?"

"Not really," Ernie said. "Just some beer cans."

"Beer cans?!"

"Yeah, probably from Mr. Crab," Genie threw out there, thinking nothing of it, especially after Grandma was so cool about the topsy-turvy comment. But then Grandma pressed her lips together into one thin line. It was clear she was trying to control her anger. She started up the stairs to the porch, leaving Genie and Ernie in the yard, unsure of why she'd called them home in the first place. Then she swung back around.

"Oh," she said, and then went into grandparent mind-reader mode. "I called y'all back here because I need one of you to answer somethin' for me."

Genie braced himself. Grandma was standing the same way their mother did whenever they were in trouble. Big trouble. *Who killed Michael Jackson?* trouble.

Grandma waved a finger back and forth

from Genie to Ernie as if she were casting a spell. Then she asked, "Which one of you peanut-heads tried to flush all that damn toilet paper?"

THIRTEEN

#471: How do you catch birds?

#472: How does a house catch a tree?

#473: How do you catch topsy-turvy?

Genie spent most of the rest of the day on the front porch, waiting, hoping — *please, please, please* — for another swallow to magically land in front of him so he could try to trap it and somehow get it into the house, and into the cage, without anyone knowing, which was a terrible plan, but . . . a plan nonetheless. When he wasn't bird stalking, he was hanging out with Grandpop, dangerously, in the inside-outside room, trying his best not to ask about the yellow house or Grandpop's father. Not to mention, the room was one bird short, and Genie was also trying not to be weird about that, especially since Grandpop hadn't noticed the one-bird-short part. Grandpop was going on and on about Ernie's fourteenth birthday and how big of a deal turning "the big one-four" was.

Turns out, it was a North Hill tradition started by Grandpop after a fourteen-year-old black boy named Emmett Till was killed for whistling at a white woman when Grandpop was younger. It scared him so bad that when he had kids of his own, and they turned fourteen, he taught them, and all the other boys around, including Crab, the only thing he knew — how to shoot. Grandpop said that back then it was self-defense, but now it was just all in good fun. Genie, however, could barely pay attention because he was too distracted with . . . well . . . being distracting. He made lots of noise, fussing with the plants, shifting pots around, turning the volume up, ever so slightly, on the outdoor sounds from the cassette player to cover for the one missing chirp. And when he wasn't hanging out at the scene of the crime, Genie was down at Tess's, using her Internet, obsessively looking up other ways to capture birds.

"I can't believe y'all really went there!" Tess exclaimed after Ernie went through the story about the birds and the cages in the backyard and the tree growing up through the house and how creepy it all was, but telling it like he was some kind of tough guy. "You gotta take me," Tess kept saying, all excited.

"Yeah, but I only saw one swallow," Genie said grimly, staring at the computer screen. Google, Genie's most loyal partner, was once again coming up blank. Well, not blank, but not exactly helpful, because most of the links were for buying birds and Genie didn't have any money, besides the ten bucks Grandma had given him. And birds cost way more than ten bucks.

"Yeah, but one is all you need," Tess said.

"Don't birds move in packs?" Ernie chimed in.

"Flocks," Genie corrected with a head shake, clicking another link. As he scrolled, read, clicked, and x-ed, Tess started coming up with her own ideas on how to birdnap.

"Look, we tie a basket to a fishing pole. Then we put some bird food — some flies — on the ground right on the side of the porch here. Then we stand on the porch with rod and basket and wait for the birds to come eat, and boom! We drop the basket right on 'im."

"That's a good idea," Ernie said. No comment from Genie.

"*Or,* we just forget about the basket and

just put some flies on a fishing hook, and go fishin' for birds. Uh . . . birdin'. I guarantee the hook won't kill it."

"Right, right. I like where your head's at," from Ernie again. Genie looked horrified, but Tess went right to another idea.

"Oh, oh, how 'bout this: How 'bout we get a sticky pad, like the kind you use to catch mice, and you put flies on *that*. The birds come and eat it and get stuck, and boom! We got 'im."

"Yo, I think that's genius!" from Ernie, of course.

I bet you do, Genie thought, steaming. He was trying to keep his head from *blowing off.* "We need . . . the bird . . . to be . . . *alive.*"

"Of course, of course. And it will be. For a while," Tess replied. What could Genie say to *that*?

Tess went on, and Genie decided to tune her and butt-kissing Ernie out and keep searching online. He changed his search from HOW TO GET BIRDS to HOW TO TRAP BIRDS and . . . bingo! Funny how something so small, like one word, could change so much. Genie scrolled through a few links before stopping on HOW TO MAKE A BIRD TRAP. His heart began to pound.

"Hey, guys, check this out," he said, moving aside.

Tess leaned in, squinting to get a better look. Then she put her hands together and dimpled. "What do we need?"

Fifteen minutes later Genie, Ernie, and Tess were at Marlon's.

"Now *what* else?" Jim the bartender topped off a beer for a woman who was paying more attention to Tess than drinking. She flashed a gold-toothed smile as Tess explained what she needed.

Buzz, went the fly zapper.

"A mousetrap. We need a mousetrap," Tess said.

"So, a liquor crate, some of them dead flies, a straw, and a mousetrap."

"Yep."

"Do I even wanna know?" Jim asked, gathering loose dollar bills off the bar and stuffing them into a pitcher full of money labeled TIP . . . OR ELSE next to the register.

"Nope. And neither does my daddy," Tess said. Jim shot his eyes from her to Genie, then Ernie. He smirked.

"Gotcha."

Genie carried the liquor crate, which was just a wooden box made of slats, which he thought was great because if they actually did catch a swallow, it would be able to breathe. He also had the Baggie of flies, because no one else would carry them. There weren't as many as Crab brought to Grandpop, but definitely enough to entice a swallow. Ernie had the straw and mousetrap. It was the old snapping kind, the kind Ma used back home to bait the mice with globs of peanut butter. The rest of the materials Tess already had at her house. Hammer, nails, glue, and string.

The assembly:

1. Cut the straw down to an inch and push one end of it around the trigger of the mousetrap (the part you normally put the cheese on).

2. Glue a few flies to the other end of the straw. A fly lollipop. Yummy.

3. Nail the mousetrap (straw attached) to the ground so it's stable.

4. Tie one end of the string to the trappy part of the mousetrap. The spring-loaded arm. The part that breaks the mouse's neck. Yikes.

5. Tie the other end of the string to the top of the inside of the box. In this case, just

wrap it around one of the slats.

6. Set the trap, carefully, by pulling the snappy-trappy arm back, setting the trigger, and propping the box up on one side so that when the trap goes off, it yanks the string and drops the box over the bird. I know, it seems confusing, but just picture every cartoon trap you ever seen.

Note: The straw connected to the trigger makes it so that when the bird eats the flies and sets off the trap, the arm doesn't snap down on the bird's neck. Instead it just snaps down on the straw. No broke-neck birds here!

Genie and Ernie couldn't set the trap up in the yard — Grandma was always out there. Tess couldn't set it up in her yard either — she wasn't worried about her mother wondering what it was, because her mother never left the house. It was her father, she told them. She didn't want him being nosy, because she didn't want to have to lie to him, but she would've because she couldn't snitch on Genie. She also couldn't put it in the yard because Crab cut the grass and would've probably run right over it. And all of this was okay, because the one place that made the most sense anyway was the yellow house. Well, not in the yellow house, but out in the yard where Genie had seen the swallow right before Ernie caused the bird-nado.

Plus Tess wanted to see the house anyway.

So back through the woods they went for the second time in one day. When they got there, Tess dropped her portion of the bird-trap supplies.

"Oh my . . . ," she said, staring up, a hand over her mouth. "I *gotta* see inside."

"I'll take you." Ernie jumped to it, all puffed up like some kind of hero. Genie wasn't impressed. His mind was on other things. Like what they had come to do.

"Y'all go 'head and I'll just do this all by myself, no problem. No problem at all." And as Genie was saying it, hoping it would guilt Tess and Ernie into hanging back, the lovebirds grabbed hands and headed for the door. Sheesh.

So Genie got to work. He surveyed the area and decided to set the trap up not far from where he saw the swallow the first time. It just made sense, and it was far enough away from the yellow house, Genie figured, that the hundreds of non-swallows wouldn't mess with it. From the front door of the yellow house, about nineteen steps forward, and twelve steps to the right. A clear view of both the front and side of the house.

He laid everything out and started constructing it. World's simplest model ever! A few minutes later, just as Genie carefully set the trap, the box perfectly propped up, *WHAM!* Ernie slammed the door, and Tess came darting across the yard, squealing, looking over her shoulder at the squawking storm of birds.

Genie, startled, tripped the string and set off the trap. Arghhh!

"That place is crazy!" Tess exclaimed, pulling up beside Genie, panting. Genie didn't respond. He just lifted the box and pulled the spring mechanism of the mousetrap back until it clicked into place again.

Tess hunkered down to get a better look. "The trap looks good, man." Ernie trotted up beside her.

"Yeah, it does," Ernie added, wiping his hands on his shorts. Genie glanced over at them and tried his best not to give them the worst ice grill ever as he slowly pulled his hands away from the box. It was like he had just finished building a house of cards.

"I know," he said, a bit cold, a bit cool. "But now, we wait."

And that's what they did. They leaned

against a tree a few feet back — Genie of course looking out for snakes, spiders, and anthills — and waited. But it didn't happen in the five minutes Genie thought it would. Or ten. Or thirty. Tess said her mother always told her that "a watched pot don't boil," so the best thing to do would be to leave it alone and go on about their business. Said they should just come check it every day, until something happened. Genie reluctantly agreed.

In the meantime, Operation Birdnap expanded into Phase Three: Operation Pretend. As in, Genie was going to just try to pretend like everything was fine. Nothing was different. Five birds? No, there's always only been four, right? Michael Jackson? What Michael Jackson? No, there's four swallows and a parrot, right? No parrot? Ah, okay, no parrot. Right. Just four swallows. Just . . . four . . . swallows.

And it was working. Every morning for the next four days Genie would have a moment of reflection (panic) about the broken red truck, before Ernie talked him down. Then breakfast. Talk to Ma and Dad, who were getting increasingly excited about Jamaica, if they called. Chores. Samantha. Grandpop. (Panic.) Inside-outside room, which, by the way, was where Genie transformed into even more of a neat-freak nut job — in addition to watering the plants, plucking the dead leaves, cleaning the poo from the cages (even Michael Jackson's cage, RIP), feeding the birds their cuisine of freshly zapped flies, vacuuming the grass carpet, Windexing the window (he even cleaned the dog poop off the outside), dusting Grandpop's cassette player and table, and even performing terrible renditions of Jackson Five performances for the Jackson Five-now-Four. Genie was determined to make that room perfect, to (panic) clean everything, even though, the thing of it was, he couldn't clean Michael Jackson out of his mind. But still, he knew that his hard work (along with Ernie's *big one-four*) was keeping Grandpop from suspecting anything, and that's all that mattered.

Next on the Everything Is Normal agenda? Tess comes up to the house. A trip through the woods. Food in trap gone. Nothing caught. Disappointment. Reset the trap. Take Grandpop out at night. Reset the guilt. Reset the panic.

In between all of this, there was another trip to the flea market, but Genie missed out on this one. The night before, Grandpop had a new job for Genie that he wanted done before their walk, and it kept them up later than ever. When Genie had arrived in the kitchen at his usual twenty-two hundred hours, Grandpop had pulled a small box from his lap and set it on the table. He'd opened it to show Genie rolls of money, each one neatly rubber-banded. Genie's eyes had bugged.

"Little Wood, you've been takin' care of everything so well, y'know, with makin' sure everything is on the up-and-up in my special room and all." Genie swallowed the need-to-be-honest that was making its way up his throat. "I really appreciate it," Grandpop went on, "and now I need you to do something else for me, 'cause I trust you." He tapped a roll like a mob boss assigning a hit. "Organize these. But here's how I want you do it. Make sure all the bills are facing the same direction. Then take the one-dollar bills and fold the top right corner down. Five-dollar bills, the top left. Tens, fold the bottom right. And twenties, the bottom left. Got it?"

"I think so." Genie repeated the instructions to make sure he had it right. Then he went through each roll, bending corners and putting the ones with the ones, the fives with the fives, the tens with the tens, and there were no twenties.

"No twenties, huh?" Grandpop asked,

scratching his chin.

"Nope." Genie flipped through the bills, double-checking. "No twenties."

Grandpop made another *huh* sound, then told him to fold each stack of bills, by denomination, rubber-band them, and put them back in the box. He didn't tell Genie why he wanted him to do all this, so of course Genie was bursting to know. But instead of answering when Genie asked, Grandpop headed for the door. Night walk time.

That evening there was a banana moon and all kinds of sky-glitter — the name Genie made up for stars. Grandpop liked it.

"Little Wood, how many you think are up there?" Grandpop had been getting more and more comfortable with the yard, and was now taking four or five steps at a time before slapping his hands back down on Genie's shoulders. But after a step or two with Genie's help, Grandpop would lift his hands again. He was like a baby learning to walk. And he almost had it.

"I don't know," Genie said, his head tilted all the way back. "Let's see."

He tried counting, but every time he got past twenty, he'd get confused about the ones he had already counted, and eventually he realized how crazy it was to try to count stars, even though it was definitely a question he needed an answer to: *How many stars are in the sky?* Finally he just stopped and took a guess. "Shoot, it gotta be at least a hundred."

"A hunnid, huh?" Grandpop said, smiling. "Well, I guess I'll have to take your word for it."

#474: How many stars are in the sky? And whose job is it to count them? Are new stars born, and if so, wouldn't that mess up the count? And as the sky gets older, does it lose stars, like teeth?

The next morning, Genie had just finished jotting down his star question when he heard Grandma's car pull into the yard. He closed his notebook and ran outside to help carry things into the kitchen.

"Hey, Grandma. Hey, Ernie. Sorry I overslept," Genie greeted them. "How was the market?"

"It was good, baby, but it would've been better if we had two extra hands." Grandma winked, setting some apples on the counter and washing her hands in the sink.

"But we did all right," Ernie said. "I took care of it." Genie could tell Ernie was feeling good about himself.

"Yeah, you sure worked *extra* hard. Probably because Miss Tess was there," Grandma said, cheesing.

"Hey, she was working hard too! Sold a bunch of earrings, man. People really like those things. Grandma even bought a pair."

"Grandma?" Grandma bought earrings made of bottle caps? Grandma never even *wore* earrings, except to church.

"Grandma," Ernie confirmed. Genie filled his plate with a second serving of something called scrapple that was sitting in a pan on the stove. It was another new food Grandma had introduced him to. He liked it even more than the grits, and it didn't even need extra sugar on top.

"Oh, so y'all think just 'cause I'm old, I can't be cool?" Grandma said, heading toward her bedroom. "Shoot, I been cool before cool was cool. Before cool was even a word." She said it loud enough for Genie and Ernie to hear it, but soft enough to make it seem like she was talking to herself.

Genie grinned at Ernie. Old people.

"So what else did you do at the market? Did the peas sell out? Get another crab sandwich?" Genie asked.

Ernie took his sunglasses off, which meant he really wanted to tell Genie something. Something important.

"Remember that crazy guy who was looking for the roller skates?"

"Yeah," Genie said. "What's his name, Mr. Binks?"

"Yeah, well, he was there again." Ernie picked a chunk of scrapple from Genie's plate and popped it into his mouth. "And guess what he was sellin'."

Genie hated when Ernie told him to guess something, because he never guessed right. But he always tried anyway.

"Light-up necklaces, like that dude at the Broadway-Nassau stop?" Mr. Binks seemed like that kind of guy.

"No, man," Ernie said. "Now guess, for real."

"What? That *was* for real! Just tell me!"

"Teeth! The guy was sellin' *teeth,* Genie!"

"Teeth, like . . ." Genie pointed to his mouth.

"Yeah, like, teeth. Chompers. Pearly whites. Teeth. Real ones. Not dentures or nothin'. That's the good luck charm Grandma was talkin' about!" Ernie started pacing around the kitchen. "Grandma claims he's been a dentist for like forty years, and whenever he pulls a tooth from someone famous, he saves it. Then he sells 'em to people. Nuts! I always hated goin' to the dentist," Ernie went on, all hyper. "Man, somebody diggin' around in your mouth, drillin' and pickin' . . . I hate it —"

"You don't hate nothin'," Grandma interrupted, coming back into the kitchen and kissing Genie on the forehead. She smelled like outside. Now he understood what Grandpop meant when he said that.

"I do. I hate the dentist," Ernie insisted. "And now look! Find out they're planning on selling my teeth whenever they take 'em out! That Binks guy — he's like a . . . a tooth jacker!"

Grandma chuckled. "I can understand that, but —"

Genie cut Grandma off. "You said he sold good luck!"

"He *does.* He sells those teeth as good luck charms. Like a rabbit's foot, y'know?"

"A rabbit's foot?!" Genie and Ernie both yelped at the same time. Then Genie said, "Don't seem like the rabbit had good luck at all."

FOURTEEN

Day fourteen started with a phone call from Ma.

Ma: Mornin', knuckleheads!

Genie: Hi, Ma.

Ernie: Hi, Ma.

Genie: You sound funny.

Ma: Me?

Genie: Yeah. Different.

Ma: Hold on, let me get closer to the speaker . . . better?

Genie: It's not that bad, you just sound different. Like, good.

Ma: Oh? That's probably because . . . Juh-mayyy-cuh, we goin' to Juh-mayyy-cuh, and ya'll ain't comin', cause ya'll gon' be pickin' peeeas.

Ernie: Ma, seriously?

Ma: Sorry boys, but it's been a long time. I don't think me and your dad have been anywhere together since our honeymoon.

Ernie: Dang!

Ma: That's what happens when you have crazy kids.

Ernie: She talkin' 'bout you, Genie.

Genie: She ain't talkin' 'bout me. You the crazy one!

Ma: Both of you crazy. Like your daddy.

Dad: I ain't crazy.

Genie: Hey, Dad.

Ma: Come closer to the speaker, Senior, so they can hear you.

Dad: Simple and Simon, Pete and Repeat, what you up to?

Ernie: Getting ready to do our chores. Wash dishes. Clean up poop. Help Grandma pluck weeds. Check the peas. Water the peas. Polish the daggone peas.

Genie: Yeah, Grandma's outside waiting for us right now.

Dad: Ouch. Now you know one of the reasons I had to leave North Hill.

Ernie: Yeah.

Genie: Dad, this Genie.

Dad: I know, Genie.

Genie: Real quick. Two questions. The first is, when are y'all *actually* leaving for Jamaica? And the second is, can you bring me a cap to fit my dreadlocks?

Dad: We're leaving tomorrow morning, for two more child-free weeks. Heaven. And we can get those hats in Brooklyn, son.

Ernie: Tomorrow's my birthday.

Dad: We know, Ernie. We were there.

Ma: Hush, Senior. Ernie, I hate that we're gonna miss it. My firstborn is fourteen. Wow.

Ernie: It's cool. Just bring me somethin' good back.

Genie: Like a dreadlock cap.

Dad: But you don't even have dreads, Genie.

Genie: But I might grow some.

Ma: No, you will not!

Ernie: Dang! Crushed you!

Genie: Shut up, man.

Dad: Chill, guys. Genie, I'll see what I can do.

Genie: Do they do Fourth of July in Jamaica?

Dad: You mean, fireworks?

Grandpop: Is that your father?

Genie: Yep, wanna speak to him? Hold on. Dad, Grandpop wants to say hi.

Dad: I can't right now. We have to go.

Genie: He's right here.

Grandpop: Son?

Dad: Ernie and Genie, you boys be good. Ernie, your birthday gift is in the mail.

Ernie: Cool.

Grandpop: Ernest.

Dad: We'll call you when we get there.

Genie, I'll let you know if there's fireworks. Take care of each other.

Genie: We will.

Ma: Love y'all!

Grandpop: Son?

Ernie and Genie: Love you too!

Grandpop: Son! Son? Hello? *Hello?*

"Old man, you in here?" Crab came busting through the door carrying his rifle, a paper bag in one hand, his hunting bag over his shoulder, and a cigar clamped between his teeth. He smelled terrible, thanks to Genie and Ernie's Olympic-level poop-flinging abilities. Genie's aim had gotten awesome, and he was thinking he could really impress his friends with it when he got back to Brooklyn. He would just have to find a shovel.

"Yeah, I'm here," Grandpop said.

Genie had just finished picking peas. Thankfully, there'd been no signs of copperheads yet, but that didn't stop Genie from keeping an eye out for them. He was also keeping an eye out for swallows, and was kicking himself for not asking Ma and Dad to somehow figure out how to bring him back a barn swallow, if they had those in Jamaica. *Question for later: Is there such a thing as a Jamaican barn swallow?* Either that, or a model fire truck, but he knew that would get Dad to digging, and he *definitely* didn't want that, since it was Dad who'd told him in the first place to be careful with the truck that was now broken. Still, of all the things to ask for — *a dreadlock cap? Really, Genie?*

Soil was caked under his fingernails, and he was trying to clean them out in the kitchen sink. When he and Ernie headed for the garden earlier, they'd left Grandpop slumped in his chair at the table; it was obvious that he was disappointed that Dad wouldn't talk to him. It wasn't his first attempt, either. Almost every time Grandpop heard their dad's voice come across the speaker, he tried to jump into the conversation, and almost every time, Dad would give the phone back to Ma, or just cut the call short. It was so uncomfortable this morning that Genie had been happy to get out the house and tackle the hot yard, even if peas were involved.

Now Crab leaned the gun carefully against the wall, then plunked the brown paper bag on the table. "Man, I was this close" — here he measured about five inches with his fingers, as if Grandpop could see him — "to hitting a deer."

"Oh yeah?" Grandpop asked, perking up.

He was at the stove, flipping hamburgers like a cook at a diner. Very "unblind-like." Genie was just glad he was feeling better.

"Yeah, but Bambi got away." Crab cackled like a bad guy in a cartoon.

"Y'know, my wife told my grandsons that I taught you how to shoot, but ever since they been here, your butt ain't shot a thing." Grandpop put his face close to the frying pan and sniffed. Genie worried that the grease was going to pop and burn him, but it didn't. "You making me look bad."

"Yeah, whatever. Then what you call this?" Crab reached in his hunting bag and pulled out three squirrels, dangling them by their tails.

Ernie had just stepped out of the bathroom. He stepped right back in.

Genie also backed away. Dead squirrels, part gray, part bloody, part . . . missing.

"See that, boys?" Crab said, all proud. "This is how a pro does it. Plucked 'em right out the trees."

Grandpop was leaning over the pan again, this time taking a really big sniff. He turned the stove off. Genie guessed the burgers were done. "What you got there?" he asked Crab.

Before Crab could answer, Grandma started yelling from the screen door.

"Marcus Crabtree!" It was always a bad sign whenever anyone in the Harris family called you by your full name. It was the call before a butt-whuppin'. "I *know* you ain't walk in *my* house before knockin' your boots clean. You got dirt, and . . ." She stopped and sniffed. "What's that, dog mess?"

Grandma said all of this before she actually got to the kitchen. Once she did, and saw Crab standing there with the squirrels, she *really* went off.

"Crab, you got ten seconds." That was all she said, and that was all she needed to say. Their dad said the exact same thing to Genie whenever he got upset with him. Actually, he combined the full name and the ten-second countdown, so it was like, *EugeneDouglasHarris,yougottenseconds.* The result — Genie booking it to his bedroom.

Crab put the squirrels back in his hunting bag, and Grandpop put the burgers between pieces of white bread. "Hold on, hold on," he said. "Mary, can you give us a minute?" Grandma looked at Grandpop like he was crazy, and even though he couldn't see her, he somehow knew that she was looking at him that way, because he added, "Please. Sixty seconds."

Grandma glared at Crab like she wanted to kill him as dead as those squirrels. But she left the room, counting backward from sixty, *loud.* Grandpop put Genie's and Ernie's burgers on the table.

"Man, she hates me!" Crab was stating the obvious.

"Yeah, she certainly does," Grandpop agreed, pouring glasses of tea as the boys took their seats. Genie, knowing exactly what was in the small paper bag on the table, moved it to the other end. "But don't worry about it. Let's just square up."

Crab pulled a wad of cash from his pocket.

"Here ya go, old man. Twenty, like usual." He slapped the money into Grandpop's palm.

"Thanks," Grandpop said, pocketing it. "So, got any plans for the Fourth?"

"I'on't know, man," Crab said. "Might take Tess and the wife down to the fairground and catch the fireworks, that is, if I can get Karen out the house and Tess away from your *grandson.*" Crab glanced over at Ernie, who was squeezing what looked like an inch of ketchup over his burger. Ernie froze. "You?"

"Well, it's my *grandson's* birthday."

"That's right, you did tell me that. Big

man, you was born on the Fourth of July, huh?"

Ernie put the ketchup down. "Yeah."

"Fourteen, right?" Crab asked.

"Right," Grandpop answered for him, adding, "The big one-four. Tomorrow. So, it's time for him to become a man."

Ernie looked up in alarm. Genie looked up too, but *he* was excited — excited to finally know what Grandpop had shushed Crab about a while back, and what he'd been so dang excited about every. Single. Day.

"You mean, he gon' learn how to shoot?" Crab guessed. "That's cool, but who gon' teach 'im? You can't see no more, remember?"

Learn to shoot? Ernie was going to learn to shoot?! What? *WHAT?* This was the best news Genie had heard since Tess's *In-ter-netttt!* Ernie was staring at Grandpop, but he didn't look nearly as excited as Genie. Matter fact, he didn't look excited at all. Surprised, yes. But mostly he looked the opposite of excited.

"Wait, Grandpop," Ernie started, "I don't wanna know how to —"

"Yeah, I been thinkin' 'bout that, Crab, and you know what I realized? That I don't need to see," Grandpop said, cutting Ernie

257

off. He smiled, sneaky, like he was up to something. "That's what I got *you* for. *You* gon' show him." Then Grandpop finally came out with it. "Surprise!"

Crab picked up his rifle and rested it on his shoulder.

"And what makes you think I'm gon' do that?" he asked, squinting at Grandpop. He took the cigar from his mouth and leaned against the wall like he was some kind of bad boy.

Grandpop dug into his pocket, then opened his palm to show Crab the cash he had just given him.

"You're going to do it because of your father," Grandpop said.

"What's my old man have to do with this? I give you what he promised, plus a little extra with the whole dead fly thing."

Grandpop's mouth formed a slant smile, clearly amused. "Ah. Well, we all know flies ain't nothin' but grown-up maggots, and hooch ain't nothin' but rotgut, but tell me, what would Marlon think about you cheatin' me, son?"

"*Cheatin'* you!" Crab put his hand to his chest in astonishment, but an awkward nervousness washed over his face. "Pop Harris, come on now. I don't owe you nothin'!" he protested, voice going high. But that didn't stop Grandpop from handing Genie the money.

"Little Wood, how much is that?"

"Now hol' on a minute," Crab started, but Genie had already begun counting. He flipped through the cash, folding the corners like Grandpop taught him. Ernie was looking at him crazy. "Twelve bucks. Two ones and two fives," Genie announced, handing the money back to Grandpop.

"Twelve whole dollars. That's funny. But at least it's better than the eight bucks you paid me last week." Then Grandpop smiled big, teeth showing and all. But it wasn't exactly a nice one. It was more like a pit bull's. Now Ernie was looking at *Crab* crazy. And Crab looked like he was going to puke.

"Wait, Brooke, I didn't." Crab hedged. "I didn't —"

"And I know you've been in that house back in them woods. The one I told you to leave alone."

Uh-oh.

Crab swallowed a huge lump of air. "I didn't mean nothin' by it. I just go in there when I'm having a bad huntin' day," he explained. "I mean, the birds are everywhere, and it's like shootin' fish in a barrel. I ain't even gotta aim to hit somethin'."

Genie was stunned. Crab hung out in that

house because it was easier to shoot birds in there? Those birds being eaten by the other ones, those were birds Crab killed just because all the other animals in the woods had outsmarted him? What the . . . ? *If I was those birds, I would've pecked his eyes out!* Genie thought. And that explained the holes all over the place! But those thoughts were trumped by another one, which was the thought of Ernie learning to shoot. Crab sucks . . . like, *really* sucks . . . but, oh man! Ernie was going to learn how to shoot!

"And what's the big deal anyway? Ain't no one else going in there. Ain't nothin' there but a big tree growin' right up the middle of it, and them broke-down bird-cages in the back that your crazy daddy built!" Crab suddenly sounded a whole lot less sorry than he had seconds earlier.

That brought Genie back. Crab sucking now trumped Ernie shooting.

"*Excuse* me?" Grandpop's voice went dangerously low. He planted his hands on the table and lifted off his seat, his head cocked to the side. "What you say? You short me and use me, then have the nerve to call my —"

"I didn't mean it like that. I'm just sayin' —" Crab interrupted, visibly shaken.

"Your minute is up," Grandpop said

tersely. "And if you don't want Mary to come back in here and turn you inside out, I suggest you make dust."

Crab looked at Genie and Ernie. Genie gave him his best screwface.

Brooklyn style.

That night Ernie was hogging the sink as they brushed their teeth before bed. "Scoot over and let me spit," Genie garbled, foam leaking from his mouth.

"Still brushin'," Ernie garbled back. Genie spit in the toilet, then positioned his tooth-brush in his hand like a gun, holding it up so Ernie could see him in the mirror.

"A'ight, so since you wanna hog the sink, give me your money, sucka," Genie said in his deepest voice.

"Quit playin', Genie."

"Hey, man, it's too bad the new Michael Jackson we catch gotta be alive, because if it didn't, you'd be able to shoot one out the sky." Now Genie pretended he was firing a rifle at the ceiling. Ernie glared at him, a nasty stink-eye, and Genie instantly felt bad. He could never *intentionally* kill a bird. The fact that Crab *could* was totally freaky. How could Tess have a father like that? Ernie glared back in the mirror, picking at his face, a big pimple in the middle of his forehead like he was mutating into a unicorn.

"Seriously, though, Ern. You excited about your birthday tomorrow?" Genie asked, rubbing his fingers along his forehead, seeing if he had any baby horns too.

"Not really. Fourteen's pretty much the same as thirteen."

"Well, *I'm* excited about your birthday."

Ernie frowned at himself in the mirror. "Why are *you* excited? It ain't *your* birthday."

"What you mean, why am I excited? You got glaucoma of the ears or somethin'? You get to learn how to shoot! Wait till I'm fourteen. I'm gonna be the most amazin' shooter ever. Like on a whole 'nother level. You think Dad'll let us come back down here then, so I can learn too?"

Ernie huffed, "You'll be on your own for that one. Plus, I'on't even really wanna learn."

"But . . . but . . . how come? It's a *gun!*"

"I'on't know, I just don't." Ernie turned back toward the mirror. Genie didn't get it — how could anybody not want to learn how to shoot?

Ernie looked at Genie from the mirror. "I mean, what is there to shoot? Not people, that's for sure."

"Of course not people." Genie didn't want to shoot people. Or birds, for that matter. He just wanted to shoot. "Maybe we just set soda cans up on the fire hydrant, and you buck 'em down. That would be cool." Now Genie fixed his fingers into a pistol and held it up to his face. He closed one eye like he was aiming at something again.

"Look, Genie, I'on't wanna shoot nothin'! Ain't no point, and I ain't doin' it," Ernie said.

Genie dropped his hand. Ernie was mad, and whenever he was upset about something Genie said or did, he had a habit of punching Genie in the arm, and Ma wasn't there to yell at him for it. Ernie slapped off the light switch and stormed upstairs, Genie following him quietly. In their room, Ernie grabbed his sunglasses off the old dresser and put them on, then climbed into bed. Genie stood by the dresser and opened the truck door, carefully, of course. How could Ernie not want to learn how to shoot? He closed the door. *He* sure wanted to learn how to shoot. He opened the door. If Ernie didn't learn, then how would Genie ever get to *see* how it was done? He closed the door again. He sure hoped Ernie would change his mind. Say he was just joking. Because if he didn't, Genie wouldn't get to watch. But by the time Genie opened and closed the driver's-side door for the sixth time, Ernie was already snoring.

#475: Why is Ernie so stupid?

FIFTEEN

The next morning — IT WAS STILL DARK OUTSIDE! — Grandma woke Genie and Ernie up crazy early. STILL DARK OUTSIDE!! Like nearly the same time Genie and Ernie had gotten up to "take care" of Michael Jackson, an event that Genie was trying his best to not ever think about again. Operation Pretend, remember? Or don't remember. Whatever. Anyway, Grandma was hootin' and hollerin' and dancing around and telling them they had to come outside RIGHT NOW and luckily Genie had on a shirt because Grandma made it clear they did NOT have time to change into their clothes. And that was the beginning of a day — Ernie's birthday and the Fourth of July — where the only normal thing to happen the next twenty-four hours was that Ernie woke up with his sunglasses on. Grandma was waving something around, and when Genie's eyes finally focused for real, he saw the last thing he ever expected to see in his grandmother's hand — a fistful of bottle rockets!

Once she got their "sorry butts" outside, Ernie stumbling in the dark, Genie trying to fake it so Grandma wouldn't notice how easy it was for him to walk around in the dark, she started hopping around like she had the best fireworks since Coney Island. "Stay over there, you hear me? Stay right there," she ordered, and just like that, lit the first one. The sun was just starting to come up, so when it went off, it wasn't really *that* cool, but it did make a great bang. Then she lit off a second. Just as Genie was wondering why Grandma didn't wait until that night, when people *usually* light off fireworks, she explained that people in North Hill get crazy and shoot random shots when it got late on the Fourth of July, and that she didn't want to be outside for all that mess.

She lit another match. "Okay, here goes another one!" Then she plugged her ears with her fingers. The thing shot off into the sky, making a weird fart sound on the way up and then exploding and bursting into what Genie assumed looked like falling stars even though they could hardly see anything. Samantha was going crazy, barking and running around in circles. Genie went over and calmed her down. Grandma didn't take her fingers out of her ears until she was sure the popping was done.

"Okay, this next one is called a cherry bomb," she told them, holding up something that actually looked just like a cherry. Genie didn't care about what the fireworks looked like as much as he loved the names. Cherry bombs, Roman candles, ground spinners, parachutes, sparklers. There was a note in his notebook from about a year ago, when a man tried to sell his mother illegal fireworks on the A train: #276: Whose job is it to name fireworks? Genie thought whoever that person was, they were doing an awesome job and that "firework namer" might've been a good career for him — see: *Poopidity* — before deciding to maybe become a detective, which would eventually lead him to life as a *questionnaire.*

Grandma lit what would've been the stem of the cherry and stepped back. They waited. And waited. Seemed like forever. She must have thought it might be a dud, because she took a step toward it to stomp it out, but as soon as she did, *BANG!* The stupid thing went off! Grandma stumbled back, tripping and falling in the dirt. Hard. Her legs went up in the air like she was doing a backward tumble. Samantha howled. Grandma howled louder.

Genie and Ernie ran over to help her up. "I'm okay, I'm okay!" she assured them, trying to get back to her feet, slapping the dust off her legs and butt. Genie was trying so hard not to laugh that it made his stomach hurt. But it became less funny when he realized Crab's jacked-up junkyard-mobile was bumping into the yard.

Tess was with him.

"Hey, Mary," Crab said, climbing out, a mug of coffee in hand, doing *his* best to keep a straight face. He lifted the mug to his mouth and took a sip.

But Tess rushed right over. "Ma Harris, you all right?" She glared at her father, who shrugged as if he were the child and she was the parent.

"Can it, Crab," Grandma snarled, pretty much shutting down anything he was *going* to say. Anything he might've even been thinking. Then instantly softening her face, she greeted Tess. "Hi, baby. I'm fine." She snatched the rest of the fireworks up off the ground, dirt all over her back.

"Wassup, birthday boy?" Crab said to Ernie, who had already thrown an arm around Tess for the kind of hug that says, *Your dad is watching, but hey,* coupled with,

What you think about these muscles?

"What you want, Crab?" Grandma said, before Ernie could answer. "It's too daggone early for your nonsense."

Crab's look got all serious. "C'mon, Mary. Listen, I just came to apologize to Brooke. About yesterday. And everything else," he said, sounding almost genuine. "And I wanted to tell him that I would teach your boy, Ernie here, how to shoot. To make up for it. Figured we could get it outta the way early; I wanna try to get Karen out the house later on for the fireworks down at the fairground." He turned to Ernie. "Might wanna put on a shirt if you gon' shoot, but whatcha say, you ready to be made a man?" Ernie looked at Crab sideways, as if he had LIAR written across his forehead. Or THIEF. Or maybe PUNK. Genie did a Repeat.

Crab set his mug on the hood of the car and popped the trunk. "You ready?" he repeated.

"Nah, I'm good," Ernie mumbled. He was looking down and kicking the dirt, like a chump, then must've caught himself feeling like a chump, especially since Tess was standing next to him, because he quickly lifted his head, straightened his back.

"Alright, so let's —" Crab didn't seem to realize Ernie had said no until he was

269

halfway through the sentence. Then it hit him. "Wait, what? *Nah?*"

"I'on't need to learn how to shoot no gun," Ernie said now, shoulders back.

"Ernie, you'on't wanna shoot?" Grandma asked, mashing the paper from the fireworks into a tight ball.

"Not really." He glanced at Tess and shrugged.

"But yesterday your granddaddy said . . . ," Crab started protesting, then headed toward the front door. "Come on, kid. Let's see what the old man has to say about this."

"Lotta footsteps I hear," Grandpop said, coming out of his bedroom as everyone swarmed into the kitchen. "And two of 'em sound like the steps of a fool." He tucked in his shirt. "Crab, you got some nerve comin' in my house after yesterday."

"My daughter's here, Brooke, so take it easy."

"Hey, Pop Harris," Tess said, throwing her arms around him.

"Hey, Tessy." Grandpop hugged back, then touched the top of her head. "Doin' okay, baby?"

"Yes, sir," she said sweetly.

"Good." Grandpop released her and

asked, "You know your daddy's a fool, right?"

Tess nodded, and Crab jumped back in. "Okay, okay, I deserve that. But I came up here to apologize."

"Well, I'm too old to hold grudges. So . . . okay," Grandpop said, all nonchalantly, to Genie's surprise. "Is that all?"

Crab glanced at Ernie. "I also came to tell you that I'll teach the boy how to shoot. But, um, he ain't interested."

Grandma was slapping her hands together, flicking off the last bits of paper into the trash, but her eyes were steely and beaming right on Crab, watching him like a hawk.

"What you talkin' 'bout?" Grandpop asked.

"Your boy here, the big man, too scared to learn how —"

"That's not what he said," Tess interrupted.

"I never said that," Ernie agreed, quickly following her up. "I said I just didn't *want* to do it."

Grandpop wove his arms across his chest. "But . . . why not, Ernie? It's your fourteenth birthday. It's . . . well . . . a North Hill tradition."

"Just because I'on't feel like it," Ernie said.

"And that's good enough," Grandma said

271

pointedly.

But Crab pushed. "Just say you scared if you scared."

"Shut up, Crab!" Grandma barked.

"I'm just sayin'." Crab put his hands up like he was under arrest.

"Everybody, hold on, hold on." Grandpop turned to Ernie. "Now, Ernie. Tell me, son, are you scared?"

"No, he ain't scared," Genie said. He felt like he had to say that because he knew it was true. Ernie was hardly scared of anything. Not scared to taste weird stuff, or walk through the woods, or explore scary places, or even fight, especially if any of those things had to do with Genie.

"Let your brother answer," Grandpop said gently.

Genie looked at Ernie. Ernie looked at Genie. Then at Tess. Then at Crab. Then he looked at Grandma. Then Grandpop. Then back to Genie. Then finally back to Crab, where he curled his lip up like a mean dog.

"No, I ain't scared. Forget it, let's just do it."

A *Yes!* firework went off inside Genie's head.

"You sure?" Grandma asked, frowning.

Ernie gave a short nod.

"Well, let's do it then," Crab said, bouncing up on his toes. Grandpop slapped his hands against the counter in excitement.

"Let me get my hat, and we can head out."

Grandma fixed him a look. "Where *you* goin'?"

"Where you think I'm goin', Mary? I at least wanna be there when the boy pulls the trigger."

"Oh *really*? And somewhere up in that brilliant head of yours, you think that's a good idea?" The volume of her voice bumped up a notch. "What if somethin' happens to you, Brooke? You haven't been out there, like that, since, well, actually, I know the last time you were out there, and you do too! You've got the scar to show for it."

Grandpop answered very deliberately. "That won't happen this time."

"You'on't know that," Grandma said, all huffy.

"Mary, please." He kept his voice kind but firm, controlled. "Calm down. I'll be fine. I can do this. I swear I can. I *want* to do this."

Now Grandma crossed her arms over her chest. "Well, if you goin', then I'm goin' too."

"Baby, Crab can handle it." Grandpop reached out for her. "Please." Grandma had that face Shelly always made whenever she asked Genie for a dollar to go to the bodega and he didn't have it. The one she made right before she went and got the money from Aaron, who always had it because he got an allowance.

"Either I go, or you stay." Whoa. Grandma just wouldn't let up.

Grandpop sighed. "Well, gentlemen, for the first time ever, I guess there will be a lady joining us in this ceremony."

"I'm comin' too," Tess piped up.

"Oh, well, two ladies," Grandpop corrected.

Grandma let out an insanely long exhale and finally said, "Okay, Brooke, fine. I'll stay." Then she came close and fixed his shirt collar the way Ma used to do for Dad before he went to the firehouse. Before he always looked guilty and she always looked tired. "Just be careful," Grandma said, which was also what Ma always said to Dad before he went to the firehouse. Before they were "having problems."

Worry in her eyes, Grandma kissed Grandpop on the cheek, then kissed Genie and Ernie.

"You sure you wanna leave an old lady here by herself, Tess?" Grandma asked.

Tess looked torn between going to be with Ernie and not leaving Grandma alone to sit and stress herself to death.

"You could maybe help me work on Ernie's birthday cake for when they get back," Grandma added, her voice suddenly high and singsongy like a little kid's, coaxing. Way different from her mad-at-Crab growl.

Tess sighed and pulled a chair from the table. "Okay," she agreed, shaking her head. She'd just been conned by a senior citizen.

"Look, I'll be outside," Crab said, heading toward the door. "All this back-and-forth is killin' me."

"Yeah, yeah, go 'head. We'll be out there in a sec," Grandpop said. He followed Grandma into their room, kicking the door almost closed behind him. Genie tried not to be nosy — in grown folks' business. And failed. He just couldn't help peering in and seeing Grandma sitting on the bed and pulling her favorite book onto her lap. Seeing Grandpop grab his hat and slap it on his head, then run his hand along the dresser until he got to a folded flag, just like the one upstairs. Slipping his hand into the pocket the folded triangle made, he wiggled out his gun. He tucked it into the back of his pants, just like Genie had seen it on that first day. Then Grandpop gave Grandma a kiss, soft and gentle, and came back out hollering, "Ernie, Little Wood, y'all ready?"

Genie could tell Grandpop was excited, and so was he. He grabbed Grandpop's arm. "Let's go!"

Ernie had run upstairs to get a shirt on, and then he had to go to the bathroom, and now Genie, Grandpop, and Crab were all outside waiting on him. Crab cracked a joke about him "peeing the fear out." It wasn't funny, and nobody laughed . . . except Crab.

He and Grandpop began discussing what exactly they were going to have Ernie shoot at.

"I'on't want him shooting at trees. Bullet might ricochet or something," Grandpop was saying.

"Right, right. Well, what you got in the house? Anything old that you won't mind getting shot up? You know, like maybe —"

"Maybe what?" Grandpop said, his voice a warning. "You better not say my wife."

"Nah man! Jeez! I was gonna say like tin cans or some of them old hooch bottles, or somethin' like that. Chill out. I ain't got no beef with your wife. She got beef with me!" Crab frowned. "Forget I asked. I got an idea, anyway."

He went to his car and popped the trunk again. First he pulled out his rifle, then, after digging around for a second, he hauled something else out and held it up triumphantly — a plastic bag full of aluminum cans and glass beer bottles. "Gotta whole lot of 'em from the bar. Gotta be at least twenty, twenty-five dollars' worth back there. Y'know, gas money."

"Don't forget to grab the ones you left in my folks' house back up in the woods."

Crab groaned. "I said I was sorry!"

Genie braced for *that* argument to start back up when, phew, Ernie came out the door.

"Now everybody be careful," Crab warned as they entered the woods.

"Man, we ain't on no battlefield," Grandpop replied, cocky.

Crab didn't reply, just made his eyes big and did some kinda hand signal to Genie and Ernie indicating that they needed to keep an eye on Grandpop.

"And watch out for dog mess. It's all over the place," Crab grunted, taking the lead. *Poopidity.* Genie had to choke down a laugh.

Ernie tapped Genie on his shoulder as they began wading through the woods. "Yo. Here." He handed him his sunglasses. Whoa. Ernie never let him touch his shades. The welt by Genie's eye had nearly faded, but Genie put them on anyway.

Crab kicked sticks and rocks out of the

way, but Grandpop was moving pretty smoothly, his hand light on Genie's shoulder. The farther they went in, though, the tighter Grandpop's grip got, and soon sweat was coming from his hands, sogging up Genie's shirt. Genie wondered how "concerned" Grandpop really was, hiking through the trees like that, occasionally tripping over ground roots that Crab couldn't kick away. And on top of that, it was daytime — copperheads were wide awake. And just because Genie, for all his watching, hadn't seen any yet, that didn't mean they weren't there.

In the distance was the yellow house. Genie wanted to point it out to Grandpop, but Grandma had said not to mention it, and when Crab *did* mention it, he almost got mollywhopped. Genie thought about how Grandpop might react if he found out about Michael Jackson. But the sight of the old house, plus all the birds chirping around him, led Genie to hope that maybe another swallow had already been caught, letting *him* off the mollywhop hook — they hadn't checked the trap today.

Genie also had the crazy idea that maybe the tweeting birds were telling the other birds to look out because crazy Crab was in the woods. Or maybe they were saying

Genie the birdnapper was coming. Genie didn't want the animal world to think he and his grandfather and brother were anything like Crab, given that Crab had probably ticked off every critter in there by shooting at them all the time. If *he* was a squirrel and saw Crab coming, he'd be pretty ticked off. But Genie wasn't an animal killer like Crab. Oh wait . . . he was.

He *was*! And what if the animals somehow knew and all banded together and launched some kind of attack? Jeez! Genie eyed the woods nervously, until, thankfully — and animal-attack free — they came to a part of the trail that opened up. It was almost like God forgot to plant trees in this one small, circular section — the forest's bald spot.

"This is it," Crab said grandly. "This is where me, y'all's daddy and uncle, and just about every other kid in town learned how to shoot, thanks to your old granddaddy here."

Genie took it all in, trying to imagine his dad and Uncle Wood as kids, getting shooting lessons from Grandpop. Grandpop, able to see, teaching Dad how to hold a rifle. Grandpop was looking left to right, right to left too, probably imagining the same thing — how it used to be. Crab set down his rifle and the bag of cans and bottles on the ground and began pulling on some of the tree branches that surrounded the area.

"You okay?" Genie asked Grandpop softly. He was still clutching Genie's shoulders.

Grandpop leaned in. "Hmm?"

"I said, you okay?" Genie asked again.

"Ah, Little Wood. I'm fine, I'm fine. What you think me and you was getting all that practice for?" he said, low, smooth.

Wait . . . what? What?! Genie's mind was erupting — Grandpop had planned this whole thing! All those night missions, why they were basically training sessions so that he could be here for Ernie's fourteenth birthday! So that he could keep up the tradition. At first Genie felt like . . . well, kinda stupid. Like he'd been pranked. But that feeling washed away as it also dawned on him that *he* was part of reason the tradition could continue. He had a big part in it, in fact!

"So, *that's* why you asked me to take you outside all those times?" Genie tried to keep his voice down, not that it would've mattered: Crab was getting the target situated, and Ernie was drifting off in space somewhere.

"Always with the questions!" Grandpop laughed. "But, yeah — I'm tired of feeling like some blind baby in a daggone playpen, and you were the only one who could do it and not treat me like one."

Well, that sure made Genie feel good, but before he could reply, Crab called out, "This one'll do," shaking a skinny limb. He let it twang back into place while he dug a Coke can out the bag. He wiggled the tip of the tree limb into the mouth of the can.

"This here's your target," he told Ernie, who was standing off to the side as if this wasn't all about him. "Now let's talk some basics, and most importantly, the rules."

Crab lifted his rifle in both hands, like he was about to demonstrate how to shoot an arrow from a bow, which would've been just as cool, in Genie's estimation. But just when Crab opened his mouth to explain what rule number one was, Grandpop interrupted.

"Rule number one," he said. "Ernie has to shoot *my* gun. He's my oldest grandson, and I think it's only right that he use the family six-shooter." He reached under his shirt and pulled out the revolver.

Crab's eyes went wide. It was an old silver beauty, with detailing in the pearl handle, a shine on the barrel. Crab looked like he wanted to kiss it. Like he wanted to *eat* it.

"Okay, old man," Crab conceded. "You got it." Then he rattled through a bunch of stuff Genie never even knew about guns.

Turned out, they were way more compli-
cated than you'd ever guess. For one thing,
you didn't just point and shoot! Crab
explained that there were only six shots in
the revolver. The bullets went in a thing
called the cylinder, which looked a lot like a
fat metal honeycomb that popped out from
the side of the gun. Genie had seen that
honeycomb thing in a bunch of movies, but
never knew the name.

Grandpop wasn't hanging on Genie's
shoulders anymore, but he stayed brushed
up close.

"No matter what, son," Grandpop interrupted again, "never, ever, EVER point a
gun at a person. Be very careful with these
things. They're not toys. Got me?"

Genie instantly had questions, questions
that weren't the kind you ask out loud, at
least not in this moment. Questions to write
down: *When were toy guns invented? When
was Coca-Cola invented? What's the difference between a rifle and a revolver? Why only
six shots in the revolver? Why not seven? Is it
because six-shooter sounds better than
seven-shooter?* What he wasn't thinking
about in this moment was Michael Jackson,
or the red truck, for a change. All Genie
could think about was how . . . friggin' . . .
awesome this all was.

"Of course, Grandpop. I'm not stupid," Ernie was saying, sort of smart-mouthed. It was the first thing he'd said since he'd given Genie the sunglasses.

"Yeah, you don't *think* you are. But it's always the smart ones, the ones who know it all, who make the most mistakes."

Crab waited until it seemed like Grandpop was done, then continued explaining what was what: the hammer, the barrel, the grip, the sight.

"And this" — Crab turned the gun on its side so Ernie could see — "is the trigger. Now I'm gonna tell you like your grandfather told me: You don't pull the trigger, son, you squeeze it, got me? *Squeeze* it."

Ernie didn't say a word. Just nodded, looking even more uncomfortable, as if that were even possible.

After about a hundred more minutes of talking about the gun, Crab finally said he was ready to let Ernie actually try it. Genie was pumped. Super hyped. But he realized something was different about Ernie. Something off. Ah! He wasn't wearing his shades. His cool was off balance.

"Ern," Genie called to him, snatching the black frames from his face. "Here."

Ernie slipped them on. And the cool was back. But only for a second.

"Uh, uh, uh." Crab shook his head. "Take 'em off. You just said you wasn't stupid, and already . . ."

"What's that?" Grandpop asked.

Ernie spat. "Nothin'." He yanked the sunglasses off, folded the stems across each other, and slipped them into his back pocket.

Crab, satisfied, proclaimed, "A'ight, then . . . Showtime!" He sort of snapped his wrist, and the cylinder of the gun popped open. He spun it, looking at all six bullets, then slapped it closed again. For those five seconds, Crab was the coolest man alive. At least to Genie.

Chick-chick, CLACK. Crab pulled back on the hammer and handed the gun, barrel facing the trees in front of them, very carefully to Ernie.

"All right, hold it with both hands. Now look down your sight and aim at that can."

Genie had the absurd thought that the branch with the can sort of looked like it had just finished taking a sip and was asking another branch if it wanted to have a taste. Then he snapped out of it and thought about how cool all this was. *Man,* did he want to try. Maybe they'd let him after Ernie.

"Keep your elbows bent just a little, but

lock your wrists," Crab was saying.

"Lock my wrists?"

"Yep, keep your wrists tight." Crab held up a weird-looking fist to demonstrate what a tight wrist looked like, which, to Genie anyway, looked just like a "regular" wrist.

Ernie held the gun up and turned toward the can. Genie studied Ernie. Studied his face, his eyes. Something was still off. And it wasn't just the fact that Ernie wasn't wearing his shades. Something else was off balance. Out of whack.

"Hold on, hold on," Grandpop said out of the blue. *That* definitely threw Ernie off — he whirled around toward Genie and Grandpop, the gun aimed directly at them. The barrel looked as big as a cannon! Genie ducked, flinging his arms over his head.

"Jesus Christ!" Crab said, pushing the barrel toward the ground. "We just went over this, Ernie. Don't point at nobody! EVER!"

Ernie looked embarrassed. "I know, I know, sorry." He'd broken into a sweat.

"It's okay, son. My fault," Grandpop said. "I just think one of us, Crab, needs to take a test shot. Show him how it's done."

"One of *us*?" Crab scoffed.

"Yeah, us, meanin' me. I should get the first shot."

Grandpop smiled wide and weird. But nobody else did. Especially not Genie, who had just had a gun aimed point-blank at his head. He almost wanted to cry. Or puke. Bye-bye super hype.

"What you talkin' 'bout?" Crab moved between the gun and Grandpop.

Grandpop just kept smiling.

"Brooke, what are you talking about?" Crab repeated, slower, clearer.

"Crab, I just wanna take a shot. It's been years since I've squeezed the trigger. Just one shot. The boy needs to get used to the sound anyway. Just up in the air." Grandpop said it quiet. He said it calm. He took a step — a brave step — forward and reached for the gun. Crab caught Grandpop's hand, and by the look on Grandpop's face, Crab must've been gripping it pretty tight.

"Please. Just one. These my grandsons, the only ones I got. C'mon . . ." Grandpop half coaxed, half pleaded. His face was a strange mix of proud and wistful. Crab looked at him for what seemed to Genie to be forever. Then he let go of Grandpop's hand and took the pistol from Ernie.

"Boys, take five steps back. That way." Crab pointed toward the trail.

Ernie and Genie stepped away.

"Okay, Brooke." Crab handed Grandpop

the gun. "Hell, it's your gun. One shot. Aim overhead, twelve o'clock." Then he took one step back. Just one.

Crab took just one step back. The way Grandpop held the gun, it was like it was made to fit in his hand. Like he was born to shoot. So normal. Nothing like how Ernie looked.

Grandpop stood there for a second, just holding his pistol. Then out of nowhere he thrust his arm straight up in the air. *Chick-chick, clack* went the hammer. *BOOM! Oh my!* Genie felt like he was standing in the middle of a thunderclap. His bones rattled in his body and his ears pulsed as if his heart had somehow jumped into them. As soon as he heard the second click, his fingers seemed to plug them on their own accord. Then, again. *BOOM!*

"You said *one*!" Crab yelled, grabbing the six-shooter.

Grandpop laughed, a laugh Genie had never heard from him. It was a real laugh. Like a kid's laugh! "I know, I know. But an old man can change his mind, can't he?"

Crab waved Ernie back over. "Let's do this thing, before your grandpop tries to take over your birthday." He held the revolver by the barrel so that Ernie could grab the grip. "Let's do it."

Ernie took the gun again and got back in the same uncomfortable-looking stance he was in the first time.

"Now, remember, keep your elbows a little bent and your wrist tight for the kickback. Aim at the can, and when you got it, squeeze the trigger."

Ernie looked a little shaky, almost like the gun had suddenly gotten too heavy for him, but he held it up anyway and looked through the sight.

"Wait," Grandpop said.

Crab flung his arms up in the air in frustration. "Now what?! Brooke, just let the boy shoot."

"I will, soon as he holds the gun right."

"Brooke, you can't even see! He *is* holdin' the gun right!"

"No. He's not. I can tell by the way he's breathin'; the gun is tippin' 'cause his wrists ain't steady. I can *hear* it." Grandpop then told Ernie, "Son, lock your wrists, as if you were arm wrestling." He held his own hand up to demonstrate.

Ernie blew breath like he always did when he was irritated. He lifted the gun again, locking his wrists, then unlocking them. He closed his left eye to aim, which made his lip curl up on one side. Sweat dripped down his forehead. He licked his lips and swallowed. The gun seemed to be kind of vibrating in Ernie's grip. Genie could tell Ernie wasn't holding the gun as tight as he was supposed to, but Genie wasn't sure that he *could.* Maybe the gun was too heavy. But it wasn't just that. Something was off. Different about him. For the first time ever, Genie could tell that his brother was scared. Really scared.

An airplane flew over them, low. Grandpop clamped Genie's shoulders with both hands.

Genie put his fingers back in his ears and got ready for the boom.

What he should've done was put his hands over his eyes.

BOOM!

The revolver jumped back, smacking Ernie right in the face, then flying out of his hands. Ernie's knees buckled as if someone had sucker punched him. He staggered backward, slamming his hands over his mouth, then crashed to the ground. Then the airplane was gone and Genie could hear him. Ernie was screaming.

"Jesus! Ernie!" Crab rushed over.

Grandpop dug his fingers into Genie's shoulders so hard it felt like he was going to break them. "Crab? What happened? What's goin' on?" he cried out. Genie yanked away from him and ran over to his brother. Ernie was on the ground, now curled into a ball, rocking back and forth.

Oh no, oh no, oh no. Had he shot himself? Had he missed the can and hit a tree and the bullet ricocheted? "Ernie!" Genie screamed.

"Ernie, you okay?" Crab was asking. He was on his knees, trying to look into Ernie's face.

"Crab! What the hell happened?" Grandpop demanded, arms outstretched like a zombie. "Crab! Genie!"

"It hurts! It hurts so bad!" Ernie was bawling now. Crab was trying to ease Ernie's hands from his face, trying to see what was the matter. Ernie fought him, shouting over and over again, "It hurts so bad, it hurts, it hurts." Genie was kneeling now too, and Crab finally got Ernie's hands down. That's when they saw the blood pouring from the sides of his mouth, down his cheeks, and into the grass.

Oh God. Please. Don't let this be happening. This can't be happening. This can't be, Genie prayed.

"CRAB!" Grandpop bellowed, dropping to his knees as well. He started crawling toward them on all fours.

"Brooke, the gun kicked back," Crab

finally told him. "Recoil. He didn't have it tight enough. Musta slipped — hit him in the face!"

Genie just started crying. The only thing he could think of to do was pull his T-shirt off to sop up the blood with, but before he could even try, Crab pushed his arm away.

"Back up, son," he told him. But Genie didn't want to back up. This was his brother. *His* brother. "Back up, Genie!" Crab barked.

"Genie!" Grandpop was slapping at the ground in front of him, trying to find exactly where his grandsons were. Genie grabbed his arm. Crab started asking Ernie a bunch of stupid questions.

"What's your name?"

"Who's your brother?"

"Where you from?"

"How many fingers am I holdin' up?"

Grandpop inched closer and started gently prodding Ernie's face, feeling, Genie suspected, for any changes, like swelling or broken bones. But Ernie whipped his face away. So Grandpop began bombarding Crab with what Genie decided were definitely better questions.

"Do you think he has a concussion?"

"Is his nose broken?"

"What about his jaw?"

"Teeth?"

Crab tried to get Ernie to stand. At least his howling had calmed to a low moan. Blood soaked the collar of his T-shirt.

"Teeth?" Grandpop repeated, more worried.

Ernie, now on one knee, heaved like he was gonna throw up or was choking on something. Then he spit out three little rocks, one by one, like pumpkin seeds. Teeth. Then he started howling again.

"Looks like . . . yeah . . . he lost three, right from the front," Crab said, picking each tooth up off the ground. He grabbed a beer bottle from the bag he brought and put the teeth in it, then gave Genie the bottle while he helped Ernie stand up. Ernie cried even harder as he got to his feet. So Genie cried harder too. Ernie covered his mouth, trying to keep some of the cry in. Genie covered his own mouth for the same reason.

It was the worst game of Pete and Repeat they had ever played.

Sixteen

Grandma: Hey, Sheila and Ernest. This is
Mama. I'm guessin' right now y'all are up
in the air headed to Jamaica. Listen, uh, we
had a little bit of an accident. Ernie did.
But don't freak out. He's fine. He's okay.
Give me a call when y'all get there. But
please don't worry. He's gon' be fine. Okay,
love you. Bye-bye.

Three teeth in a beer bottle is a weird thing
to look at it, but what's weirder is when your
grandmother takes that bottle, tips it so all
the teeth roll out into a glass of milk. Yes,
milk. And then gives that milk to her youn-

gest grandson to hold in the backseat of her car, with strict directions not to spill it, as she rushes him and her other grandson to the hospital. A dentist would've made more sense, but it was the Fourth of July. No dentists' offices open.

Genie stared at the teeth — he couldn't really see them anymore, because they were submerged in milk — but he still stared into the glass, concentrating on not spilling it, as if he were carrying the Holy Grail. It was better than staring at Ernie, sitting in the front seat, holding an ice pack on his mouth. Grandma said the ice would keep the swelling down. Everything Genie wanted to do to help he knew probably wasn't a good idea. Like saying anything. What was there to say? *I'm mad at myself for wanting you to learn how to shoot? I'm mad at Grandpop for making you do it?* Which was exactly the way Grandma was feeling — she made that clear as she laid into Grandpop in their bedroom before they left the house.

"I knew this was a bad idea, Brooke. I *knew* it," Grandma had said, her voice, shaky, coming from behind the old wooden door. Tess had already left with her father. She had looked so excited when Genie'd burst through the door with Grandpop, standing in front of a big ol' birthday cake, clearly ready to brag about it, ready to hear Ernie brag about shooting. But instead of smiles and laughter, she got blood, tears, and teeth in a bottle. And then Crab hauling her home, quick-fast.

"It was an accident, Mary. He'll be okay."

"But it didn't *have* to happen," Grandma went on, fuming. "That's what you don't get. The boy didn't wanna learn how to shoot. He was scared. You knew it. I knew it. Hell, even Crab knew it."

Grandpop mustn't have responded fast enough, because Grandma barreled on. "But you *pushed* him. You pushed him like you *always* do."

"I didn't push the boy, Mary, I —"

"You did, Brooke!" Grandma shouted, then brought her voice back down. "You did. Just like you pushed Wood. Is your grandson a *man* now, Brooke? Is he?" Then came the jingle of car keys, and Grandma swept Genie and Ernie out the door.

As Grandma tore down the bumpy hill, then over and through the winding roads to get to the hospital, Genie did his best to hold the glass of milk steady. Ernie did his best to not look at himself in the side-view mirror. Grandma did her best to keep her eyes on Ernie and Genie both, checking Genie in her rearview and glancing over to the passenger seat, occasionally patting Ernie on the knee. She turned the radio on but changed the station from gospel to hip-hop, which on any other day would've been totally cool. But today, Ernie couldn't bob his head. Neither could Genie. Today, rap music meant nothing.

Twenty minutes later Grandma wheeled the Buick into the hospital parking lot. Inside, people were sitting in Pepto-pink chairs with purple diamonds on them, almost every person leaning on the armrests, their chins planted in their palms, their eyes focused on a TV in the corner of the room.

"We're still hours away from the fireworks show down here at the fairground, but people are already coming in droves. Come on down and claim your spot on the lawn and get ready for North Hill's — no, America's — brightest night!" The newscaster flipped a burger on a grill before they cut to commercial.

A man in the waiting room coughed. It sounded like there was broken glass in his throat.

A young woman held a bloody towel over her hand; an older woman sat beside to her, flipping through a magazine. She glanced up at the Harrises as they came into the lobby.

"Hi. My grandson knocked his teeth out,"

Grandma told the receptionist. Straight to the point.

"Fill this out, please," the lady said in a voice that must have to say that very same thing fifty times a day. Not nice, not mean. Genie figured she couldn't have wanted to be spending her day at work on the Fourth of July.

"What's the wait?" Grandma asked, taking the clipboard the lady slid across the desk, her voice still stinging with Grandpop anger. She did a quick glance around the room, then added, "Ten, fifteen minutes?"

"Ma'am, I'm not sure," the lady said. But she should've said "Forever" because that's what it felt like for Genie, who was doing his best not to spill the teeth-milk while Grandma filled out Ernie's paperwork.

"Hope they call us soon," Genie said, growing more and more impatient as doctors and nurses came back and forth escorting patients through the double doors to the emergency room.

Grandma patted Genie's knee to comfort him. "They will."

Genie sighed. "Just seems like we been here for a month of Sundays."

"Mary?" a voice called from across the room. A doctor. "Mary Harris? Is that you? Why, I haven't seen you since you retired."

"Grandma, you know her?" Genie asked hopefully. The answer came immediately as the doctor walked right over to Grandma, and they went into a hug-fest.

"Oh my goodness. You look so good, Mary!"

"You too!" Grandma said. She turned to Genie and Ernie. "Boys, this is Dr. Maris. I been knowin' her a long time. Matter fact, I remember when she started here."

"This where you used to work?" Genie asked.

Grandma smiled. "You got it. Thirty years in nursing, right here," she said. "This old lady seen a whole lot. Even worse than what's goin' on with you, son," she added, now to Ernie. He kept his gaze on the linoleum as she rubbed his back. "Way worse."

"Mary, who these handsome babies?" Dr. Maris asked, beaming at them.

"These are my grandbabies: Genie . . ."

"Hi," Genie said.

"And Ernie. Ernie's had a bit of an accident." Nothing from Ernie. Normally Grandma would've checked him about being respectful, especially to elders, but not this time.

Dr. Maris's smile disappeared as she went immediately into doctor mode. Must be a hospital thing. "What happened here?"

"Well, Ernie, he's fourteen — today's his birthday," Grandma explained, forcing a frown. "He was learning to shoot and the kickback hit him in the mouth. Knocked a few of his teeth out."

"Oh *no,*" Dr. Maris said, hissing as if she knew how painful it was. "Do you have the teeth?"

Genie held the glass of milk up as if he was making a toast.

"Nice to see you haven't forgotten the tricks, Mary!" Dr. Maris said, and now Grandma beamed.

"Girl, I'd be lying if I said I haven't lost a step. But I'm still pretty sharp." Grandma ran her hand along her head, brushing her hair back, cool.

"Listen, you're family around here. Come on back."

"No, no, I know you're headed to lunch."

"Mary, lunch ain't goin' nowhere. C'mon."

Dr. Maris led them through the white, hand-sanitized, beeping world of the emergency room. Grandma waved at and spoke quickly to some of her old friends.

"Okay, son, have a seat right there," Dr. Maris said, nodding to a bed and yanking a curtain to create a fabric wall around them.

She took the glass from Genie. "Now, I might be able to reimplant his teeth — I'll splint them to make sure they'll hold steady until they've stabilized in the gum, which could take a while. But it won't be pretty, and you're still gonna want to take him to see an orthodontist, eventually, to make sure things are healing properly once the teeth are secure."

Grandma nodded as Dr. Maris slipped her hands in plastic gloves. She poured the milk slowly into a plastic bin, making sure the teeth stayed in the glass, then tapped the glass on her palm until the teeth came rolling into her hand. She set them in a small metal dish, examined them closely. Finally, she gave a nod.

"Ernie, I need you to help me out here," Dr. Maris said. "Be brave. Lift your head for me."

Ernie did so, and Dr. Maris pressed her thumb against his chin, opening his mouth. "Head back, a little more, a little more," she coaxed. She shined a small light in his mouth, lifting his top lip, studying his gum line and the sockets where the teeth had once been. At least the bleeding had stopped. Still, Genie looked away. Grandma patted him on the knee again to try to calm him down.

"Okay, two of them can go back in. Your centrals, or as you know them, your two front teeth," Dr. Maris declared, looking pleased. She turned the mini flashlight off. "But the left lateral is chipped. A piece of the tooth is still there. So that one you'll definitely have to take up with a dentist, but I'm gonna go ahead and reimplant the others."

From the corner of his eye, Genie watched as Dr. Maris grabbed one of Ernie's teeth and pinched it between two fingers. It reminded Genie of how he'd picked up the pieces of the broken wheel, and he hoped Ernie's tooth didn't slip from Dr. Maris's grip, hit the floor, and roll somewhere, never to be seen again.

"Ernie, this is going to hurt a bit," the doctor warned. Ernie immediately winced and tensed, his hands closing into tight fists as Dr. Maris pushed the first tooth back into his gum, like a plug into a socket. Then the other. She glued brackets to them, then attached those to what she'd called the "lateral" to the right, and the "upper left cuspid," which is that tooth that looks like a fang. Genie watched, fascinated — it was kind of like building a model car. Connecting pieces to other pieces. Gluing things together to make them work. Repairing

301

something that was accidentally broken. Now Dr. Maris was attaching wires to the brackets, and suddenly, Ernie, the boy with the perfect smile, had braces. Sorta.

When they finally got home, Grandma had no sooner sent Ernie upstairs — with the beer bottle containing the half tooth — to lie down with a double dose of pain reliever when the phone rang. Ma and Dad. Grandma quickly filled them in, Genie helping with the specifics of what had happened that Grandma wasn't so sure about.

"Did he take his eye off the target? I mean, was he aimin' the gun right?" Grandma asked Genie, who stood attentively right beside her.

"Yeah, he was aimin' right, but the gun, I mean, his wrist just wasn't locked enough," Genie explained.

"His wrist wasn't" — she looked at him — "locked?"

Genie nodded.

"Locked," she repeated to Ma, who then repeated it to Dad, who Genie figured must've taken the phone immediately, because then Grandma said, "No, he's okay, Ernest. He'll be okay. We got him situated right away. Saved the two front ones." Grandma paused. Then she said, "Did

Ernie ask to go shootin'? Well, no, not directly — what?" Another pause, then a heavy sigh. "It was a freak accident, but I knew the poor baby was scared. I could see it all over him. He said he didn't wanna do it, but you know how it is with your father."

And that was when Dad started yelling. Genie couldn't make out what he was saying, but he was saying it loud.

"I know, son," Grandma kept repeating. "I know."

Grandpop, who'd been hovering nervously over Grandma's other shoulder, now tapped it. "Give it to me, Mary," he whispered. "Lemme talk to him. Please."

Grandma gave him a cold stare, but relented, saying, "Hold on, son," and passing Grandpop the phone.

"Ernest, I'm sorry," Grandpop said, first thing. "I was wrong and I'm sorry. I'm sorry," he repeated a few more times. But apparently Dad, at the mere sound of his father's voice, had given the phone back to Ma. "Hello?" Grandpop called into the phone. "Ernest?" Then his face dropped into disappointment. "Oh. Hey, Sheila." He waited while his daughter-in-law asked something. "Yeah. No problem. Hold on."

Grandpop handed the phone back to Grandma, who then explained, for the second time, that she had already taken Ernie to the hospital and had him checked out and splinted, and would take him to get all checked out again and that there was no need for them to leave Jamaica — they had just gotten there. Even though Genie pretty much felt ready to go home at this point, it seemed like that wasn't going to happen. So Grandma fixed him a quick ham sandwich and left him in the kitchen while she disappeared to her bedroom, where she started flipping through the book she was always flipping through. Grandpop retreated to the inside-outside room, which was fine with Genie as he didn't want to be anywhere near him. It was like Genie was suddenly on an island too. A deserted one.

Maybe everybody in the house was.

Later that day, Tess came to visit, all kinds of worried, wanting to see Ernie. But Grandma turned her away.

"I'm sorry, sweetheart, but he's really, just, y'know, kinda low right now," Grandma explained gently.

"Yeah," Tess said, her voice sad but understanding. "Well, can you just tell him I said hey? And that I hope he's okay?"

"He is, baby. He is," Grandma assured her. "And I'll tell him."

In addition to running interference, Grandma also gave Ernie aspirin to help with the pain, and she made sure there was no extra swelling. The only other thing he really needed would've been a TV with some fighting on it. And, in fact, there was a TV, one Genie and Ernie hadn't even bothered to watch, the one in the living room, which to Genie was just the *land of the missing wheel piece.* Or the room with the door leading to Grandpop's inside-outside room — *bird-murderville.* Actually, there were two TVs. A big one that was like a piece of furniture, like a cabinet with a screen in it. And a smaller television sitting on top of it. The big one didn't work. And the small one was fuzzy, because Grandma and Grandpop didn't have cable. After he finished his sandwich, Genie went over to it and wiggled the antenna. Only one channel came in, some kind of weird repeating infomercial with a woman selling letter openers that looked a little like *katana* blades, which was *not* going to make Ernie feel any better. Plus, there was no remote. So TV was out.

Desperate to help Ernie out *somehow,* Genie decided to joining him up in the bedroom and imitate his ninja interpretations, leaping off the bed, kicking the air, pretending to chop the wall, which Genie thought would be pretty funny. But Ernie didn't laugh at all, not until Genie tried to do a roundhouse kick and hit his foot on the dresser. Then Ernie started chuckling and shaking his head, but he threw a hand over his mouth first so that Genie couldn't see his teeth.

Genie fell onto the bed, rubbing his foot. It felt like he had been stung by a giant bee.

"It hurt?" Ernie asked.

"Not much — how about your mouth?"

Ernie shrugged. "Not so bad anymore."

"Can I see?"

"No." Ernie said it like there was no way Genie could get him to change his mind.

Still. "Come on, Ern. Lemme see. I won't laugh. For real."

Ernie put a fist up. "I swear, Genie, if you laugh —"

"I won't. Promise."

Ernie pulled his hand away and opened his mouth just enough for Genie to see. At first Genie *did* want to laugh. Not because it was funny. It wasn't. Not at all. But because he was nervous, and sometimes when he was nervous and he didn't know what to say or do, he got the giggles. Luckily, he held it in. But it was tough. The perfect picket fence now had a gate over the top of it, and one of the pickets was broken, jagged. It was a mess.

"Not so bad," however, is what Genie said.

"What are you, blind? I look crazy!" Ernie fumed. "I never shoulda shot that stupid thing!"

Genie just sat there quiet. Didn't really have anything to say. Plus he was scared that anything he said was going to make Ernie even madder. So he just listened to Ernie go on and on about how his face would never be the same, and how Tess wouldn't like him anymore, and how people in school would probably give him a stupid nickname like "Tooth Lee" and he'd probably get suspended all the time for kicking their butts even though he wasn't sure if he still wanted to take classes, because people would have to see him this way, and to top it all off he was mad (he said *pissed*) because his sunglasses had broken as a result of the fall, as if having three teeth knocked out wasn't enough. He was pretty much planning to never be seen by anyone ever again, which didn't seem like a good plan to Genie, but that was how Ernie was talking. And Genie was just listening and listening until Ernie finally stopped.

Then Ernie repeated, "I shoulda never shot it. It didn't feel right."

"What you mean, it didn't feel right?" Genie asked.

"You know how it was with you and Samantha at first? Like, for some reason you just didn't trust her. Like there was just somethin' about her."

"Yeah, her teeth," Genie joked. Ernie didn't laugh, so Genie followed with, "The difference is, I was scared." Then, he went for it. "Ernie, you were scared too, weren't you? With the gun?"

"What, when the gun hit me in the face? Of course! You woulda been too!" Ernie sat up a little.

"No, not that part. Before. When you were aimin'. You were scared, right?"

Ernie didn't say anything. He just stared straight ahead, like he couldn't get enough of that blue dresser. Genie thought about how Grandpop told him that he was afraid of being outside, and how even though they did all that practicing, the old man was still squeezing Genie's shoulder hard when they were in the woods. And Grandpop was even tougher than Ernie. So if he was scared, anybody could be scared. Realizing he wasn't going to get an answer, though, Genie said, "Well, if you were, it's okay," just as Grandma came waltzing into the room carrying a tray with an envelope and a bowl on it.

"It sure is okay," she said, sliding right into their conversation. She was always doing that. Sneaky, sneaky Grandma. "We all get a little scared sometimes. There's nothing wrong with it. Nothing at all." She set the tray on the dresser, then held the card up. "This is from your parents. Came in the mail yesterday for your birthday. I'm gonna put it right here." She set it on the dresser, between the red truck and the bottle holding Ernie's leftover tooth. Genie instantly thought how cool it would've been if Grandma pulled out one of those *katana*-looking letter openers and handed it over to Ernie too. Would've been a small victory. Instead she brought the bowl over to him.

"Here," she cooed. "It's chicken soup without the chicken or the noodles or the vegetables. Now, your gums are going to be real sensitive, so use this straw."

Ernie leaned forward and took a sip of what was just broth. His eyes got big all of a sudden, and Genie could tell he'd burned the back of his throat.

"Good?" Grandma asked.

Ernie caught his breath and nodded.

"Good," she said, going back over to the dresser. "You were brave out there, Ernie. That's in your blood. Your grandpop, he's a brave man too," she clarified. "He ain't perfect, but he's brave, livin' his life trapped in the dark, gettin' on. Your daddy's brave too, fightin' fires, riskin' his life to save other people." She paused and picked up one of the medals on the blue dresser. It swung from a purple ribbon, glinting. "And your uncle was brave too. This is what they gave him — what they gave Wood — when he was killed." She brought it over to Ernie. "They call it the Purple Heart. It's very special." *It's very special,* Genie thought. *Like the broken truck.* Uggh.

Ernie covered his mouth before saying, "But he died, so what's the point of giving it to him when he wasn't even here to see it?"

Genie could tell Grandma was thinking of how to answer. It was a good question.

"I guess to remind us that he was brave, even though he was scared."

"Uncle Wood was scared?" Genie asked, trying to push the thought of the fire truck further back in his brain. Back, back, back behind the thought of Grandpop telling him about Uncle Wood whupping on that dude, Cake, to protect Dad. To Genie, Uncle Wood didn't sound like the scared type.

"Oh Lord, yes. He was terrified. Before he went to Kuwait he sent me a letter, and I could barely read it because he had cried all over the daggone thing. Ink was everywhere." She swallowed hard. "He was *so* scared."

"You still have it?" Ernie asked. "The letter."

Grandma turned away, but Genie saw her blinking hard. Blinking away tears. She put the medal back on the dresser, lining it up nice and neat. Then she turned back to them, her face so sad it made Genie's stomach hurt.

"Yeah," she said softly. "I read it every single day."

Seventeen

#476: Teeth can reconnect to the gums? How? The doctor said when they are connected to the other teeth around them, they can do it. Weird.

#477: Why did Grandma make me put Ernie's teeth in milk? To save them? Should I have put Michael Jackson in milk?

#478: Should I be drinking more milk? I hate milk. Makes me poop.

#479: Why are the fang teeth called cuspids? Cuspid is almost cupid. Love bites.

#480: What if Ma and Dad's trip was ruined? If they get divorced, is it my fault because I was the one who really wanted Ernie to shoot the gun?

#481: What causes kickback, anyway? I wish Ernie could kick kickback back.

#482: How much do real nice sunglasses cost? Ernie got a hundred bucks from Ma and Dad for his birthday, so at least he'll be able to replace his broken ones with better ones. Or maybe he can fix that chipped tooth.

Genie set his pen down and snaked the spiraled wire out of the first few holes in his notebook, holding it up to his mouth trying to imagine what it felt like to be Ernie. He'd stayed upstairs with him most of the day — he figured that if it were him who'd had his teeth knocked out, he would want Ernie around even if he didn't want to talk. And Ernie didn't want to talk. And that was fine with Genie. He spent the rest of the day thinking and scribbling questions in between running down to the kitchen for snacks. Soft snacks, like applesauce and pudding. Man, even with a busted mouth, Ernie *still* ate a lot.

Ernie fell asleep early that night, and for the first time ever, Genie was glad to hear him snore. He had been fourteen for one day, and it was the worst day of his life. So to hear him calling the hogs, as Dad always said, and not be in much pain thanks to the medicine Grandma had given him, was good. But it was still loud, and in between each snore Genie could hear a familiar clicking coming up through the floor, from the kitchen.

Grandpop was up. And Genie didn't know if Grandpop would be in a talking mood, and actually Genie wasn't sure if he even *wanted* to talk to Grandpop after everything that happened, but he was kinda hungry, so maybe he'd just have some ice cream, just sit down there until he got sleepy.

When Genie got downstairs, there Grandpop was, just as Genie suspected, sunglasses on, disassembling his gun again, twisting the screws, yanking and pulling at the revolver.

Genie stood at the entranceway. All of a sudden he was kind of nervous.

"What is it?" Grandpop grumped.

"You wanna be alone?"

Grandpop stopped fooling with the pistol. He kicked Genie's chair out from under the table. "You sure you want my company?"

Genie didn't answer, because he wasn't sure if he actually did. As far as he was concerned, this was pretty much mostly Grandpop's fault. How come Grandpop couldn't tell Ernie was scared? How come he couldn't hear that? But as mad as Genie was at Grandpop, the truth of it was he was also mad at himself. He *knew* Ernie had been scared, but he'd egged him on anyway. So Genie knew that *he* had messed up too, and not just with Ernie. The only difference was Grandpop didn't know about some of it. About Michael Jackson. So Genie figured he and Grandpop could be the bad guys together, and he slid into the seat.

Grandpop went back to breaking the gun down. Genie could smell the liquor. He looked at the pieces of gun on the table and realized that it was the first time he didn't want to touch it. Not even a little bit. He didn't have any questions that he wanted to ask about it. He didn't even want to learn how to shoot anymore. And he came to the conclusion that if he had to do that to become a man, get his teeth knocked out, then he was fine with being a kid forever.

Once Grandpop had the gun completely apart, he lined the screws and bits of metal all out on the table like Genie always did when he was about to start building a model car. Grandpop ran his fingers along them. Then he guzzled the rest of his drink, and he cleared his throat.

"Little Wood," he whispered.

"Yes?"

"Could you take me outside?"

Could, but Genie wasn't sure he wanted to now. But then the image of Grandpop crawling around in the grass and leaves, slapping his hands against the ground, trying to get to Ernie, came back. How all Grandpop's fear of outside, of the unknown, disappeared when he heard his grandsons cry out.

"Don't you wanna put the gun back together first?" Genie asked.

Grandpop tipped his glass nearly upside down to get the last few drops.

"No."

Down the porch steps and into the yard, Grandpop barely held Genie's shoulder, except for the occasional touch for balance. He counted each step, as usual. Seventeen to the middle of the yard. And now they were twelve steps to the left, putting them right around where Crab always parked.

They paused. The crickets were crazy loud, which was a good thing because otherwise it would've been weird with neither Genie nor Grandpop saying anything. Finally Grandpop asked what he always asked. "Little Wood, tell me, are the stars out tonight?"

Genie looked up. Not one star. Even the

moon was mostly covered by clouds.

"No," he said, blunt.

Grandpop grunted. "Good. Let's just stand out here till it rains."

"Until it rains?" Genie wasn't really into getting wet for no reason. "What if it doesn't?" he added, also worried they'd be hanging out outside all night.

"It will." Grandpop took a deep breath. "I can smell it."

And sure enough, it did, not five minutes later. It came down hard and cold, and Genie wanted to go in, but Grandpop wasn't budging. So they just stood there, letting the rain wash over them. Genie couldn't tell for sure, because they were both soaked, but he didn't think all the water on Grandpop's face was from the sky.

Things at Grandma and Grandpop's were pretty awkward for the next few days. Crab didn't show his face, a good thing; Grandma might've jumped on him if she saw him. Ernie eventually came down from the bedroom, even started going back outside again, but he refused to see Tess, even though Genie was pretty sure Tess wouldn't give a hoot about how Ernie looked. He spent most of his time with Samantha, playing fetch with the rubber toy. Genie could tell he was keeping an ear out for Tess, just in case she decided to come up the hill, so he could make it back into the house before she saw him.

Genie didn't wait around for Ernie to get out of his funk. He couldn't afford to. He still had things he had to take care of, like figuring out how to fix that wheel on the model truck, and the even more important task of catching a new Michael Jackson. So while Ernie let Samantha lick his sadness away, Genie, on Day Sixteen, ventured off to the yellow house to check the trap. This was the first time he'd be going by himself, and he was kinda nervous, and went a little crazy swinging his trusty stick in front of him, swiping away invisible webs that might have been homes to poisonous spiders, scaring away any lurking poisonous snakes.

And, big bummer, the trap was empty. The box was down, but nothing inside; it was most likely blown over by a breeze.

Day Seventeen: The trap was still standing, as if not even the wind was interested in it.

Day Eighteen: Genie had, in fact, caught something, but not what he was hoping for. It was, go figure, a squirrel. If only Grandpop had taken a liking to squirrels and not birds, this would've been a much easier task.

318

Luckily, squirrels didn't seem to be interested in flies, so at least the bait was still there.

Whenever he wasn't traipsing through the woods, which was less and less scary each time, Genie would pop in and out of the inside-outside room to keep up with his duties. Grandpop was practically living there now, like he was hiding from everyone. Like . . . a broken bird in a birdcage. And whenever Genie came in to tend to the plants, clean up a little and feed the four birds, pretending there were five, Grandpop would ask him to leave. One time he even barked at Genie, scaring him half to death.

"I'm sorry, son. I'm sorry," Grandpop said, running his hand across his own forehead. "I'm just . . . I . . ." Grandpop couldn't find his words. "I know you're just helpin' out. And I appreciate that. So come in and do it, but once you done, you gotta let me be, okay?"

Let him be? Let him be what? Sad? Guilty? Part of Genie didn't want to really be around Grandpop anyway, but another part of him did, because he understood those feelings too.

It seemed to Genie like Grandpop and Grandma sort of switched places, and now Grandma and Genie were together most of the time, mainly because they were the only two people in the house who were talking. Grandma was on a cooking frenzy, making all kinds of crazy soups so Ernie wouldn't hurt his teeth on anything hard, and turned Genie into a sous-chef, she called it, which was just a fancy word for helper. When Grandma had finished up whatever soup she could make out of whatever was growing in her garden, she and Genie would play M.A.S.H., a game his mother had taught him, where the point was to randomly decide your life — who you're going to be with, your job, where you'll live, your car, and the best part, whether you will live in a mansion, an apartment, a shack, or a house. M.A.S.H. The rules were simple:

1. Create a list (of four) for each category.
2. Choose a random number (something above ten).
3. Count through the list, crossing out whichever item your number lands on.
4. Repeat the count until only one item in each category is left. That's your life!

M.A.S.H.
GIRLS-JOBS-PLACES-CAR
Shelly-detective-Brooklyn-'71 Mustang-mansion
Shelly-firework namer-China-Dad's Honda-shack
Shelly-mechanic-Jamaica-spaceship-apartment
Shelly-firefighter-Brooklyn-school bus-house

Genie's best future life according to M.A.S.H. (with a count of twenty-one) was the one where he lived in a mansion in Brooklyn, driving a Mustang, working as Detective Little Wood and married to, of course, the one and only Shelly. Not bad at all.

Then one morning, Day Twenty-One, after Genie and Ernie had picked peas (yes, Ernie was still expected to do chores!), Genie was in the kitchen, ripping a page out of his notebook for M.A.S.H. version #8, when Grandma plunked something in front of him. Genie did a double take. It was the BOOK. The book Grandma was always reading in her bedroom.

"Let's have a look-see," she said, opening the cover. Inside, it was full of pictures of Dad and Uncle Wood when they were kids, pictures of Grandma, and Grandpop when he could see — weird seeing him without sunglasses — and even some pictures of Genie and Ernie when they were little. But most importantly, there was a letter — *the* letter, the one from Uncle Wood when he was heading for Kuwait, a crinkled piece of paper with blue writing on it.

"See if you can read that," she said to Genie, moving the book closer. It was hard because the words were smudged and smeared, just like she said. *Plus,* he felt kinda nervous.

But Grandma was watching him expectantly. So Genie started. "It says, 'Dear Mama.' " That was the easiest part to make out. "I hope you and Pop are —" He got stuck. The next words looked like *on fire,* but that didn't make sense.

"Are fine," Grandma prompted. She leaned against the refrigerator and continued on without even looking at the book. She had it all memorized. "I'm writing because I have bad news. My unit got called, and in a few days, I'm going" — Grandma paused — "I'm going into battle." Her voice started to wobble, and Genie didn't want to hear any more; he didn't want to see her cry.

"He goes on about how he feels trapped

because there was no way out of the decision, and down at the bottom he says, 'Whatever you do, don't tell Ernest I'm scared. Just tell him I love him.' " Grandma pressed at her eyes, then came back to the table and closed the book. "He was your daddy's hero. Sometimes I think he went into the army just so that Ernest wouldn't have to. He took the hit."

Genie thought about Ernie. About how Ernie always did everything first, just to make sure it was okay. From simple things like tasting the weird foods first, to being in the front when they were walking through the woods. Or even back in Brooklyn, how Ernie always took up for Genie, fought his fights. Even the ones that didn't have to be fights, Ernie fought those, too. And now Genie wondered if Ernie had taken the hit for him. If Ernie knew that because Genie was fascinated by learning to shoot, he would test it out for him. Make sure it was okay. Even if that meant doing something he didn't want to do. Something he was *scared* to do. He wondered.

About an hour later, Grandma announced they were going to the market — she had enough peas. But Ernie refused.

"Why not? I need both you boys," Grandma said.

"I ain't goin'!" he repeated, his words muffled by his T-shirt, the neck of which he'd pulled up to his nose. "Genie can handle it."

Genie perked up.

"Well, can you at least help me pack it all up and get it in the car?" she asked. Then she winked at Genie. "Genie is strong. He is. But you're stronger. Just help me get it all in the car, and I'll take Genie with me." See, all Ernie had been doing, besides his chores, was moping around, playing with Samantha, still saying really nothing, and when he did, he pulled his T-shirt up over his face like a ninja mask. So Grandma was smart — she was trying to get Ernie off his duff.

So Ernie helped load all the peas in Grandma's backseat, the sun blinding him, making him squint. Ernie without sunglasses just wasn't Ernie. And he still refused to actually go to the market.

Once Grandma and Genie got there, which of course involved super-loud church music and Grandma saying, "Gotta play it loud enough for God to hear it, so he can send people to come buy up these peas," they lugged the baskets over to the table. That Mr. Binks guy was setting up his table too, right next to theirs. This time he had on sweatpants that were way too small, and a pink shirt with a red tie. On his feet, roller skates! He was pulling wooden boxes out of a bag, as well as a whole bunch of glass jars, the kind that Genie drank sweet tea out of. Once the old guy caught Genie looking, he flashed a smile. Then he opened the boxes. Genie craned his neck to see. The boxes were full of TEETH! Genie'd forgotten all about that! Teeth on top of teeth on top of teeth! Mr. Binks rolled around the table, setting the teeth up in cases like rings at a jewelry store. In the glass jars were even more of them.

"Hey now, Mary," Teeth Man (which Genie decided at that moment to call him) said.

"Mornin', Binks. You remember my youngest grandson, Genie." Grandma set her scale down on the table.

"Genie, of course I remember." He held his hand out. "Remember your promise, the first one was a shake, so from now on fives, right?"

Genie smiled, and he and Binks did the most awkward five ever, but it was still a five. The guy was weird, and selling teeth was definitely creepy, but Genie still kinda liked him.

"Where's big man?" Teeth Man asked.

"Ernie?" Grandma frowned. "He couldn't make it today. He had an accident about a week ago."

"An accident?" There was genuine concern in Teeth Man's voice.

"Yeah, he was learning how to shoot, and the gun accidentally jumped out his hand and punched him in the mouth," Genie blurted. Then it was like he couldn't control himself. He just kept going. "It knocked out three of his teeth." Then, realizing that that wasn't the complete truth, he corrected himself. "Really, two and half teeth."

Genie glanced over at Grandma, who was glaring back at him with the strangest look on her face.

"Sorry." Genie shrugged. "That *is* what happened, though."

"I know that's what happened, Genie." She turned to Teeth Man and frowned. "There it is, Doc. All the family business laid out like Sunday dinner."

But Teeth Man seemed more concerned with whether Ernie was all right.

"He's fine," Grandma said, snapping a pea in half. "It was July fourth, so I had to take him down to the emergency room, and they got it taken care of. But poor thing is too embarrassed to leave the house, so it's just me and peanut-head here today."

Peanut-head? Jeez!

"What'd they do, splint them?" Teeth Man asked knowingly.

Grandma nodded.

"How many?"

"Two. A third one was chipped. They said they couldn't do anything with that one."

"Ah. Gotcha now." Teeth Man nodded at Genie. "That's the *half*."

"Right," said Genie.

"Are the teeth stable in the splint? He's not complaining about any movement, right?"

"No, no, it seems pretty sturdy. An old friend of mine did it. I trust her. She said it should be fine," Grandma explained.

"Ohh, that's good, good, Mary, that's good. If she splinted him already, he should be as good as new in, I don't know, maybe a month." Teeth Man's voice was so warm, so concerned. He shook his head and added, "I'll tell you one thing, thank the Lord for old friends." Then he began turning the jars of teeth a half inch in one direction, an inch in another, until they were all lined up perfectly. Every jar had a different label, like ATHLETE, or MOVIE STAR. Genie was glad he didn't have one labeled LITTLE BOYS, because then he would've had to talk to Teeth Man the rest of the day with his hand over his mouth so he didn't get any ideas about adding one of Genie's to his collection.

Grandma watched, opening her mouth, then closing it, then opening it again. It was like she was trying to say something else, but the words weren't ready yet. Then finally, "Binks, I don't know how to ask you this, but, see, my old friend who rigged up the splint said Ernie would eventually need to see somebody just to make sure that —"

"You want a second opinion," Teeth Man cut her off, catching on. "Of course I'll take a look." Teeth Man cheesed and rolled to the other end of the table. His smile looked like something out of a toothpaste commercial, even though the rest of him looked like something out of a circus.

"I would really appreciate it," Grandma said, relief in her voice. "Just for a double dose of peace of mind. I know you're probably very busy, but I just wanna make sure."

"Happy to. Call my office; as soon as I can get you in, I will."

Grandma was nodding yes, yes, yes, and Genie was trying so hard not to shake his head no, no, no. He liked the guy, but he didn't know if he liked him enough to trust him with his brother's mouth. Dude sold teeth! So he couldn't help himself, he had to ask: "Is he gonna take more teeth out of Ernie's mouth?" He tried to say it low so Teeth Man wouldn't hear.

"No, baby," Grandma said.

"Well, is he gonna add any teeth to Ernie's mouth, like one of those old ones he has lying around?" Again, he tried to keep the words under his breath.

But Teeth Man heard him and laughed. "No! Of course not! I just want to make sure that everything is going smoothly. And look at that chipped one to see if we can put a crown on it. That's all. Mary, let's set it up before the day is over."

A *crown*? Well, *that* sounded pretty promising, actually. Ernie would have a . . . king mouth? Awesome.

Then it was back to work. "Not in the store, not on the street, you ain't never seen a pea this sweet!" Grandma hollered with her usual cheer.

And just like last time, people came rushing over to Grandma's table, snatching up all the peas, which Genie carefully weighed. In an hour, the baskets were nearly empty. Teeth Man, however, hadn't had the same luck with his collection. But he was showing a couple this one tooth, telling them the story behind it.

"Yes, yes, Michael came in and said that it

329

was bothering him so bad he could barely dribble the ball," he was saying. The guy peered close at the tooth Teeth Man held up.

"That's crazy! So you took it out?" he asked. He kept looking over at his girlfriend, his eyes buggin'.

"Not me. I wasn't Mike's dentist. A buddy of mine was. I traded him for a Miles Davis," Teeth Man said. Genie didn't know who Miles Davis was, but the people at the table sure did.

"So, how much for the Jordan?"

Teeth Man rolled the tooth around the palm of his hand, examining it.

"It's just a wisdom tooth, so nothing crazy. Twenty bucks sound fair?"

The guy forked over a twenty-dollar bill, and Teeth Man put the Jordan in a tiny bag and handed it over.

Soon as the couple walked away, the guy already opening up the bag to stare some more at the tooth, Genie asked in awe, "You can really sell teeth for twenty bucks?"

Teeth Man lit up, shifted a wooden case two inches to the left. "That's a cheap one," he said. He picked another one out of the case. "This baby could go for two thousand!" So for Teeth Man, teeth were his babies. Made sense. At the same time . . .

"Two thousand . . . dollars? Two thousand bucks for somebody's old nasty tooth?" Dang!

"Not just *somebody,*" he said, lifting the tooth to the sun like it was some kind of diamond. "This is one of Babe Ruth's front teeth. Got knocked out by a bartender."

"Whoa. Babe Ruth! But how did *you* get it?" Genie asked.

"My grandfather was the bartender." He showed Genie a few more cool ones, mainly from people whose names he had heard before but didn't really know. Finally, Genie asked, "You got any ninja teeth?"

"Ninjas?"

"Yeah, like fighters, or karate people, or anything like that?"

Teeth Man's eyes lit right up. "Why, yes I do. Right here." He pointed to a yellowish one. It was small. "This one here is Bruce Lee's."

Must've been one of Bruce's baby teeth or something. It was tiny!

"You a fan?" Teeth Man asked.

"Yeah, but not as much as my brother, who someday is gonna be able to fight just like him," Genie explained. "Better than him." He appraised the tooth. It looked like a cuspid. Cuspid. The word he learned from Dr. Maris. "How much for it?" Genie asked

331

like a big man, even though he only had ten dollars — the same ten dollars Grandma gave him the first trip to the market — on him. But he wanted to know.

"I'll tell you what." Teeth Man leaned close. "I'll trade you. You get your granny to give me some of those peas, and the tooth is yours."

As Grandma and Genie were closing down their table, the last of the peas going to Teeth Man, Tess appeared.

"Hi, y'all," she said, bopping up, setting her can of earrings down.

"Tess!" Grandma squealed. "How you doin', sweetie?"

"Fine. Y'all need some help?" And she immediately began stacking the baskets.

"Thank you, darlin'," Grandma said. When they'd carried the baskets, the scale, and the sheet all to the car, Grandma asked Tess, "How you get down here, Sugah?"

Genie wondered if Grandma was worried about running into Crab. Not that Grandma would be worried. *Crab,* on the other hand . . .

"My mama brought me," Tess said, passing the scale to Genie. He put it in the backseat.

"Your *mama?*" Grandma looked shocked,

then fixed her face quick. "Sorry, I just mean . . ."

"I know, I know," Tess said, brushing it off.

"So," Grandma began more carefully. "How'd you get her to bring you?"

"I had her Google hypochondriac," Tess said, raising her eyebrows at Genie. He couldn't hold in his smile.

"Ahhhh," Grandma said, nodding.

"Right. So, I basically had her look it up so that she could know what was *really* wrong with her. I told her yesterday, 'It's not glaucoma, Mama. It's *you*!' " Tess bounced up and down on her toes like her father. "She read about it for hours, then this morning she decided to take a step. I couldn't believe it. She drove me here and everything. But then she got a little freaked out by all the dirt and dust and took off."

"Baby steps," Grandma said knowingly.

"Exactly."

"Well, good for her," Grandma enthused. "So, how you gettin' home?"

"Ms. Barnes was gon' take me. You know Ms. Barnes? Sells the white socks?"

Grandma nodded. "Yeah, I know her."

"Yeah, so, I'm not gon' hold y'all up," Tess said, seeing the car was packed. "But could you give this to Ernie?" She dug into her

333

can and pulled out a face mask. The kind doctors wear. The kind Tess's mother had been wearing every time Ernie and Genie saw her. A certified mouth hider.

Grandma smiled wide. "Why'on't you come give it to him yourself?"

Tess squished into the backseat and Genie sat up front. He squeezed the Bruce Lee tooth in the palm of his hand, peeking at it every few minutes. He just couldn't believe it — Bruce Lee's tooth. He told Tess about it and made her promise not to tell Ernie. He knew she was great at not snitching; she had already proven that with the whole dead bird thing, which Grandma and Grandpop still had no clue about. Which reminded him — he needed to check the trap.

"It could be like a good luck charm," Grandma agreed, the church music playing low on the radio.

"When should I give it to him?" Genie asked.

"That's up to you, son. You could give it to him right away, or you could save it for when he might really need it. Your call," Grandma replied.

Genie thought about it. "I'll wait and surprise him."

"Sounds good. I won't say a word."

Ernie was outside rubbing Samantha's belly like she was a baby when they bumped up the driveway. When he saw Tess, the look on his face made it seem like he wanted to make a run for it, but he didn't. Genie and Grandma made a swift move to the house, Genie heading straight upstairs to hide the tooth. He took a good look around before his eyes locked on the flag on the dresser. Next to the Purple Heart. Next to the red truck, the half wheel. Next to the bottle holding Ernie's chipped tooth. The flag was folded into a perfect triangle of white stars just like the one in Grandpop's room, where Grandpop hid his gun — well, before he broke it all apart. Along the side was the same pocket, and if it was perfect for Grandpop's revolver, Genie figured it would be even perfect-er for Bruce Lee's tooth. He pushed the tooth into the tight fold. Perfect-est. Then he ran back downstairs, zipped past Grandma, who sat at the kitchen table with her feet in a bucket of steaming water — standing too long caused them to swell, she complained — and jetted outside.

"Sweeeeeet!" was what Genie said, mimicking Grandma's voice, when Ernie asked him how his first solo trip to the market was. He and Tess were tossing the squeaky toy back and forth, just out of Samantha's reach, and she was running back and forth frantically. Tess laughed. Ernie, now wearing the mask that Tess brought him, actually laughed too. He looked like a total ninja.

"Let me guess, everyone came runnin', right?" he asked.

"Yep! It was wild."

"Wait, wait," Tess said, cutting in. "What's goin' on with the ichael-May, ackson-Jay, ird-bay, ap-tray?"

"Really? Pig Latin?" Genie said, zinging Tess.

"I mean, we like twenty feet from the front door," she said, and she was right. Even *if* Grandma was busy soaking her feet.

"Well" — Genie turned around to make sure the front door was closed — "there are, uh, no new discoveries," he said cryptically.

Tess looked disappointed. But Ernie was more interested in Genie's trip to the market, the trip he'd *refused* to come on.

"So wait, was the crazy guy who sits at the table next to Grandma there? The one with the roller skates and all the teeth for sale?" Ernie asked.

Genie glanced at Tess and swallowed hard — had to get the secret about Bruce Lee's tooth all the way down to the bottom of his stomach so that it wouldn't come out. "Yeah, he was there. Such a cool dude. I think Grandma talked to him about checking your mouth out. Just to make sure everything was okay."

"What?!" Ernie shouted, whipping the toy at the ground. Samantha lunged.

"What's the big deal? He's nice."

"And he only gon' do a checkup. Trust me, I have braces. It ain't that big a deal," Tess added.

"No big deal? That dude is nuts. He sells teeth that he says are famous people's!"

"Maybe some of them *are* famous people's, and anyway, like Grandma said, they're like good luck charms," Genie said, trying to calm him down.

But Ernie's panicked look didn't go away. As a matter of fact, it got worse. "I can't believe she's gonna try to take me to that psycho. I'll probably have no teeth by the time I leave his office! He'll probably put them all on sale, and say they're Martin Luther King's or somethin'," he went on. "She can't. No way!" And he stormed toward the house, Genie and Tess scrambling after him. He slammed through the door, scaring Grandma, who kicked the bucket of water over.

"Dammit!" she shouted, jumping up and grabbing a towel off the sink. "What in the blazes is going on?" She used her foot to move the towel around, sopping up as much water as she could. It was everywhere.

"Sorry, Grandma," Ernie said, crouching down to help. "But Genie said you were gonna take me to see that weirdo who sells the teeth at the market!"

Grandma just kept mopping with her foot. "Yeah, he's just gon' check the splint. Nice of him," she said, flat. Grandma told Tess to look under the sink for another towel.

"Nice of him? Grandma, he's crazy! What if he takes my teeth?"

Grandma fixed Ernie a look, then took the towel from Tess, thanking her before laying back into Ernie. "Listen, he ain't gon' steal your teeth, boy."

"You'on't know that," Ernie replied.

"Yes, I do know that. I know this man, Ernie. He ain't no stranger. Besides, he's a dentist. Fixin' teeth is his job."

"I'on't wanna go."

The door to the inside-outside room swung open. Genie and Ernie froze. Grandpop came stepping out into the kitchen like a man risen from the dead. It had been days since he'd come into the kitchen while the sun was up.

"What's all the fuss out here?" Grandpop demanded. Ernie glared at him and readjusted his mask. It was as if Grandpop opened the door and a cloud of awkwardness came out. Shame made the kitchen stink worse than greens.

"Nothin' you need to worry about," Grandma said quick. "The floor is wet, Brooke. I don't want you to slip, so maybe you should get yourself back in your room."

"Ernie, what's the fuss?" Grandpop pressed.

Ernie just kept glaring.

"Okay," Grandpop said, annoyed. "Genie?"

Genie had to say something. "Ernie doesn't wanna get his mouth looked at by the man at the market who sells the teeth."

"What?"

"Genie!" Ernie cried in fury. Genie looked away fast.

Grandma sighed. "Brooke, you know Dr. Binks, down at the market. He told me he would look at Ernie's mouth. I trust his opinion." All the while Ernie was shaking his head, no, no, no.

Grandpop bit down on his bottom lip, like he was embarrassed. Guilty. But before he could respond, Ernie rushed back outside, the screen door slamming behind him. Motioning for Genie and Tess to go after him, Grandma picked both towels up off the floor and wrung them out angrily over the sink, twisting them like she was trying to strangle them, if a towel could be strangled. Grandpop's face seemed to crumple as he stepped haltingly back into the inside-outside room. He fumbled to find the doorknob, then closed the door behind him.

EIGHTEEN

"I'm not goin'," Ernie repeated over and over again, his voice muffled by the face mask. He, Genie, and Tess tramped down the hill.

Genie really didn't see what the big deal was, and really wanted Ernie to come with him to check the trap — y'know, do something that *really* mattered — but he knew Ernie well enough to know that once he got this mad, it was best to just wait it out until it passed. Saying something could mean a karate chop. But Ernie wouldn't chop Tess.

"Okay, Ernie. We get it. You're not goin'," she said, which was interesting because that made Ernie stop saying it. Just shut him down. It was like she performed some sort of southern reverse psychology that Genie had never witnessed before. He'd have to remember that the next time he and Ernie got into it. Better yet, when he and Ma got into it.

As they reached the base of the hill, Genie noticed that the front door of Tess's house was open.

"Uh, Tess," Genie said. "Your mother is . . . doin' somethin'."

Her mother was heaving a huge armload of clothes out of the front door onto the porch.

"What now?" Tess moaned, crossing the road, hopping over the ditch, and running to the house. "Ma!" she called. "Ma, what you doin'?"

Tess's mother dashed in and out of the house, each time returning with another armful of clothes, grunting and sweating as she tossed each bunch onto a growing pile.

"Tessy, baby, I'm so glad you're here. Ever since I drove you over to that market today, I've been itchin'. I think it might be ticks or fleas or somethin'. I'on't know. But I know it was in my clothes, and so I want you to take all this stuff and check it closely. See if you see anything."

"See if I see *what*?" Tess said, climbing the steps warily.

"I don't know. Itchy things." Tess's mother disappeared back inside, Tess trailing her. Genie and Ernie waited at the edge of the porch, uneasy. Should they stay? Go? Genie decided "stay," and sat down. Ernie, for once, played Repeat.

A few minutes later Tess was back, her arms cradling at least fifteen pairs of shoes. She dropped them between Genie and Ernie. Then she went back for more. When she returned, she dropped a load of dresses.

"So much for bein' healed," Tess griped.

"Remember, baby steps," Genie said.

"You want us to help?" Ernie offered.

"Help what? Help pretend there's something wrong with her clothes?"

"Um . . ." Ernie was stuck. "If you want?" Tess's frustration slowly turned to a quivering laugh. She shook her head like even she couldn't believe this one.

"I'll be right back. There's only a few things left. Then we'll . . . pretend to check for bugs. Or somethin'."

Genie looked at the garments next to him. Southern church-lady clothes. The fancy blue silk. The patterns — polka dots, stripes, weird designs. Flappy collars and mismatched cuffs. And buttons. So many buttons. Triangles and squares and circles. Yellow and green and . . . wait . . . wait . . .

"This is the last of it." Tess dropped five or six dresses onto the pile. Then she noticed Genie with a jacket held up not six inches from his face. "What you lookin' at?"

Genie glanced up, *Oh . . . my . . .* all over

his face. "This button." He turned the jacket around — it was all satiny and super dressy and looked like it cost a lot. There were only three buttons on it. But those buttons were plastic. Shiny silver. With black trim.

"What about it?" Tess asked.

Ernie looked as confused as Tess sounded.

"It's the *wheel.* The wheel to the truck." Shiny silver like the rim. Black trim like the tire.

"What?" from Tess.

Ernie leaned over. "It is! It's so close!" he cried out. The button looked like the wheel on the red truck. Not identical, but very similar. He filled in Tess, who just listened with a *tsk-tsk-tsk, city boys* look on her face. Then, as if it were no big deal, she grabbed the jacket, put the button in her mouth, and used her teeth to nibble through the thread. Grinning, she spit the button out, wiped it on her shirt, and dropped it into Genie's hand.

"It's all yours."

"Really?" She was giving it to him, just like that?

"She won't even notice it's gone." Tess laughed. "Plus, this makes us even, for the whole hypercognac thing."

"Hypochond—"

"Jokin', man. Jokin'. Hypochondriac."

They didn't check the trap. And for once, Genie didn't mind because at least he had that button. So that night, while Ernie complained himself to sleep, Genie found glue — white glue — in the top drawer of the dresser. He applied one single drop to the button, then pressed the gluey button to the axle, sat on his bed, and held it there for what seemed like hours. Finally he gingerly released his grip and . . . the wheel stayed put! Hallelujah! He'd finally solved one big problem. The truck was fixed. He wanted to run outside and scream it to the moon. To the stars. The truck was fixed! Instead he lay in bed and dozed off with a grin.

Now the only thing left hanging over his head was Operation Birdnap.

NINETEEN

"Little Wood, listen to me when I tell you that life ain't nice to nobody. *Nobody.* Not me, not Mary, not Ernie, not your daddy, not Uncle Wood. *Nobody.*" Grandpop's words were slurring. Genie could tell he had been drinking. "You're born and you're sad, crying and ugly, and you live crying and ugly, and someday you die, and all you can do is hope you ain't crying, 'cause you damn sure still gon' be ugly."

"Nine, ten, eleven, twelve," Genie counted under his breath. Now it was Day (Night) Twenty-Four, and he'd gotten so he didn't get freaked out when Grandpop started rambling. After the Dr. Binks discussion, Grandpop practically barricaded himself in the inside-outside room. He even refused to eat with the family, so Grandma had to take his plate to him. He'd only come out late at night, and he'd never say much, not in the house. He'd just sip his liquor, which, by the way, Tess was now delivering along with the dead flies, and sit with his gun stripped into pieces like Legos, which he now kept in a ziplock bag. But once he and Genie got outside, Grandpop would let loose. Turned out Grandpop was pretty much mad about everything, and had been for a long, long time.

"And that's just the way it is, son." Grandpop spoke like his tongue was too fat for his mouth. "Wish I could tell you life is easy, but it ain't. Wish I could tell you you won't hurt nobody, but you will, and guess what, people gon' hurt you, too. We all trapped in this game of hurt. Trapped in this game of . . ." His words slurred into just sound.

"Sixteen, seventeen, eighteen, nineteen," Genie said, stopping.

"I can guaran-damn-tee it," Grandpop picked back up. "But you know what's not guaranteed? Not one thing. Except for cages. Cages . . . everywhere!" He wasn't really making much sense. "Nope, I can't even guarantee you that you won't go blind or that your kids won't be killed in a war, you know what I'm sayin'?"

"Nineteen, Grandpop."

"And where are we?"

"The side of the house."

Samantha lifted her head, then stood up.

Her eyes flickered green and yellow in the moonlight. She took a few steps forward, her chain dragging in the dirt, her tail still.

"What's that?" Grandpop asked, reaching out and touching the siding. It was their first time to that part of the yard. They usually stuck to the front, but on this night, Grandpop said he wanted a new count.

"Samantha," Genie whispered.

Grandpop's mouth went from smile to a scowl.

"That ain't Samantha." Grandpop growled like a crazy man. "Samantha's dead. That's . . . that's . . . that's an impostor." But he crouched down, started to whisper, "Sammy. Sammy." Samantha looked and looked, almost like she was trying to remember who he was. Then all of a sudden she burst into a bark-fest.

"Shhhhhh," Genie shushed frantically. Grandma would come looking if Samantha didn't chill out, and it would've been bad news if she caught them spookin' around outside in the middle of the night.

"Come on, Grandpop, we gotta go," Genie said, tugging his arm.

"No, not yet," Grandpop said, pulling away, stumbling back against the house. He cocked his head, listening, as if Samantha's barks were a sweet song.

"Grandpop, Grandma is gonna catch us," Genie begged. "Please, let's go."

Grandpop rested there for a few more seconds, his chest swelling every time he breathed in.

"Nineteen, that way" — he pointed toward the middle of the yard — "and seventeen that way to get to the front door." He chanted the counts until he and Genie finally got back to the porch, but at least he let Genie get him back there. And at least Grandma didn't meet them at the door with her angry face on. Samantha finally stopped barking as they slipped back inside. They crept quietly into the kitchen, Genie finally daring to let his guard down, when he jumped a mile. Grandma. Sitting there at the kitchen table. She had taken Grandpop's gun — the pieces of it — and had removed them from the ziplock. The bolts and springs were in a pile on the table.

"Grandma, I — I —" Genie stuttered, but she cut him off.

"What in Sam Hill were y'all doin'?"

Grandpop straightened up just like Ernie did whenever he got caught doing something he had no business doing. "Just gettin' some air."

"It's eleven thirty at night, Brooke."

"The air is better round this time, Mary,"

Grandpop said, trying to get her to smile.

"And you're drunk."

"He's not drunk," Genie said.

"He is," Grandma retorted. She pointed toward the staircase. "You. To bed. Now!"

Genie started for the bedroom. Grandpop did too.

"Not you, Brooke. *We* need to talk."

"We can talk tomorrow."

"No, we can't. Right now."

Grandpop mumbled something and continued heading toward the room.

"Brooke, I'm not playin'. We're talkin' tonight!"

Genie froze at the base of the staircase. Grandpop was flinging his hand around dismissively, like he was swatting at a mosquito. That really ticked Grandma off.

"Brooke Harris." She grabbed the trash can from the corner of the kitchen and, with one huge sweep, brushed the pieces of the gun off the table as if they were crumbs, the metal knocking against the plastic of the garbage bag.

Now Grandpop froze. "What's that?"

"You know what that is," Grandma said, steely. "It's gone."

Grandpop rushed for the can, thrusting his arms in, frantically digging. Out came broken egg shells. Coffee grinds. Chicken bones. But no gun pieces. They must've sunk to the bottom. Grandpop fell to his knees, digging farther.

"Stop, Brooke," Grandma said. "Stop. Stop." She tried to pull him up as he panted, wet tea bags in his hands. "Let it go."

But Grandpop couldn't stand. He wrapped his arms around Grandma's waist, pressed his head against her stomach, and slowly, drunkenly, painfully started sobbing. And Grandma, over and over again, like to a child, whispered, "It's over now."

Twenty

#483: Is there an age limit for divorce?
Old people like Grandma and Grandpop
can't get one, right?

Go to bed. Go to bed. Genie hated when
his mom told him to go to bed after he'd
seen something that was going to keep him
awake, for like, the rest of his life. Go to
bed for what? It wasn't like he could sleep.
It was like when his mother used to say go
to bed so Santa could come and leave him
gifts when he was younger. Who could sleep
knowing that some magic man is coming to
bring you presents? Nobody. Didn't old
people know that? It wasn't fair. Genie went
to bed anyway. Once he got under the covers, it was like his mind was a TV flipping
channels by itself. Channel One: Samantha
barking. Channel Two: Grandma yelling.
Channel Three: Grandpop crying after
Grandma swiped the gun pieces into the

trash can. After everything that had happened, Genie wanted nothing to do with guns anymore anyway. EVER. He was over it. No guns. He figured he would just ask his mom and dad to sign him up for karate class too. Y'know, Pete and Repeat style.

And as if sleeping wasn't hard enough, the crickets and frogs were out too, and for the first time their chirping was annoying. Man, they were loud. Almost as loud as Ernie. Finally Genie just pulled the pillow over his head, but then he realized he didn't want to go to sleep because the morning would come sooner, and then he'd have to deal with whatever strangeness was going to follow Grandma throwing away Grandpop's gun. Grandpop was probably going to nail himself into his room. Have to slide food under the door! Flat food. Did Grandma even know how to make pizza?

That was the last thought he recalled, because the next was that it was morning, and everything was stranger than Genie had even imagined. Grandpop was sitting right there in the kitchen! In his chair! He was poking at the scrambled eggs on his plate and listening to the radio buzzing with old-school music. Grandma was sitting across from him, still in her nightdress, sipping tea, flipping through her old book, straightening up photos. It was like the night before had never happened.

"Mornin', Genie," she sang out.

"Mornin'," he said, not sitting.

"Mornin', Genie," Grandpop said, also sounding all happy.

Genie hesitated — why was everyone acting so normal?

The screen door creaked as Ernie came in, already sweaty, the doctor's mask the only thing reminding Genie that things were still real.

" 'Bout time you got up, man," he said, wiping pea garden dirt on his shorts. He headed straight to the sink, filling a glass to the top with water, pulling the mask down and guzzling the whole thing down. Then he headed right back outside.

Grandma got up and set a plate on the table in Genie's place. Grits, sausage, and toast. "Sit down and eat, then go help your brother."

"I'm not really hungry," Genie replied uncomfortably. He just wanted to get outside, maybe snap peas in half, toss poop around. Anything besides sitting at this bizarre table.

"Hold on, Little Wood," Grandpop said, reaching for Genie's arm. "Lemme just say somethin' to you." Then he looked over at

Grandma like she was supposed to give him the words. "I, uh," he started. He swallowed hard and cleared his throat. "Look, I just wanted to say, I'm sorry. About last night. About everything."

Genie's mom had always said that when a person says they're sorry, to do your best to forgive them, no matter what.

"Me too, baby," Grandma followed, with a lopsided smile.

"Okay." Genie didn't really know what else he was supposed to say. It wasn't like he could say, *My mother and father argue. I don't want you and them to get divorced. Then I'll have to figure out which parent to live with and which grandparent to visit.*

Grandma nodded, then pulled Genie's head down so she could kiss the top of it.

"Now eat," she ordered, gently pushing him into his chair. She laid a hand on Grandpop's shoulder. He reached up and laid one of his on top of hers. Genie guessed whatever they talked about last night when he was upstairs praying for his own deafness and the end of Grandpop's sobbing — the sound of black sheep — went well. Well enough for them to hold hands. Well enough for them to say sorry. And he couldn't help but think that if Grandpop and Grandma could do that after what had happened, then maybe, somehow, Ma and Dad could too.

Outside, Ernie was in the garden, snapping pea pods off left and right. He and Genie didn't even have to look at what they were doing anymore; they could tell which pods were ready just by the feel of them. When Ernie saw Genie coming toward him, his cheeks lifted the mask enough for Genie to know he was smiling. The sun was turned up. God had put the heat on high, as Ma always said. The hose lay curled in the grass like a giant worm. The mosquitoes were thirsty and flies flew around Genie's face, buzzing so loud he felt like he had stuck his head into Grandpop's radio.

"You a'ight?" Ernie asked, slapping at a mosquito on the back of his leg. "Before we got here, you never slept later than me. Now you just be snoozin'."

"Yeah, I'm good." Genie shrugged. Then he decided then and there that he was going to tell Ernie what happened; now that Grandma knew, technically the secret was out. So it wasn't really wrong to tell Ernie. "Just got in trouble last night."

"Trouble? With who?"

"Grandma."

Ernie gave the head shake. "For what?"

Genie squeezed a pod. Nothing in it. Not

yet. "You gonna keep it a secret?" It wasn't really a secret anymore, but still.

" 'Course I will," Ernie said. There were little sweat drops all over his forehead. Like see-through pimples.

"Okay." Genie lowered his voice. "Grandpop and I come outside, late. Almost every night. In the dark."

"What? You and Grandpop. Come outside. At night?" Ernie said like a robot.

"Yeah."

"What! Why?"

"At first because he just wanted to get used to being outside again, so that he wouldn't be afraid to go in the woods when it was time for you to learn how to shoot." Genie pressed at another pod. Ready. "But now, we just do it because he likes to. That's all. We just come out and walk to different parts of the yard. We talk." Genie caught himself. "Well, these days mostly he talks. It's cool." He squeezed another pod. It was another good one, so he picked it off, slow, because for some reason he felt a little shy about telling Ernie the next part. "But last night, well, he was drunk, and Samantha started barkin' and woke Grandma up."

"And she didn't know y'all were doin' this?"

"Of course not," Genie said.

Ernie's eyes got big. "What she do?"

"She threw his gun in the trash."

"Why?!"

"Because he wanted to go to bed and she wanted to talk."

"So she just threw his gun away?" Ernie's eyes were totally buggin'. "Not that I care, but what did she wanna talk about that was *that* important?"

"I'on't know. Maybe she was just tired of him being all weird and stuff. But it was crazy, man. Grandpop was cryin'. Like *cryin'* cryin'. She sent me to bed, but I couldn't sleep after all that."

"No joke? And that's why you slept so long this mornin'." Ernie shook his head. "*Wow.* You good?"

Genie thought about it for a second. "They said they were sorry. So, yeah. I'm okay."

Ernie extended his hand and gave Genie a five, pulling him in for a hug. Then he hunkered back down between the vines. After a few seconds he popped back up empty-handed.

"Wanna see something? What I've been doing all morning?"

Genie nodded, hoping it was more dog tricks, like Samantha learning to talk. Better yet, maybe Ernie taught her how to shut up. That would've been nice last night!

Ernie pointed to a cluster of peas.

"See these?" He tapped one of the pods. "Watch."

He stepped back, then came forward and did a karate kick, the crane kick, and — *hi yah!* — knocked a whole bunch of those pods right off the vine. Genie had seen him do some sweet karate stuff, but this was definitely one of the best. And now he noticed that loose peas, like little green marbles, were all over the ground, like a hundred pods had just exploded. Ernie picked up a handful of them and held them in the air like a warrior, and Genie knew that his brother Ernie was back.

Well, he was, for that day, and for the next two — Day Twenty-Six and Day Twenty-Seven — but on Day Twenty-Eight, when Grandma dropped the bomb on him that the next day was when he had to go see Teeth Man, Ernie went right back to being weird.

"This is not a big deal, son," Grandma kept saying. "Tomorrow, he's just gon' look. Probably won't even touch nothin'."

Ernie retied the strap of his face mask before replying. "I just don't get why I even have to do this. Ma and Dad will be here in, like, a few days, and in Brooklyn I can just go to my dentist, Dr. Wilson, who I don't like, but at least I know he doesn't sell people's teeth."

"We're going because I told your parents we would. And because I need to know that you're fine *before* you go home. For my own sanity."

The lamp was on and the whole bedroom seemed to glow orange. Ernie sat on the edge of his bed while Grandma folded up clothes that she had just washed for them. She brought a stack of T-shirts to the blue bureau and glanced at the truck for a moment, but didn't seem to notice it had been fixed, maybe because the piece of the original wheel was still on the dresser. But that was fine with Genie, because it wasn't like the truck was back to normal. It wasn't like Grandma was going to be able to ignore the plastic button that was slightly larger and slightly thinner than the original wheel. Genie just wanted to fix it, and let it be fixed. Just to correct the mistake. And he'd done that. Best as he could. So he was good.

Grandma patted Ernie's knee. "Dentists see kids who've had their teeth knocked out all the time," she assured him, tucking the shirts into a drawer. "It's what they're trained to deal with." Ernie stayed scowling, and Grandma moved to the shoes and jeans, telling Genie to start matching the socks.

"Puffs or knots?" Genie asked.

"Your call," she said, folding a pair of dingy jean shorts.

"Puffs," he said. They were easier.

Around puff number six there was a light tap on the door. It opened and Grandpop stepped hesitantly into the room, running his fingers along the wall.

"Safe for me to come in?" he asked, looking toward Genie, who imagined him winking.

"Yep," Genie said.

"You built the house," Grandma said, smirking.

Ernie didn't say anything.

"Good." Grandpop walked forward until his leg bumped the dresser. "Mary, let me get a second with the other men of the house, please."

Grandma's nostrils flared, but she laid the shorts next to the shirts and left the room, giving Grandpop a little nudge as she did.

Genie couldn't help but wonder if this was it. If he was caught. He knew everyone was focused on Ernie, but he was still a bird killer. Ernie lost a tooth. Grandpop lost a bird that most likely, Genie *decided,* symbolized Uncle Wood. Ernie got two of his teeth back. But Michael Jackson was probably somewhere in Grandpop's backyard being eaten by a snake! This was it! This was *it*!

Grandpop waited until he was sure Grandma was all the way downstairs, and then he said, "I understand you goin' to see old Binks tomorrow, Ernie."

The cat released Genie's heart and got Ernie's tongue instead.

"Well, I want you to know that ever since the accident happened, I been thinking about how I could make it up to you. At first I thought maybe I could just give you *my* teeth." And he reached into his mouth and . . . yanked. The. Whole. Top. Row. Out. Spit strings dangled like cobwebs, and Grandpop's smile was in the palm of his hand. *In his hand!*

Arggggh! Genie hadn't even known the man had fake teeth! *That's* how he was chomping those apples!

"But I figured you wouldn't want 'em, 'cause you still got your own." Grandpop's voice sounded different without teeth, and his top lip tucked itself behind his bottom like a bulldog. Brooke the blind bulldog. Genie choked back a laugh.

But Ernie didn't. Grandpop shoved his top row back in his mouth, clicking them against the bottom until the fit was right.

"Dang. I thought that would at least get a smile," he said, clearly to Ernie, who stared stonily at the window. Genie didn't know how Grandpop knew Ernie wasn't smiling, but at this point, Genie had stopped questioning how Grandpop did most of the things he did. Why, the other day he even saw Grandpop write a list of things he needed from the grocery store in a notebook. Every word was on the line!

"*I'm* smiling, Grandpop," Genie offered.

Ernie shot Genie a look. Genie shrugged and mouthed, *What?*

"Okay, no more jokes." Grandpop brushed his hair with his hand a few times. "Ernie, I know right now you hate me, and if you're anything like your daddy, you'll probably feel that way for a long time. And I won't say that I don't deserve it. But I will say that I'm sorry. I know you don't wanna go see that old crazy dentist —" Grandpop stopped, must've realized that that probably wasn't the best thing to say. "I mean, he's a good dentist. He's just . . . peculiar. But he knows what he's doin'." Grandpop leaned his head in Ernie's direction. "I know you're scared," he went on. He made his way slowly toward Ernie's bed until his knees bumped the mattress, and then he sat down, his back to Ernie. "And here's what I want you to know. I'm scared sometimes too. It's funny" — he rested back on his arms — "I've been livin' in the dark for a long time now, and sometimes it still scares me to death. But times when I can't see the old photos, or the letters from my oldest son, or I can't see that look of anger on your daddy's face, and now on yours, I think to myself that bein' blind ain't always so bad."

To Genie, that was one crazy statement. Being blind *had* to be bad. You couldn't see. And when he thought about all the things he was lucky to see, like stars, and model cars, and Shelly, he knew for a fact Grandpop couldn't have meant that. But then again, after seeing Grandma's face when she was disappointed, and his mother's always-exhausted expression, and imagining how Grandpop's face was going to melt when he found out about Michael Jackson . . . Genie could sorta understand.

Grandpop rocked forward and stood back up. He reached for the dresser, ran his hand across the medals and the flag. "I'm gonna leave you guys alone, but first, Ernie, I wanted to give you these." Grandpop took off his sunglasses but kept his eyes closed. "Should've given them to you days ago. Take them. I have others. I know yours are broken, so . . . here."

Genie gave Ernie a *Take them* look. Since they'd been there, Genie had never seen Grandpop take off his glasses, even once. And now he was *giving* them to Ernie? Whoa. Ernie finally turned toward Grandpop. He hesitated, put a hand out, hesitated again, then grabbed Grandpop's sunglasses. And when he did, Grandpop opened his eyes.

Holy. Moly!

Grandpop's eyes . . . oh man. They were . . . *strange.* Like fogged-up windows. They almost didn't even look real. It was almost like there were clouds inside Grandpop's head, floating just behind the glass.

Genie couldn't stop staring, all the while praying Grandpop couldn't tell he was staring. He tried to get himself together but couldn't help thinking about how if Grandpop took his teeth out and his sunglasses off, he basically looked like a zombie. Whoa.

"Thanks," Ernie said, cool, trying hard to pretend like he wasn't shocked by Grandpop's eyes or the fact that he was giving him his shades. Genie couldn't pretend at all. And *he* was glad Grandpop couldn't see *him* at that moment, because he couldn't stop looking.

Grandpop reached his hand out, searching for Ernie's. Ernie met his, and they shook on it. Grandpop squeezed and said, "Let's start over." He gripped Ernie's hand tight. "The first one is always like this, the rest are fives."

Ernie nodded, and right as Grandpop was leaving, Ernie said, "And I don't hate you."

Grandpop paused. But he didn't turn around; he just took a breath, then under that breath started counting the steps.

#484: Why do Grandpop's eyes look like ice?

#485: Why do young people lose their teeth, just to get new ones, and then get old and lose those, too? And why do teeth only grow back once? Seems like they should just keep growing back like fingernails.

#486: How come teeth ain't called mouthnails? Or maybe fingernails should be called fingerteeth.

#487: Do old birds ever lose their beaks? Do they ever crack them pecking hard things? If they do, does that change the way they sing?

#488: Why do they sing anyway? And is the song of a bird different if the bird is in a tree, in the sky, or in a cage?

TWENTY-ONE

Day twenty-nine — like déjà vu. Everyone, including Tess, waiting outside for Ernie to come out, the same way they had waited for him on his birthday.

"What's takin' the boy so long?" Grandma, wearing the earrings she bought from Tess, groused. She popped the elastic waistband on her dress. "I don't wanna be late. Binks doin' us a favor as it is."

"He's comin'," Genie said, staring down the front door. "He was puttin' his sneakers on." Truth was, he was wondering what was taking Ernie so long too. This was the moment when he was going to give Ernie Bruce Lee's tooth! He had it tucked into the little pocket in his shorts, ready for when Ernie burst through the door so he could wish him luck at the dentist and tell him to tuck the tooth into *his* ChapStick pocket for the protection of Bruce Lee — the dragon. But Ernie was taking f-o-r-e-v-e-r.

Grandpop was wearing different shades, big black ones that looked like they belonged to one of the characters from the *Back to the Future* calendar on the wall Genie had been looking at for weeks. With one hand on Genie's shoulder, as usual, Grandpop suggested, "Maybe the boy got the poopsies."

"Gross!" Tess said, snickering.

"The what?" Genie asked.

"The poopsies," Grandpop repeated. "You never heard of the oopsy-poopsies?"

"Brooke, please," Grandma pleaded.

Grandpop laughed and ran his hand along Genie's face until he found his ear. He whispered for a few seconds.

"Ernie don't have that!" Genie yelped.

"He might. When you nervous about something, sometimes it just happens."

Grandma squinted at her watch. "Let me go get this boy." But she didn't need to because the door flew open, slapping against the side of the house.

"Told you," Genie said, up-chinning at Grandpop.

Ernie stood on the porch looking like old Ernie — like he used to look before he learned to shoot. His hands were in his pockets and he didn't have on the mask. But the best part was that he was wearing

Grandpop's sunglasses. The ones he gave him. He looked cool again.

"I was just comin' to get you," Grandma said. "It's almost two o'clock, and I don't wanna be late."

Ernie trotted off the porch, and Tess was right there to hug him. Ernie smiled, wide, the metal from his splint-braces glinting in the sun as he headed to the car. Tess smiled too, flashing all the colorful rubber bands in her mouth.

Genie wiggled his finger into his Chap-Stick pocket. "Ernie, hold up! I got somethin' for you."

"What?" Ernie waited, half in, half out of the car. He held his hand out.

Genie dropped the tooth in his brother's open palm.

"A pebble?" Ernie said, with some attitude.

"Nope" — Genie felt his chest swell — "that's one of Bruce Lee's teeth."

Ernie looked closer. "No way."

"Yep, I got it from Teeth Man. It's a good luck charm."

Ernie closed his fist around the tooth. "Bruce Lee? Really? Well, a'ight, man." He put his arm around Genie's neck and yanked him close like he always used to do when it was headlock time. "Thanks." Then he dipped into the passenger side of Grandma's Buick, which now was cranked up and rumbling, ready to go.

"He got the shades on?" Grandpop asked Genie as Ernie slammed the door.

"Yep."

Genie could feel Grandpop smile behind him. He didn't even have to look.

Once Ernie and Grandma were gone, and Genie had walked Grandpop back to the house — actually, Genie took a few steps, then pretty much just watched as Grandpop walked *himself* back to the house — he and Tess decided this was the perfect time to go check the trap. They weren't sure when they would have another moment when Grandma would be gone, and they could sneak the bird right past Grandpop, easy.

Genie yelled to Grandpop that he'd be right back, grabbed his swatting stick, and then asked Tess what the heck she was doing: She had her hands pressed together and her head bowed.

"Prayin' to Big Bird for a miracle. What you think I'm doin?" she zapped. "If we don't catch this bird, you're a dead man, and I'm just prayin' that when you go to heaven you don't bump into your long-lost feathered friend, Michael Jackson, up there. 'Cause I'm sure he's *PO'ed.*" Then she nudged him. "Joke!"

And once again they headed through the woods toward the strange yellow house, swiping limbs from their path and jumping over thick roots bursting through the earth. As the brush began to thin, and the yellow house was in plain sight, Genie could hear something. Something different from the normal nature sounds. The sound of something trapped. The short, choppy fluttering of wings slapping against wood. It was a bird! Had to be.

Genie broke free from the forest, Tess right on him, skidded to his knees, and peered through the slits in the slats at a bluish bird strutting back and forth. He knew right away. Head was hooded in blue. The chest, orange. Just like Tito and Jermaine and Marlon and Jackie.

"It's a barn swallow!" Genie cried, grasping Tess's arm. "We did it!"

"Well, let's get it," Tess said, as if "getting it" was no big deal.

Huh. They didn't have a bag. Okay. That was dumb. Soooo . . . Plan B. On the fly.

"Well, there's really only one way I can think of," said Tess, the first to have a Plan B. "We block both sides of the box, then lift it real slow and grab it." Genie paused. He'd been afraid of touching a dead bird, and honestly, he was pretty scared to touch a living one too, especially knowing he'd have to then walk it all the way back through the woods. But he knew it had to be done. This was his time. This was his chance. And he was ready. He gave Tess the *okay* nod.

Once they positioned themselves across from each other, Genie glanced at the yard in front of him, the rickety birdcages all cracked and mangled and peeking from just behind the house. He thought about how birds were once in each one, but how those same birds were let go when they were strong enough to fly.

"Okay, I'll lift. You grab," Tess was saying, holding the sides of the box.

"Got it." Genie refocused and readied his hands like a quarterback before calling hike.

"All set?"

Genie nodded.

Tess slowly lifted the box, and Genie slid his hands in, his fingers first touching the feathers, then wrapping around the body of the swallow. "Okay . . . okay . . . I got it. I got it!"

Tess lifted the box completely and there

Genie was, swallow trapped between his palms.

For four whole seconds.

The bird began to struggle, to flap its wings, and as soon as it lurched in its fight to fly, pecking at Genie's hand, he got scared.

And he let go.

"Genie!" Tess cried as the swallow took off. Genie's eyes pricked with tears, hands still cupped, watching in disbelief as his good luck flew away.

The walk back through the woods was a slow trek. He'd been so close to catching that bird and setting things right. *So close.* At the same time, he couldn't stop thinking about those cages. And how the bird fought. And how nothing was wrong with it. It wasn't hurt, it was free, and Genie had wanted to trap it. And how would the new Michael Jackson feel? Genie felt kinda silly thinking about the feelings of a bird, especially since this was a serious situation, but he couldn't shake it. And he knew he needed to do something — something else — but he just wasn't sure what.

He was so busy beating himself up in his head that he didn't even notice Grandpop on the porch — *sitting on the porch, all by himself,* until he'd reached the porch himself. Grandpop was outside! He'd come outside, by himself! And even though it was only the front porch, outside was outside.

"Listen, there's still time. We'll get it," Tess whispered before giving Genie a hug and heading down the hill. She probably would've stayed and hung out, but Genie was clearly not in the mood, plus Grandpop had two mason jars of tea at the ready. Not three. Genie took a seat, a little surprised that Grandpop's tea was . . . tea.

Grandpop took a sip. So did Genie.

"Too sweet?" Grandpop asked.

"Nope. Just right," Genie said, sitting awkwardly next to Grandpop like they were on a first date or something. Like how Ernie and Tess used to sit next to each other when they first met. A *squeak, squeak* came from Samantha's house. She was chewing on her Bite Buddy.

"So, Little Wood," Grandpop started. "Tell me about Brooklyn."

"What about it?"

"I'on't know. Tell me a story."

Genie thought for a moment but couldn't come up with any stories, at least not about Brooklyn. He could've told the story about how he killed a bird, and tried to catch another one, but . . .

"I'on't have a story, Grandpop. But I do have a question," Genie said.

"Ah. Of course you do. Okay, well, shoot."

Genie thought back to the first breakfast when he asked Grandpop about wearing sunglasses in the house. How it was awkward at first, but afterward, Grandpop was honest with Genie about everything, including him being crazy, which Genie now figured was just a family trait.

"Well, what's the deal with that yellow house back in the woods?"

Grandpop pressed his lips tight, then said, "You know what I like about you? If you wanna know, you just ask." Not really. Genie had all kinds of questions that he'd written but hadn't actually asked. Questions Google couldn't answer. Questions like, why all the birds and the birdcages? What about Great-Grandpop's suicide? But he figured now was the time to go straight to the source.

A breeze came out of nowhere and swept across the porch. Genie imagined him and Grandpop were sitting on a giant spoon, and God was holding them up to his mouth and blowing on them like hot soup. "So that old house . . ." Grandpop began, but before he could get into it, the *squeak, squeak* from Samantha's house turned into her

376

barking, and the rickety sounds of a nearly broken-down car came up the hill.

Grandpop straightened up as the driver's-side door swung open. Crab swung himself out of the car.

"Now, if I had a cat, I suppose she woulda been draggin' you in, huh?" Grandpop said, like an old cowboy.

"I suppose," Crab said, loping over to the porch.

"Well, I got a dog." Then out of nowhere Grandpop hollered, "Sic 'im, Samantha! Sic 'im! Sic 'im!" Samantha stopped barking, almost with perfect timing, then made a few circles before lying back down in the hot sun. "Ah, I agree, Sammy. It ain't worth it. We'll just wait for Mary to get back."

"C'mon, Brooke." Crab looked pained.

"What you here for, Crab?"

Crab pulled the cigar from his mouth, spit, then put it right back where it had been. "I came by to check on the boy," he said. "And to drop off some goodies." Crab tossed the rolled-up paper bag to Genie and set a brown-bagged bottle on the porch.

"Thought that was your daughter's job now."

"Yeah, well, it is. But that's just 'cause I knew she was gonna be comin' up here anyway. Plus, to be frank, I felt so dern bad

I ain't know what to do. I guess I just thought it'd be better for me to lay low and hide out for a while. Especially from Mary. Shoot, it was bad enough havin' Tess mad at me."

Grandpop took a sip of his tea and nodded. He'd kept a straight face, a cold one, since Crab pulled up. But he let it slip, his mean-mug relaxing, as he admitted, "I can't blame you for that. Truth is, it ain't been much better for me up here on the hill. But Genie's been here to keep my head on."

Crab nodded. "And Ernie?"

"He's fine. At least he's gonna be."

Crab nodded again.

"A'ight, well I'm a head on back down the hill. Just stopped by to drop that stuff off," Crab said, heading toward his car.

"Crab," Grandpop called, getting up from his seat and inching forward, swinging his arm low until it touched the bottle. "Take this with you."

Crab paused, puzzled. He glanced at Genie then back at Grandpop before grabbing the bottle and toe-bouncing back to his junker.

As Crab's car left in a cloud of smoke and dust, Samantha snapped back into action, jumping around and barking. The breeze picked up even more, and the sky rumbled like an upset stomach. Genie was buzzing about the whole Crab/Grandpop interaction, trying to figure out what it all meant. It seemed like it was some kind of amends, but Genie couldn't be too sure. He took a peek into the bag — whoa — a fly mother lode! Crab was *definitely* trying to make amends.

"Now where was I?" Grandpop asked.

"You were gonna tell me about the yellow house," Genie said.

"Right, right." Grandpop sniffed. Genie immediately thought it was another stinky armpit moment, but Grandpop put that to rest by saying, "I smell rain. And this is gonna be a long story, so how about we go back in the house." Samantha finally stopped barking. "Matter fact, Samantha's a part of the story. But not this Sam. The *original* Sam."

Genie wasn't exactly sure what Grandpop meant but followed anyway, mason jars and bag of flies in hand, as Grandpop headed for the door.

Once inside, Grandpop, to Genie's surprise, moved through the kitchen, right past the nunya bidness door, and right into the living room. Then he felt around and eased down onto the couch, a couch Genie had never seen Grandpop sit on. He reached out to grab his drink from Genie, then patted the cushion next to him. "Sit."

Genie sat. He lay the bag of flies between them, and before he could take a sip of his own tea, Grandpop ripped right into the story.

"When I was a youngster livin' in that old yellow house back there in them woods, there was a man named Barnabas Saint, used to live at the bottom of the hill, not too far from Crab and Tess. Barnabas was probably the only person my daddy called a friend. They used to work together, and back in them days, black men down here worked the tobacco fields. Times were different, ya understand? This was early Jim Crow days."

Genie had learned some of this in his social studies class — racism, slavery. Question for later: *Who was Jim Crow?*

"My daddy and Barnabas Saint worked a field two or three miles down the road owned by this man with the last name Bristol," Grandpop continued. "Now old man Bristol used to love dogs, and he kept them in his barn. Same barn that he made all the field hands, my daddy, Barnabas, and a whole bunch of other men, keep the farm tools — up in there with the dogs and dog mess and all that." He leaned forward and

Genie could tell that the story was about to get good, even though he was still waiting for Grandpop to tell him about the yellow house. "Bristol was a mean son of a gun. I mean, just a nasty you-know-what, always threatenin' the men, and yellin' at 'em like they weren't people. Like they were his dogs too. So one day, not long after one of Bristol's mutts gave birth to a litter, the men all went to the barn to put their tools away. It had been a hard day and Barnabas had had enough and decided that he was going to steal himself a puppy. So he reached down and snatched one of the little rascals up, stuffed it in his hat, tucked his hat under his arm. Barnabas and my daddy ran the whole three miles home, laughin' their heads off."

Grandpop leaned back again. The rain had finally started, gently tapping against the roof.

"What happened?" Genie asked, now all in.

"Well, turned out old man Bristol knew exactly how many pups was in that litter. And after questionin' all the men the next day, well, threatenin' them really, one guy broke and said they saw Daddy and Barnabas run out of the barn suspiciously."

"Oh man."

"Oh man is right," Grandpop said. "Bristol showed up at the yellow house, all in my daddy's face, askin' all kinds of questions. I was just a kid. I came to the door to see what was goin' on and Daddy told me to go to my room. I ran to the top of the stairs, but then stayed there and listened. Listened to Bristol tell my father that either he tell him the truth, or he would have our whole family killed."

"What?" Genie gasped, not believing his ears. "He could do that?"

"Back then, a lot of people could."

"So what did your dad do?"

Grandpop looked at Genie, square. "He did what he had to do. He told Bristol that Barnabas stole the puppy." Grandpop lifted his right leg and rested his ankle on his left knee, so he could scratch the snake bite scar. "Bristol fired my daddy on the spot. The next day Barnabas came to the house upset because he had gone to the field and Bristol had fired him, too. But my father didn't tell him that he already knew what had happened. My father just couldn't face him, couldn't admit what he'd done, couldn't apologize for what he knew full well was coming next to Barnabas. And when he finally had the courage to make it right, it was too late. Bristol and his boys set Barnabas's house on fire." Grandpop nodded slowly. "Burned to death. The house smoked for two days. On the third day, my father, who had become a ghost himself, went down to Barnabas's. I always felt like he went to pay his respects to Barnabas's spirit or somethin'. But when he came back from the burned house, he had that puppy. My mother named her Samantha."

Genie gasped again. "You mean, the puppy lived?"

"Yep. The dog lived," Grandpop replied. "And that wasn't the only time my pop went down to Barnabas's house. He would go all the time, and come back home with pieces of wood from the floor of the house, and screen wire from the doors and windows. That's what he used to make those bird-cages you and your brother found behind that old house." Genie froze — caught! "Yeah, that's right, I know all about that. Your grandma told me." Grandpop flashed a slick grin. "Some of them very same cages are in my room, but you already know that too, don'tcha, Little Wood?" Genie's breath caught in his throat. Grandpop dropped his leg back down. "Anyway, why am I even tellin' you this story again?"

"We were talkin' 'bout Samantha, the yellow house . . . ," Genie reminded him.

"Ah, right. The point is, my old man was never the same. He was already a little scattered from his time in the war, and everybody thinks the war is what drove him over the edge, but after the whole thing with Barnabas, it *really* got bad. It was what broke him, because he couldn't forgive himself — not for making the decision that he made, but for not apologizing and being honest with his friend when he had the chance. The old man was locked in guilt for the rest of his life." Grandpop circled the rim of his jar with a finger. "And that's why I keep Sam — a version of Sam — around. As a reminder."

"But what about the tree, and all those birds?" Genie asked, trying to keep the conversation going a little longer, hoping to shake the weird feeling that was creeping into his stomach. Plus, he really wanted to know. "I mean, what made that happen?"

Grandpop crossed his legs. "I'on't know. What you think?"

Genie did have a thought, one that came instantly. Probably from every scary movie he had ever sneak-watched, combining with the story Grandpop had just told him. A thought about whether people could die and then come back. If Grandpop's dad could be that tree, still trying to break free from the guilt. Or maybe Barnabas Saint was the tree, tearing the house apart, and Great-Grandpop was the birds, sitting in all that mess, eating themselves. Either way, Genie knew he couldn't actually say this to Grandpop. He wasn't even sure he knew *how* to say it, without sounding silly, or mean. But what if it were true? Could that happen to Genie? Or to Grandpop? Or Dad? *But it can't be true. It can't be. Don't be stupid. Too . . . many . . . scary . . . movies! But what if . . .*

By now Genie had a lump in his throat the size of, well, a small bird. Thoughts were coming every which way — the death of Michael Jackson, the disposing of the body, the constant fear that Grandpop would find out, the fact that he wasn't sure anymore if he should catch another one, and he realized that he also felt . . . trapped. Trapped in a deep hole he'd dug all by himself.

"I'on't know," was all Genie could say, his head spinning. But he knew. He knew what he needed to do to keep himself from becoming a nasty bird eating other birds, or a tree growing in a scary house.

He knew it was time to come clean.

"Grandpop, I need to tell you somethin'."

"What's that, grandson?"

And then the front door opened.

"How could you let this happen?!" Dad's voice came through the house — his dad? His dad! His parents were back! — and it sounded like he was storming into the kitchen, followed by Grandma, Ernie, and Ma. Dad was totally going off. "I knew sendin' them down here was a bad idea," he was fuming.

"Ma? Dad?" Genie called out in confusion, hopping up. "What y'all doin' here? Y'all three days early."

Ma met Genie in the kitchen entranceway, hugged him tight. "We just needed to get back to our boys. Missed you too much." He missed her, too. He really did. He studied her face to see if it was still tired, if she looked sad. Because if there was any sadness on her face, Genie would know that he'd have to get back to figuring out which parent he was going to live with. He'd also know to never take Shelly to Jamaica. "*Woo*, you stink. Smell like outside," Ma zinged him, scrunching her nose up so Genie couldn't tell if there was a smile with it. But she didn't look tired like she usually did. That was a start. Genie kept his eyes on his mother as she went over to the couch, bent down, and kissed Grandpop on the cheek. "It's good to see you, Papa Harris," she whispered. Grandpop smiled sheepishly.

"Um . . . how was Jamaica?" Genie asked, his brain bouncing back and forth between being happy to see his mother and totally freaking out. Because, yeah, he was excited to see her, but he was about to confess something — maybe the biggest mistake he'd ever made — and he didn't want her to be there when he confessed it. Because then he'd have to confess it to *everyone.* And the difference between parents and grandparents was that parents were allowed to get *real,* real mad.

Ma broke into a smile, but before she could answer, Grandpop called out for Dad. "Son."

Genie quickly shifted his gaze as Dad stalked into the living room with Grandma and Ernie, who was holding the suitcase, following behind. Dad gave Genie a big hug, but his face was tight, his eyes narrowed and lasering in on Grandpop.

Grandpop rocked forward, slowly getting to his feet, Ma reaching out to help him but then pulling back, knowing that wasn't what Grandpop would've wanted.

"Um, boys, why don't we go upstairs and get your stuff ready to go," Ma said, her eyes darting back and forth between Dad and Grandpop.

"Yeah, that's a good idea," Grandma followed up. Ernie, who had set the suitcase down, picked it back up, and Grandma grabbed Genie's shoulders, moving him around his father. The rain was picking up.

Grandma hung back as Ma led the way upstairs. Halfway up, Genie asked Ernie about what had happened at Teeth Man's.

"He said everything's lookin' good and that I should be fine by the time school starts," Ernie explained, lugging the suitcase step by step.

"Cool." Genie nodded. "But what he say about the chipped one? He said they might be able to put a crown on it? Like a king? That would be *sweet.*"

"I'on't know," Ernie said, now at the top of the stairs. "Maybe."

As they entered the room, he turned to Genie and gave him a look. A *What's up with the bird?* look. Genie just shook his head. Ernie grimaced.

In the room, Ma started pulling all the clothes from the old blue dresser.

"So, I guess I don't need to ask if you boys had a good time, huh?"

Ernie helped stack the clothes neatly into the suitcase. Genie folded up the blanket.

"I did," Ernie said. Ma looked at him in surprise. "I mean, learning how to shoot was wack, but I still had a pretty good time, when I think about it."

"I did too," Genie said. And he wasn't even playing Pete and Repeat. He really did.

Ma looked at them as if she didn't recognize them. "Well, that's good," she said, smiling at last.

All of a sudden, there was a whole bunch of noise coming through the floor, from downstairs. Dad and Grandpop. Ma told Genie and Ernie to finish packing and dashed off to keep their father from "doing something stupid." Genie looked at Ernie, Ernie looked back at him, and they both booked it down the stairs behind her.

And Dad was there, standing in front of Grandpop, all puffed up. Probably what Uncle Wood looked like when he stood up to Cake, Genie thought. But this was *Dad* and *Grandpop.* Grandma was planted between them.

"You did it to us, and now you've done it to them! Are you happy?" Dad was shouting.

Grandpop didn't respond, and Grandma tried to speak for him, but Dad cut her off.

"No, Ma, let him answer. Let him tell me why he can't get it through his head that his job was to protect, but he's done a lousy job of it! He didn't protect Wood, he didn't protect me, and he didn't protect my boys!"

Dad stalked to the other side of the living room and slammed the wall, the bang making everybody jump, especially Grandpop, whose hands started shaking. Ma ran over to Dad as he pressed his head against the peeling wallpaper, and put her arms around him.

But Genie's eyes were on Grandpop. He wondered if it all sounded and felt worse to Grandpop because of how they say people who can't see can hear and feel more than people who aren't blind. What did Dad sound like to him? Because if he sounded scary to Genie, he must've sounded like a monster to Grandpop.

Dad turned back around and started raging again. "And what if a bullet ricocheted off a tree and hit him? Or Genie? Did you think about that? What if it hit *you*?" His voice started cracking.

"Then at least I would've done something to make you happy!" Grandpop blistered back. He put his hand on the arm of the couch, as if his legs were going to give out. He crumpled onto it, and in that moment, Dad suddenly shattered. He took a seat next to Grandpop. He looked at his wife, all the anger draining from his face. He looked to Genie and Ernie, hurt, embarrassed. Then he reached over, slowly taking Grandpop's hand. Grandpop didn't resist. Dad dropped his chin for a few seconds, then lifted his face and quickly whisked tears away from his cheeks.

The rain poured.

Then Grandma, who was staring directly at Ma, cleared her throat to get her attention, nodding toward the stairs.

Ma nodded back. "Boys, why don't we go back upstairs and finish packin'? Leave Grandpop and your dad here to talk."

That seemed like a good idea to Genie, because things were getting *weird. Again.*

Grandma followed them up this time. Ma started cramming shirt after shirt into the suitcase, telling the boys to make sure they had everything, Genie his notebook, Ernie his cell phone. And as she went on about how she couldn't understand why it seemed like her sons had more stuff leaving than they had coming, Grandma came over to the dresser and shooed her away. "You've been drivin' half the night — and these boys know a thing or two about work, now — they got this." And that was when she noticed the truck.

"Wait a minute," Grandma said, picking it up, her eyes watering as she flipped it over. "Who? How?"

Genie smiled hopefully. "I fixed it."

A tear fell from Grandma's eye as she looked back and forth from Genie to the truck. She set it back in its place in front of the flag and medals and bottle with Ernie's chipped tooth and, yes, the piece of broken wheel. She stepped back and looked at it, gazing at it as if she were remembering Wood playing with it when he was younger. Then she picked it back up, nodding her head.

"Take it," she said, pushing it into Genie's hands and wrapping his fingers around it.

"You serious?" Genie asked.

"Baby, we all gotta learn to let things go sometimes. So it's yours." She kissed him on the forehead. "Plus, I don't think Uncle Wood would mind if you added this one to your collection. As a matter of fact" — Grandma grinned wide — "I think he'd be honored."

Genie lit up. "Thanks, Grandma."

"And what we gon' do with this, Big Ernie?" Grandma wiped the tears from her eyes and held up the beer bottle with the chipped tooth in it.

"Oh my," Mom gasped. "Ernie, is that . . . yours?"

"Yep. This guy, Crab —"

"I know who Crab is."

"Oh. Well, yeah, he saved it for me. And

then we went to the doctor but she said —"

"Uh-uh." She wagged a finger. "I'on't wanna know." Grandma passed the bottle to Ma. She held it up to the light, like she couldn't believe what she was seeing. "Just lookin' at it gives me the willies," Ma said at last. "So you takin' this back to Brooklyn with you? Show it to all your friends, tough guy?"

"Nah," Ernie said. He turned to Grandma. "You and Grandpop can keep it. As a good luck charm."

"A . . . *what?*" Mom looked even more horrified.

Grandma, on the other hand, gushed. "Aww, thank you, Ernie."

Ma looked at them like they were all crazy, then said they had to get a move on because Dad wanted to avoid Richmond rush hour, so they doubled down on the packing and Grandma called through the floor to make sure it was okay to come down.

"Is there still fire in the hole?" she yelled.

"No, Ma, it's fine," Dad called back.

On the way downstairs, Grandma hit Ernie and Genie and their mother with everything she had to get them to stay the night.

"Just stay for dinner, then," she persisted when Ma turned her down. "Y'all shouldn't get on the road hungry. These are growin' boys."

"I know, Mama Harris. We'll stop on the way."

"But it's gettin' late. Y'all don't wanna rest your heads just for a few hours? Avoid that traffic?"

"Can't. I mean, we'd love to but it's just . . ." The pause was awkward as Ma tried to find the right words, but Grandma seemed to understand. She nodded warmly. Ma exhaled and continued. "I slept the whole way down, so I can take over if he gets tired."

And on and on, while Genie clunked the heavy suitcase against the shaky steps, going down them for the last time. And even though he knew that in a few seconds he'd be about seventeen steps to freedom, there was no way he could leave without somehow talking to Grandpop.

In the living room, Grandpop and Dad were sitting side by side. They were drinking sweet tea and listening to the radio, Grandpop's box of money — the rainy day stash — in Dad's lap. Ma hugged Dad's neck and Grandma did the same to Grandpop. Everybody loved Pete and Repeat. Even old people.

"Time to go," Dad said, clapping his

hands together, standing up, the box in hand.

"What's that?" Ma asked.

Dad smiled. "Gas money."

"Enough to get you there. And back." Grandpop dimpled, rocking a little, and Ma, glassy-eyed, grabbed his hand to help him to his feet. "All right. I know you gotta get these knuckleheads back to the concrete jungle."

"Wait," Genie said, handing the suitcase to Ernie. "Um, Grandpop, we didn't get to finish what we were talkin' about. I mean, I . . . uh . . . I still need to just . . . tell you somethin'."

Dad looked at Genie, curious, concerned. "Son, we really gotta get goin'. You can call him when we get home."

"Ernest, just give us a second," Grandpop said. "It's still raining a little, plus I *know* Ernie has someone he'd like to say good-bye to."

Dad and Ma looked at Ernie, who gnawed the side of his jaw trying to hide his embarrassment. But it was true. Dad sighed and nodded at him. Ernie immediately broke for the door, heading, Genie knew, straight to Tess's, while Grandpop, sensing Genie's need for privacy, asked, "Our room?"

In the inside-outside room, Genie and

Grandpop took their usual seats. Genie took one last look at the birdcages, one without a bird. His heart started jumping around, and he couldn't get his right leg to stop tap-tap-tapping. He took a deep breath. "Grandpop, Michael Jackson is . . . dead."

"Yeah, he died a few years back. Somethin' crazy 'bout a doctor, and too many meds." Grandpop shook his head. "Is that what —"

"No, I mean Michael Jackson, the bird," Genie clarified, then decided to really get to it. "One of *your* birds. In this room. One of them is . . . dead. He's gone. We were out of flies . . . and I didn't know what to do because I had already fed the others, so I just gave the smallest one a few apple seeds to hold him till Crab brought more flies. And it killed him. I . . . killed him."

Grandpop drew a long breath, seemed to last forever. Then he simply said, "I know."

"Huh?" Genie thought he'd heard wrong.

"I said, I know." Grandpop knew? How long had he known? *What in Sam Hill was going on?!*

"But — but —" was all Genie could manage.

"Because of these, son." Grandpop tapped his earlobes. "I heard a change in the room a long time ago. It was as if there were five

396

people talking at the same time, and then suddenly one stopped talking. Everything changed. I knew right away that something had happened, but I been waiting for you to come clean. To speak up. But . . . you never did. Until now." Grandpop put his hands together, squeezed and massaged his fingers. "What took so long?"

"I've been tryin' to fix it," Genie said, now staring down at his beat-up Converses. "But I just couldn't. I'm sorry. I'm so sorry. Sorry for killing Michael Jackson and lyin' about it. I'm sorry for stealin' his dead body from the cage before it was light outside and puttin' it on a shovel and flingin' it into the woods. I'm sorry for settin' a trap and tryin' to catch another barn swallow to sneak into the house and put it back in the cage, and I'm sorry for even thinking about callin' the new stolen one Michael Jackson too, but then I would've been sorry to the new Michael Jackson for catchin' him and trappin' him in a cage, so I guess I'm not sorry for that part, so . . . I'm sorry for that too."

The truth practically vomited out of him. All of it. The whole thing.

Grandpop looked stunned. Genie worried his apology wouldn't be enough, even though he was already starting to feel a little better. But after a few seconds, Grandpop smiled. It was slight, but it was enough, enough to let Genie know he was okay.

"Anything else?"

"Well, actually, I do have *one* more question."

"Your last question." Grandpop stood, reached his hand out to Genie.

"My last question." Genie grabbed Grandpop's hand, standing. "Would you ever let the rest of the Jacksons go?"

Grandpop went back over to the door, sighed, and yanked it open. He *looked* looked at Genie again, the smirk still on his face. "Maybe."

And as Genie left the inside-outside room, he stepped on something. He looked down to see what it was. A small jagged piece of plastic, black, with a bit of silver in the middle.

ACKNOWLEDGMENTS

As always, I have to acknowledge my editor, the great Caitlyn Dlouhy, who, for some reason, never gives up on me. And my agent, my friend, Elena Giovinazzo for always championing my crazy ideas. My grandfather Brooke; my older brother, Allen; and my father for inspiring this tale. I also have to thank my cousin Tracie Smith Furgess, for her help with all the dental stuff. I had no idea! And lastly, I just want to acknowledge everyone who has supported me — all the librarians, teachers, students, friends, and anyone else who has spent a moment or two with my colorful characters. It truly means the world to me.

ABOUT THE AUTHOR

Jason Reynolds is crazy. About stories.

If you ever want to know what a perfect peanut butter and jelly sandwich tastes like, he's your guy. And if you ever want to know what the worst selfie in the world looks like . . . he's still your guy. So he'll trade you: a sandwich for a selfie lesson. And maybe, just maybe, he'll even throw a story or two in there. He's already written a bunch: *All American Boys* (which he wrote with Brendan Kiely) and *The Boy in the Black Suit,* both of which are Coretta Scott King Honor books; and *When I Was the Greatest,* for which Jason won the 2015 Coretta Scott King/John Steptoe Award for New Talent. And he's working on more. Check him out at jasonwritesbooks.com.